Femmes Fatal

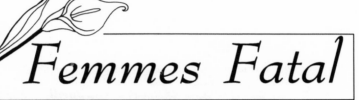

Femmes Fatal

DOROTHY CANNELL

Bantam Books

NEW YORK · TORONTO · LONDON · SYDNEY · AUCKLAND

FEMMES FATAL
A Bantam Book / October 1992

Library of Congress Cataloging-in-Publication Data

Cannell, Dorothy.
    Femmes fatal / Dorothy A. Cannell.
        p.   cm.
    ISBN 0-553-08846-7
    I. Title.
PS3553.A499F4   1992
813'.54—dc20   92-10745
                                                                  CIP

Published simultaneously in the United States and Canada

Bantam Books are published by Bantam Books, a division of Bantam Doubleday Dell
Publishing Group, Inc. Its trademark, consisting of the words "Bantam Books" and
the portrayal of a rooster, is Registered in U.S. Patent and Trademark Office and in
other countries. Marca Registrada. Bantam Books, 666 Fifth Avenue, New York, New
York 10103.

PRINTED IN THE UNITED STATES OF AMERICA

BVG   0 9 8 7 6 5 4 3 2 1

For Meg Ruley, my friend, agent,
and partner in crime

Coupon

☞ *Ladies, has the love light gone out of your marriage?*

☞ *Are you asking, Where have all the flowers gone?*

Become the woman he always wanted by phoning **FULLY FEMALE** today for your **FREE** confidential consultation with one of our fully accredited staff members.

The first one hundred who remit this coupon also receive as gifts our very own black satin sleep mask and sample size Peach Melba Love Rub.

☎ **34366** today and be in your hubby's arms tomorrow!

Must be 18 years or older. Not valid where prohibited by law. *Peach Melba Love Rub* is a trademark of Fully Female Ltd.

Chapter One

He was a dark and stormy knight. A latter-day rake with eyes the colour of emeralds worth a queen's ransom. His smile promised voyages to the moon. And heaven alone knew how many females lay littered in his wake.

To a rousing burst of Rachmaninoff, he swept into my London flat one January evening and, with the hauteur of his greeting, captured my virgin heart forever and a day.

"Miss Ellie Simons? My car awaits. Shall we splurge on dinner or parking tickets?"

Never mind that he had no intentions honourable or otherwise, my existence as an overweight, underpaid interior designer would never be the same. The man wasn't just a handsome face. He could do more than raise a dark sardonic eyebrow. He could cook. And not just baked beans on toast! Bentley T. Haskell was a first-class chef.

In the grand tradition of paperback romance, we went from loathing to loving with all unseemly haste. My first two years as Mrs. Haskell were a rapturous journey with all the thrills and spills of white-water rapids. Our lovemaking blew enough fuses that one night all the lights went out. Our quarrels were glorious. The making up marvelous. Could any woman ask for more?

On a glowing April morning, I awoke in my bedroom at Merlin's Court to the woeful realization that the honeymoon was over. Ellie Haskell was no sultry siren straight from the pages of a bodice-buster romance. I was a thirty-year-old matron, weighing almost as much as when the twins, daughter Abbey and son Tam, were born four and a half months before. Worse, my marriage had turned flabby.

At one time the sight of Ben putting on his socks had been enough to make passion's flame set my nightie alight; now late-night feedings and stretchmarks that refused to fade with the application of S'Mother Cream had taken their toll.

"Good morning, Sunshine." Ben stood at the foot of our four-poster bed, clad in a black silk dressing gown that did wonders for his complexion. Tossing a coin in the air, he clapped it down on the back of his hand. "Heads, you cook dinner tonight. Remember, I will be home this evening. We have that meeting of the Hearthside Guild at the vicarage. And I am program chairman of the Full-Time Father Committee." A woeful glance down at the coin. "You lose, my dear."

What had become of the man who once refused to let me

sully my hands tossing a rasher of bacon in the frying pan?
To outward appearances he remained totally adorable. The
black hair was tousled, a smile lurked in those jewelled eyes,
and the need for a shave hinted at gentleman turned bandit.
No one would guess he had worked until midnight at Abigail's, his restaurant in the village.

"Full-time father?" I queried.

"Ellie, we are talking about an attitude." Again Ben spun
the coin in the air, this time catching it in his pocket. "Parenting is my number-one occupation. Work is something I do"—
he grinned—"to get out of the house when the nappies need
washing."

Smile in place, I tossed back the bedclothes and rose to face
the day. As yet there was no clarion call from the nursery.
Sunlight darted accusing fingers at the haze of dust on the
mahogany furniture. But this remained a proud, handsome
room, its copper fireplace giving off the rich glow of Harvey's
Bristol Cream. Merlin's Court—dear to me as the day I first came
here, a podgy child with a chip on my shoulder the size of a
tablet from Mount Sinai. The good old days when I hadn't been
expected to lift a finger except to ping the bell for tea.

"Something wrong, Ellie?"

"Just daydreaming." I whirled to face him, if flannel can be
said to whirl.

A hopeful gleam lit his eyes. It had been days, weeks since
we had . . . well, you know . . .

"Sorry, dear, mornings are off-limits. I have to get the babies up, bathed, and fed before I take a break and fix the
washing machine."

"No need, I rang the plumber." Typical male, clouding the
issue by being helpful.

"Thanks. I'll have Mr. Fixit cluttering up my kitchen all morning."

"You don't have to entertain the man. A cup of tea perhaps. But definitely no cake. These days cake undoubtedly constitutes sexual harassment."

"What a blessing."

"My apologies for gadding off to work."

We studied each other, Ben with hands sunk in the black silk pockets, I sunk in gloom. Was love's minuet reduced to this? Each of us tiptoeing around the other's feelings? He moved to the door, hand on the brass knob.

"Coffee's made and the babies . . ."

"I know." A half hour earlier I'd heard him go in to change Abbey and Tam. All things considered, he deserved better than a love life that had gone from gourmet to thaw-and-serve.

"How about frozen dinners tonight, dear?" I said, but he was gone in pursuit of the bathroom.

Time for the mistress of the manor to get going. Motherhood had taught me a minute saved is a minute earned. Nudging the wardrobe open to unhook my dressing gown, I backed away from the mirror on the door, my raised hands warding off the evil vision in the manner of a vampire assaulted by sunlight. Lucky vampires! *They* cast no reflection. Was that flannel-faced, flannel-garbed woman really me? Had youth and beauty fled without a backward glance?

My poor hair, what there was of it! I could stuff a sofa with what had come out on my brush since the birth of the twins. Twisting the now pathetic strands into a plait, I honed in on the bags under my eyes. Mouth quivering, I reminded myself there are worse things—baggy knees, for instance—and then made the mistake of looking down. The case was desperate. Time to get serious about my diet. No meals between meals, no more hedging. How could I face the handsome Reverend Rowland Foxworth tonight at the Hearthside Guild with a nose like this? The mirror drew me back with all the hypnotic power of the one belonging to Snow White's stepmum.

"Ellie . . ." Ben's reflection rose up behind me, handsome as all get-out in his cuff-linked shirt and pleated trousers.

"Oh, God! My nose. It's moved so far over to the left I should never wear anything but red."

"My adorable nincompoop!"

Great, now my mind was going. Peering around me, Ben bared his teeth at the mirror. Concerned, I suppose, that they weren't a perfect match for his ultra-white shirt. A false alarm, needless to say.

Those lips now met mine in a kiss of sorts. But neither of us had our hearts in it. Mentally, he was already at Abigail's, plotting a curry that would prove the cure for the common cold. I was lost in bitter reverie. Damn, life is a sexist institution. Pregnancy had not achieved the ruinous effect on Ben that it had on me. If anything, his manly charms were enhanced. His shoulders had broadened and I could swear he was a couple of inches taller. Careful, an inner voice warned, as sure as the winning raffle ticket is always the one lost, you will lose Ben.

One morning I would awake to find a note posted on the bedroom mantelpiece, informing me that he had gone home to Mother. The next forty years would be spent forwarding his mail and explaining to the twins why I had driven their father from the nest. "Daddy was all growed up, my sweets, he was too big to go on living at home."

Dear God, something must be done! Perhaps if I took lots

of steaming hot showers ... These pathetic musings ended when I turned to find Ben gone. His footsteps echoed with a dreadful finality on the stairs. Some muffled words floated up to me before the front door thumped shut.

"Have a nice day, hubby mine." What an idiot I was! Did I suppose my words would chase after him to the car? Were I a wife worth the name, I would rush after Ben and stand in the courtyard beneath the blaze of mullioned windows. The wind would ruffle my nightgown about my ankles and play tag with my hair; my eyes would turn the colour of the sea on a rainswept day, and he would take the memory with him. A sweet and secret thing, a rose pressed within the pages of a book. Memories maketh marriage.

Perhaps I wasn't dead from the brain down, but I wasn't about to find out. When I sped from the room, it was in answer to a cry from the nursery.

"Coming, my darlings!" Amazing that some N.S.P.C.C. official had not already come banging on the door. Never could I convince myself that the babies cried because they were hungry or had wet bottoms. Almost putting my foot through my flannel hem, I entered that Mother Goose room with my throat full of butterflies. True to form, I fully expected to find a masked man with a bulging sack tossed over his shoulder— a latter-day Mr. McGregor, that dreadful man who made away with Peter Rabbit's papa. Does a mother ever learn to feel safe where her offspring are concerned? Would I be fretting that Abbey and Tam were at the mercy of a wicked world when they were sixty? Would I ever let them go downstairs alone, let alone outdoors?

My heart turned over at the sight of their drooly sweet faces pressed against the bars of their cots. Abbey's stood at the daytime side of the room, under a sky-blue ceiling, painted with Smiley Sun and clouds with lambs' faces. Tam occupied the nighttime side, where the Cow, sporting a buttercup necklace, jumped over the Moon. Oh, to have arms long enough to scoop up both my babies at once! What's a mother to do? Tam's squeals competed with the springs of Abbey's cot as she did push-ups.

"Gentlemen first today." Avoiding my daughter's eyes, I stepped past the window alcove wherein stood the toy box that Jonas built, cleverly disguised as the Old Woman's Shoe. There—I have mentioned the man's name. Jonas, who goes by the title "gardener" at Merlin's Court, had bunked off the previous week with Dorcas, our erstwhile housekeeper. This wasn't a spree to Gretna Green, for Jonas is in his seventies and Dorcas has foresworn men. Purportedly they were helping out a friend of Dorcas's who was laid up with a bad back— or a good book, more like. Dorcas I could believe; she is a great one for pounding the sickbed pillows and ramming a thermometer in your mouth—or wherever comes handiest. But Jonas? I hadn't bought his story of feeling impelled to pitch in with his pitchfork in Mrs. What's-Her-Name's garden. I had spied a furtive look in his eyes and for one shocking moment actually suspected him of running away from home. He told me some cock-and-bull story about Mrs. Pickle, the vicar's daily, having designs on him. Ridiculous! But what other reason was there? Jonas lived the life of Riley here at Merlin's Court. I coddled him along with the twins and never took advantage of his affection for them. When he offered to fetch them down from their naps, I told him to stay put and drink his Ovaltine. When he offered to take them for a wheel in the pram, I went with him to make sure he didn't get out of puff coming up the hill. Jonas must live forever, for the thought of Merlin's Court without him was unbearable.

"Right, Tam, my darling?"

My clever boy was in my arms almost before I reached for him, his grip on my nose explaining why it was off-centre.

"I'll trade you a finger."

He grabbed the one I held up and crowed with delight. Nuzzling him close, I crossed to pick up Abbey. They were squirmy as seals and getting too big for me to hold both at once, but as I breathed in the milky-new smell of them, I told myself I was the wickedest woman on earth.

Your life is a fairy tale, Mrs. Haskell, you ungrateful witch. You live in a castle straight from the realms of the brothers Grimm. So what if sometimes you feel like the princess who turned into a frog? Some sensible exercise, a change of shampoo, the removal of all edible food from your diet and you might begin to feel Fully Female. Now where had I heard those F words? Probably some advert for a douche.

The twins, straphanging from my ears, gurgled replies that made a lot of sense to each other. Occasionally I did feel something of a third wheel. Maternal pride aside, they were adorable with their periwinkle blue eyes and red-gold hair, just beginning to turn from down into feathers of the real stuff. Neither looked much like me or Ben. But I didn't worry that they were changlings; they were born in this house on a snowy evening not fit for man nor beast to be abroad. Ben had been a tower of strength, reminding me when it was time for a contraction. Heaven forbid we should miss one.

Speaking of Daddy, he would now be at Abigail's, too busy among the stainless steel pots and copper bowls to cling to the memory of my wanton indifference. Suffused with shame and the inability to breathe with my wee ones choking me, I settled on the window seat and embarked on our geography lesson for the day.

"See the garden with its pretty trees? Beyond the iron gates is Cliff Road. And below the cliffs is the sea. Sometimes the sea sounds like a growlly tiger, other times it sounds like Tobias Cat slurping milk, and sometimes the sea cries like you do when you are hungry. This morning . . . shhh, the sea is sleeping. Mustn't wake it."

Applause.

"Ouch!" I removed Abbey's hands before she made bone-meal of my face. "Our closest neighbour, a quarter of a mile down the road, is nice Reverend Foxworth. He is vicar of the historic St. Anselm's church which dates back to Norman times. Understand, my darlings, I am not speaking of Norman the Doorman, star of kiddy television."

For those unacquainted with said character, he was by day the mild-mannered doorman of Tinseltown Toyshop, but when shadows lengthened and the Closed sign appeared on the door, he turned into Norman, Defender of Wronged Toys. Decked out in his Hermes helmet and waterproof cape (only soap or water could bring his undoing) and chased by goblins with—you've got it—water pistols, he scaled buildings and shinned down chimneys, proclaiming "Never fear, Norman's here!" Yesterday I'd missed the rescue of Dolly Dimples because Miss Thorn, the church organist, had knocked on the door at the crucial moment. Ostensibly she came selling raffle tickets to raise money for a new altar cloth, but I knew her prime motive was to find out why I had missed services three . . . or it could be four . . . Sundays in a row. Miss Thorn is one woman who does have eyes in the back of her head.

Her spectacles had misted up when she spoke of the reverend's most recent sermon, while her thin, knobby face achieved a kind of radiance.

"A moment of epiphany, Mrs. Haskell. Reverend Foxworth's text was St. Paul to the Corinthians, you know the one—faith, hope and love, and the greatest of these is love. I had goosebumps everywhere, Mrs. Haskell, even on my . . . derriere. I could hardly sit still on my stool." A titter behind her hand. "I wanted to rise up, clench my fist and shout 'Right on, Vicar!' "

I told her I really would have to get to church more often.

"Such a *freeing* experience!" Miss Thorn's eyes were now magnified to mushrooms behind those specs. "I felt like Eve after the Fall, throwing off her fig leaves and crushing Adam to her breast. For the first time I feared I had been wrong not to marry. One does what one can spreading joy here and there . . ." A pause, during which we both paid homage to all those who had fallen in the line of duty at Miss Thorn's feet. What her secret was I didn't know. She had to be the most excruciatingly plain woman I had ever seen, but even Jonas admitted to a quiver below the belt when Miss Thorn tittered. "What I am saying, dear Mrs. Haskell, is that when I was a girl, I spoke as a girl and loved as a girl, but now that I am a woman, I must cast off girlish things."

Like other women's husbands? And for this I missed Norman the Doorman.

"*You* are responsible, Mrs. Haskell."

"Me?"

"Yes." A blush stained her cheeks a delicate shade of chartreuse. "It was at your wedding, seeing you so radiant, that I knew the time had come to blow out my old flames and strike a match." Hands clutched to her concave breast. "You and your Heathcliff are still as much in love as ever?"

Words wouldn't come, even to ask who was the lucky chap destined to win her hand. Now, as I sat on the window seat in the nursery, Miss Thorn's words still rang in my head, echoing my own dismal sense of failure. Ben was a man in a million. Somehow, somewhere, I had to find my way back to him, to the passion that once was ours . . . but first things first. The babies. The difficulties inherent in carrying them downstairs in one armload would be obvious to Pooh Bear. Naturally, the double trek appealed strongly to the exercise fiend in me, but would have been tough on the baby left clinging to the bars of the cot. So, Necessity being a mother too, I had taken to using the twin pack—a front-and-back pack, given to us by my cousin Freddy who works for Ben at Abigail's.

"Won't be a tick, my loves!" I stashed both babies in the nearest cot, fished the pack off the changing table, and looped it over my head. I felt like a parachutist ready to jump for God and country. A deep breath to inflate my lungs before positioning Tam in the front pouch, then hoisting him around to the back. If this didn't beat pumping iron any day! Now in with Abbey. A jostle to get them even, a moment to adjust Tam's foot, a final check to make sure my flannel nightdress was hitched above safety level, and with Abbey sucking on her fist, all systems were go.

We headed out onto the landing, that wainscotted gallery lit in daytime by the stained-glass window at the turn of the stairs and further brightened by the photo of my mother-in-law, Magdalene Haskell, on her prie-dieu. Were her eyes more reproachful—make that *resigned*—than ever this morning?

Taking the first stair, I remembered! That letter I wrote to her and Pop Haskell last week was still on the study desk, waiting for Ben to add his imprint. Me and my scruples! I should have forged his kisses. My half-dozen pages were now hopelessly dated; Ben no longer had a cold, the twins were no longer sleeping through the night and I was no longer going on the shopping trip to Peterborough with the Hearthside Guild.

Any fool knows a staircase is no place to let one's mind doodle. Halfway down, Abbey jerked on my nightdress, Tam grabbed my hair—snapping my neck like an asparagus stalk—and all three of us squealed as I swayed and grabbed for the brass rail of the iron staircase. In that moment my life flashed before me. I don't mean past glories and despairs, but the ongoing now—the twins' breakfast and bathtime, the grocery shopping that must be done if we were not all to get scurvy, and the ironing of all those adorable little outfits that must not be left languishing in the airing cupboard an hour longer if they were to be worn twice. Clutching the banister as if it were the mast of the *Hesperus,* my vision cleared. Why, whatever was that at the foot of the stairs?

A strange man was standing in pooled shadow by the front door. But no need to blow things out of proportion. Bless his heart, he wasn't a great hulking fellow brandishing a Colt .45. My intruder was a shortish chap sprouting a Charlie Chaplin moustache and flexing an iron wrench the length of his arm.

"Morning, Missus." His furry thick speech and puckered left eyelid caused me to wonder if he were a family man, devoted to his godfather. Releasing a breath that set the wall tapestry swaying, I reached a casual hand for the bronze urn, conveniently placed in the niche to my right. The trick was to employ the calm, reasoning voice that worked when getting the babies to go night-night.

"Move a muscle," I trilled, "and you're dead."

"No call to take that tone, Missus! I wiped me feet when I come in the door."

"*Good Housekeeping* should give you a medal." How dare he look outraged. Crushing the neck of the urn, I backed up a step. "Waltzing in here! Just who the hell do you think you are?"

"Jock Bludgett."

"Not Sammy the Slug?"

"Eh?" He strained at me with his good eye as though I were a talking kangaroo. Abbey wriggled in her pouch, bringing me to my senses. Attack is not the best defense when you are an out-of-condition female who gets winded standing still and who, moreover, has one baby yanking on her hair and another sucking on a collar button, almost choking one in the process. Guile was more my speed. I would offer the burglar a cup of Earl Grey and, while his back was turned, pour in a bottle of teething medicine. Didn't the label promise to turn a cross face into a smiley face or your money back? A pity I didn't have any arsenic handy, I could have used that. But beggars can't be choosers.

"Time's money, Missus." The burglar was warming up the wrench on a ham-sized fist. "I got a couple of big jobs after this one."

"You don't want to overdo, Mr. Bludgeon."

"Bludgett."

"Pardon me." The urn tucked under my arm, I inched down the stairs, counting my blessings like crazy in one of those bargaining sessions with God. The twins seemed to be asleep and my flannel hem had stayed hitched above the ankle. Suddenly I saw the funny side. Entertaining a burglar in my night attire, whatever would the neighbours say? The bubbles were rising in my throat, and any moment they would explode in a cacophony of lunatic mirth.

Strange! The peals which rang through the hall seemed to emanate not from me, but the trestle table which occupied the stone dais across the flagstone hall. The telephone. So near and yet so far.

"That's my husband. If I don't answer, he'll . . ." The urn fell from my grasp, drowning out thought. It thudded and thumped down the stairs, slammed with metallic force onto the flagstones, and rolled with gathering speed—like a bowling ball about to make a strike—toward the skittles—I mean, the legs—of Burglar Bludgett. The moment was mine. My infallible clumsiness had saved the day.

Forget the cheering. Victory was about to be snatched from my clutches. Hopping nimbly over the urn, which ran to earth under a table, our villain headed for the phone.

"The call's for me, Missus."

"No!"

"I'd know that ring anywhere." His ugly face softened horribly. The Charlie Chaplin moustache quivered into a smile that flattened his features. Tucking the wrench in his back pocket, he thumbed up his trouser belt and smoothed a hand over his godfather hair, before lifting the receiver and placing it caressingly to his ear.

Was I to be granted a second chance? Terrified the twins would awake and sound the alarm, I edged toward the front door and—heart-stopping moment—almost tripped over the newspaper that lay spreadeagle under the letter box. Was fate setting booby traps? Usually *The Daily Chronicle* arrived before Ben left the house and he read it over his cup of coffee. Freedom was within my grasp, my fingers were inches from the doorknob, when the grandfather clock boomed the half hour. The vibration moved up through my feet and hot-rodded toward my heart; I couldn't move in case I stepped on a land mine and blew up. Oh, my darling babies! For a second I thought that queer rasping sound was me, then realized it was Burglar Bludgett's heavy breathing. He stood fondling the telephone cord, a glazed look in his eyes.

"Little Miss Muffet, I'll sit on your tuffet any day. You get yourself all perfumed and pretty and, if you've got a mo, stick a bottle of that massage lotion in the microwave, just to take the chill off like, and I'll be 'ome in two shakes . . . of me tail."

Click. He had replaced the receiver and was heading blindly toward me.

"That was my Moll."

"So I gathered."

"Sorry to rush off like, but it's this way. She—the wife— wants me"—Burglar Bludgett licked his moustache—"wants me 'ome for lunch. So if it's all the same with you, I'll be back tomorrow to finish up the patch job on the washing machine. Then I'll do me sums and see if I can't come up with a price to suit."

"Yes!" I was caving in under the weight of the babies and my own folly.

"Lady, you need a new pump."

"You're the plumber!"

I'd stopped him in his tracks.

"Seems to me, Missus, you need more than a new pump." His good eye swerved away from me, but not before I caught a glimpse of pity. The next moment he ducked down, picked up the newspaper and whirred through the pages, then finding what he wanted, he folded it over and shoved it in my hands.

"There, Missus, do yourself a favour and read the column on top page sixteen. My Moll did and it's changed our lives. She's a different woman and I'm twice the man I used to be. I've started sending 'er flowers and a thank-you card the morning after. Cheerio and best of British."

And off he went without a backward glance, through the door, down the steps, and across the courtyard to his van, which he boarded in a single bound, for all the world as though pursued by some madwoman who had mistaken him for a burglar.

I closed the door on a glimpse of the van hurtling down the gravel drive, past the cottage where cousin Freddy lives, through the wrought-iron gates onto Cliff Road. And I am ashamed to say the nasty thought crossed my mind that if he went over the edge, he would never get to have a laugh with the Missus about the grouch with the pouch. Rolling the newspaper into a cudgel, I wished Ben were here this minute, so I could whop him over the head for not shouting up at me that he had let Mr. Bludgett in on his way out. As for taking a look at page sixteen, I'd be blowed if I'd do anything of the sort. An advert for iron pills I did not need. Dr. Melrose already had me taking so many my mouth tasted like a foundry. Besides, why in the world would I harken to the advice of Mr. Bludgett, a crackpot plumber who raced home for lunch at eight-thirty in the morning? The Missus must have quite a way with fish paste sandwiches.

There I stood, knowing the twins were dozing, and suddenly it was as though the hall lost all sense of familiarity and became a chilly antechamber in one of the great cathedrals. The twin suits of armour standing against the staircase wall became St. Rufus and St. Raoul. Buried under the flagstones would be dames like me—women who had spent their lives chasing dust and were now dust themselves. A place where all doors lead to the confessionals. If I were to kneel behind the grille, what would I say? "Help me, Father! In the blink of an eye my babies will be grown and I will be a grey-haired woman colliding in this very hall with a handsome stranger who introduces himself as my husband. 'How do you do, Mr. Haskell. Didn't we meet once years ago? Perhaps we can get together to renew the acquaintance over a glass of wine and a romp under the covers? And please don't get me wrong, I don't usually do this sort of thing on the first date in twenty years but . . .' "

The Daily Chronicle fluttered from my grasp. And when I grabbed for it, I found myself glued to page sixteen.

BEDDED BLISS

Want to put the lust back in love? Our village of Chitterton Fells is gripped by a new craze which threatens to turn wives into vamps and husbands into sex objects ready to flee the boardroom for the bedroom in answer to the siren call of black satin sheets and Peach Melba Love Rub. Police constables are abandoning their beats and bus drivers their routes in order to rush home for five minutes of stolen pleasure with their wives.

The goal of Fully Female is to enable every woman to fulfill her physical, emotional, and sexual potential. Clients are urged to participate in all phases of the program. These include

Working Women Workouts, Heart Happy Holistics, and Retro Relaxation. At Marriage Makeover, participants discuss such compelling issues as when they discovered they had a G Spot . . .

Abbey stirred in her pouch before I could finish the article. "Load of twaddle," I murmured, stroking her silk hair, the colour of barley sugar in the sunlight, which darted like Tinkerbell about the hall. "Mummy would be a complete nincompoop to phone up this Fully Female." But even as my lips did the talking, my legs did the walking over to the trestle table up on the dais. With a bit of luck, Directory Inquiries wouldn't be able to provide the number.

Efficiency will be the downfall of this country. The telephone number was promptly supplied. Frankly fearful, I dialled the number and began counting the burps. Seven rings and I would hang up. No one need ever know that I had momentarily embraced the archaic notion that Man is Head of the Household.

Brrrp, brrrp.

Heaven help me, what might I be getting into? A ghastly vision filled my mind—me on a stationary bike, called a Sexercycle, pumping away for dear life while my face broke out into a map of broken veins and my exploding heart yearned for the good old days before we all started killing ourselves keeping fit. Who was I kidding? There have always been nutty females.

"Mummy, why can't I grow up to be a galley slave like big brother Ethelwolf?"

Brrrp, brr . . .

Chapter Two

"Good morning, Fully Female here."

The snooty-tooty voice nabbed me as I was about to hang up. I could picture the speaker as clearly as if she had been flashed before me on a screen. A super-efficient mannequin in fashion spectacles, wearing a smile that clipped on like a bow tie, and blessed with more arms than an octopus, capable of juggling a dozen phones at once.

I gave up lying, the way people give up cigarettes, when the twins were born, but every so often I weaken and tell a major fib. "Sorry, wrong number," I mumbled.

Instant retribution. The straps of the twin pack were cutting into my flesh and Abbey kicked out a foot, getting me below the belt.

"Who were you dialling?"

"Uhhhmmm—"

"Signing up is the hardest part, dear."

"But I don't want—"

"I quite understand, Mrs. . . . ?"

"Haskell." Bother! Talk about giving the name away! Now I'd be on their mailing list. A pair of pasties would arrive in the mail; Ben would get curious and I'd have to tell him they were eye shades.

"Fully Female is very soft-sell, Mrs. Haskell."

"That's nice."

"If you would be so kind as to spare a few moments to answer our questionnaire, we will send you free of charge our heart-shaped Do Not Disturb sign to hang on the bedroom door when your mother-in-law visits."

An offer no red-blooded Englishwoman could refuse. "Well," I hedged, "if it won't take too long. I have four-month-old twins who want their breakfast."

"Busy Lady, our forty-five minute beauty routine, could be a life-saver, Mrs. Haskell." A rustle of papers, then: "Ready for question one?"

"I . . ." What was I getting myself into? Already I felt like a prisoner, bound hand and foot by the telephone cord, unable to move a finger to hang up. I, who am the sort of person who tries to find euphemisms for "making love," was about to be trapped into talking about nitty-gritty stuff like peekaboo underwear and multiple orgasms.

"Question One: Are you as much in love with your husband as the day you married him?"

Resignation surged through me. "I'd like to make an appointment."

"One o'clock this afternoon. You won't be sorry."

Famous last words. I was sorry the moment I hung up, even without benefit of a crystal ball. At that moment I felt I had the weight of the world on my shoulders, which wasn't too surprising since the twins were growing by leaps and pounds. Who could I find to babysit that afternoon? Freddy was my only hope. He was always off on Mondays, and despite his madcap, motorcycle ways, he was surprisingly wonderful with Abbey and Tam. Even so, I hated palming off my responsibilities. And then there were the nappies to wash, the kitchen windows to wash, and my hair . . . there weren't enough hours in the day.

Fortunately, inadequacy tends to empower me. Glaring at the suits of armour, I snapped, "To work, you lazy louts! There is brass to be polished and floors to be scrubbed." Bother! Couldn't I have waited to remind myself at least until I had fed the babies?

MY AUNT Astrid, who never lifts a finger to butter her own toast, let alone make her bed, is a great believer in the efficacy of making lists. Seeing my day set out in black-and-white exhausts me, however. I prefer conning myself that I'm a junior housemaid who will be dismissed without a character if X number of jobs aren't completed in X amount of time. The trouble with this method is that occasionally I outfox myself. That particular day it completely slipped my mind that this was, in a manner of speaking, my day off. For on Mondays Mrs. Roxie Malloy came to help out at Merlin's Court. She typically arrived at whatever time suited her fancy, so there was nothing unusual in her not having been on hand to give Mr. Bludgett the third degree.

Mrs. M is quite a personage. We became acquainted at my wedding reception, where she had been hired to hand round the champagne. And very conscientious she was, too, taking a slurp from each glass to make sure there were no slops on the crisp white doilies. Admittedly, it is wrong to judge by appearances, but the word Madam suits Mrs. Malloy better than it does me. Maybe it's her hair—jet-black with two inches of white roots. Or the plaster-of-paris makeup. Or the beauty spots that make her look as though she's recovering from a bout with the Black Death. Whatever, on that first meeting I suspected her of moonlighting in a house of ill repute, the sort of genteel establishment where the gentlemen always take off their shoes before getting into bed and leave the appropriate tip for extra-special service. But I couldn't have been more wrong. Mrs. Malloy had confined her favours to three, or it may have been four, husbands and adhered to a strict moral code—no boozing before work. When she took me on as a client—strictly on a trial basis, you understand—I discovered that she had more hats than the Queen Mum, owned at least four fur coats—parting gifts from the hubbies—and was given to sequins and taffeta frocks with plunging necklines.

By ten o'clock on the morning in question, I had the babies settled in their playpen in front of the kitchen fireplace. I had already taken one of the quickest baths in history, swigged down a cup of cold coffee and flipped on the telly, which was presently seated on the ironing board because I'd had to move it from the working surface to make room for the basket of washing.

The screen flared to life, becoming the front window of

Tinseltown Toyshop. On came the familiar musicbox jingle, and I pushed away all thoughts of the dreaded interview with Fully Female, my day instantly brightened by the sight of Norman the Doorman hanging up the Closed sign on the glass door.

"Highly educational!" I informed the twins. "It will put you way ahead of the pack in prenursery school." What a shame. My darlings were too busy playing with the beads on the playpen to gurgle a comment for or against.

Norman opened the shop door and held it wide. "Why, bless my spectacles, just the people I was hoping to see. My favourite boys and girls. A little bird told me you would be popping by . . ." A cockatoo with scarcely visible marionette strings fluttered onto Norman's braided shoulder and sat preening and batting his eyes through spectacles just like the Doorman's. "I've had a bit of worrying news. Word from the grapevine . . ." In the toyshop window a smiley-faced potted vine with leaves for hair and bunches of grapes for earrings began hopping and bobbing. "Word is that a little girl named Annabelle Fandangle hasn't been treating her toys properly. Who wants to come with me and rescue them?" Norman cupped a hand to his ear, and Mr. Cockatoo fanned an encouraging wing.

"Count me in!" I pumped a fist in the air.

Mercifully the twins missed seeing me make a fool of myself. They were snuggled in the middle of the playpen, terry-cloth rumps in the air, sleeping the peace of God's little lambs.

"Splendid!" Norman tipped his cap at the camera, revealing a head as bald as Humpty Dumpty's. "But before we step aboard the magic escalator, let's recite The Tinseltown Toyshop Motto in your best big voices. Ready, set, go!"

Seated on a corner of the kitchen table, legs swinging, I forgot all about being a parent and became a child again.

"Teddies and dollies,

Stuffed rabbits too,

All have feelings,

Like me and you.

Don't leave on the floor,

Nor out in the rain,

Lest dear old Cuddles

You don't see again."

"Brings tears to the eye, don't it?" I hadn't heard the garden door open to admit Her Mightiness, but there stood Mrs. Malloy. Unbuttoning the leopard coat that looked as though it had been ironed on the wrong side, she thumped her supplies bag down on the china cabinet shelf, to the annoyance of Tobias Cat who was there taking a snooze.

"Who the hell does he think he is, the Chat of Persia?" This was one of Mrs. M's standard quips; her second—or it could have been third—husband had been from the wrong side of the Channel, as well as the wrong side of the blanket, and had left her naught but a smattering of *parlez-vous Français* when he abandoned her for another.

Scrambling off the table as if caught on the headmistress's desk, I switched off the telly and looked wildly around at the chaos. "Heavens! Are you sure you're meant to be here?"

"This is Monday unless someone's been tampering with the calendar."

The grim reply should have warned me that Mrs. Malloy was not her usual merry self but I was too busy stacking up the breakfast dishes to look for nuances. Having friends catch me on the hop doesn't bother me. But Mrs. Malloy, never! I always have a whip round before she sets her high-heeled foot in the door. I feel I've let her down if she doesn't find the house the way she left it—the pile vacuumed off the carpets and the windows buffed spotless with newspaper and her fool-proof cleaner. A mixture of gin and the secret ingredient—*It*.

"If you don't need me, Mrs. H, say so." Mrs. Malloy stood by the ironing board, coat still on, holding her feather hat in her hands as though it were a church collection plate.

Offend Mrs. M and her hourly rate tends to go up. "Of *course* I need you."

The washing machine had been pulled out from its cubby hole at a crazy angle in the room, along with the dryer, which Mr. Bludgett in his wisdom had also disconnected. His tools were strewn on the table along with the breakfast dishes. The newspaper lay tossed on a chair, the sink was full of soaping nappies, and the broom leant against the pantry door as if taking five minutes out for a cigarette break.

The babies alone would pass inspection. Daisy-fresh in their terry-cloth suits appliquéd with bunnies, they were awake, faces pressed to the bars of the playpen, their coppery hair a match for Ben's collection of jelly and blancmange molds.

"Sorry about all this!" I gave the nappies a stir with a wooden spoon (not the one I use for soup). "Why don't I straighten up in here, Mrs. Malloy, while you get going in the study?"

The token protest wasn't forthcoming.

"Suits me, Mrs. H." She sidestepped Tobias, who was buttering up to her on account of the feather hat, picked up the supply bag and tottered on her four-inch heels past the playpen without a sideways glance. Peculiar. Mrs. Malloy had developed a sneaking affection for the twins, whilst still insisting she'd prefer a canary.

Wasn't she feeling up to snuff? Shaking my hands free of suds, I dropped the noose of an apron over my head and began tying the strings. Mrs. Malloy turned back from the hall door.

"Remember, I don't do ceilings, Mrs. H."

If Michelangelo had taken that tack, where would we be? Never mind. Her face told me there was more here than keeping me in my place. The beauty spot above her damson mouth was all atwitch and her pancake makeup looked ready to crack at the seams.

Reaching for the kettle, I said, "How about a cup of tea before getting started? And there's some of that cherry cake you like."

"I'd as soon get going." All the spark had gone from her voice. And her bosom, which would have done double-duty as a flotation device were she ever lost at sea, heaved. But I felt a little reassured when she changed the subject. "By the way, I saw Mr. H as I was getting on the bus. He was outside the post office."

"Really?"

"Chatting away with Miss Gladys Thorn."

"Was he?"

"Never say I didn't warn you! That woman would lie back and give the V sign to anything in trousers. You know it was her what caused the break in my marriage to François."

Before I could proffer sympathy, Mrs. Malloy's leopard coat twitched out the hall door. But at least I knew why she was out of sorts. As for Ben . . . did it say something about the state of our marriage that I could not work myself into a froth over his being seen with Miss Thorn? Our church organist's sexual magnetism was legendary—the more so because the women couldn't explain it and the men wouldn't. In a rare idle moment, I had toyed with the idea that Miss Thorn might be one of those Plain Jane secretarial types who to save their Cary Grant bosses from some fate worse than death—usually another woman—whip off their spectacles and unloose their hair. But somehow that didn't work for Miss Thorn. I'd seen her without her glasses with her mousy locks stirring in the breeze, and it was a reminder that Mother Nature is not always kind.

After picking up Abbey and Tam, cuddling them for a bit, then resettling them, I got busy with the nappies. They would have to be hung out to dry in a hurry if I wanted to miss the rain which, from the way the lilac bushes had begun shivering and the clouds glooming overhead, might not be far off. And this had started out as such a picture-perfect day.

The great thing about housework is that your hands scurry about like moles, leaving the mind stuck in the same old place. I tend to get some of my best worrying done at such times. One bugaboo on this morning's agenda was, needless to say, Fully Female. For the life of me I couldn't think why I'd made that appointment. Admittedly, the meeting with Mr. Bludgett on the stairs had brought home the realisation that life at best is short and we had better make the most of it, but did I have to rush into self-improvement? Surely by the time I was ready for a complete revamp, science would have come up with all sorts of shortcuts. Such as, The-More-You-Eat-the-More-You-Lose Diet and Armchair Exercise.

Piling the rinsed nappies into the basket, I dropped in a

handful of pegs and switched over to Mrs. Malloy's problem. Was I jumping the gun in assuming the blight was Miss Thorn? Spotting her on the street couldn't be anything unusual. Chitterton Fells is a small place. Could the trouble be something as simple as losing at bingo last night? Or might Mrs. Malloy have had bad news about her health? Oh, the evils of drink! Was her liver now paying the price or ... perhaps her heart? Who would have thought it! Despite an occasional unsteadiness on her pins, she always seemed so robust. At nearly twice my age, she could run rings around me with the Hoover. Pity the burglar Mrs. Malloy met on the stairs.

Sighing at the memory of my poor showing in the face of Mr. Bludgett, I was overcome by one of those mad urges to rebuild my body in five minutes. Gritting my teeth, I contemplated pushing the table back against the wall and doing some aerobics; then I remembered that walking is believed to be one of the best forms of exercise. Before pegging out the washing, I would jog briskly down the hall to the study and give Mrs. Malloy the newspaper for cleaning the windows.

"Mummy won't be a moment." Leaving the babies lying on their tummies, sleepily chewing on their blanket, I crossed the hall to the study. Its door is one of those round-topped oak ones, studded with heavy nails, that you know must have been taken from a dungeon about to be modernized. The ring handle creaks with the turning and sometimes the door jams, so that you have to give the old heave-ho to get it to budge. Inside is a small room with latticed panes set into deep sills. A dreadful oil painting of an Irish wake looms above the fireplace. But I am a great believer that every house should have its share of eyesores or everything gets lost in perfection. The study has another blooper—a hospital-green gas fire, installed donkey's years ago because the chimney smoked.

Wedged in the doorway, the newspaper in my hands, I said, "Sorry to burst in on you, Mrs. Malloy."

How embarrassing! I felt such a snoop. She wasn't hard at work buzzing around the room with the Hoover or scattering ornaments with her duster. Still in her leopard coat and feather hat, she was slumped in the easy chair by the gas fire, arms trailing, neon lids closed.

"What is the matter?" I dropped the newspaper in a flutter of pages and rushed toward her, cracking my hip on the desk in the process.

"Mrs. H," she said, her shoulders heaving, "I've come to the end of me rope."

"Don't tell me I'm out of Johnson's Lavender Wax again?"

"I can't go on in this hell-hole."

"You don't mean that!" Dropping on my knees, I grabbed her hand. Her perfume, Tequila Sunrise, rocked me on my heels and made me choke up. "Mrs. Malloy, you can't let it end like this. I'll do anything, give you anything!" Frantically, I looked around for something to press into her hand, some piece of family silver that did not need cleaning.

Her eyes cracked open and the butterfly lips fluttered into a sad smile. "Mrs. H, you mustn't blame yourself."

"But I do."

"Flatter yourself, don't you?" Mrs. Malloy straightened up, her voice strengthening to its usual rasp. "My working for you one day a week don't mean you own me body and soul."

"I never thought anything so feudal." Outraged, I stood up, almost putting a knee through my apron.

"You may be queen of the castle up here at Merlin's Court,

Mrs. H, but the world spins all on its ownsome without you giving it a poke."

"You said something about a hell-hole."

"Life, Mrs. H."

"Oh!"

"If I choose to kill meself, that's *my* business."

"Quite." In the relief of hearing she wasn't handing in her notice, I didn't quite grasp the horror of what I was hearing.

"Mrs. Malloy—Roxie, dear!" My eyes zeroed in on the hospital-green monster. "You weren't going to use the gas fire?"

"Ever know me to take liberties?"

"Never!" I lied.

Her sigh blasted me halfway across the room. "I'll have you know, Mrs. H, I'm of legal age. No need for parental permission norways an excuse slip from the boss."

"But why?" Standing there wringing my hands like the village idiot, I watched as in ghastly slow motion she lifted the supply bag from the far side of her chair and cracked open the catch. Oh, my heavens! She had pulled out a gun. Between the gaps in my fingers I watched her raise it to her temple.

What sort of a monster was I? At that moment my mind escaped to safer ground. I thought of the nappies waiting to go on the line and the threat of rain. I pictured Abbey and Tam alone in their playpen. If only one—or both of them—would start crying. That sound might break the spell.

"Why?" Mrs. Malloy asked, and it took a moment to sink in that she was echoing my question of a lifetime ago. "Why take me farewell bow at Merlin's Court?"

I tried to say *Why do it at all?* but I couldn't get my tongue around the words. She was buffing the gun on her cuff. "No need to say nothing, Mrs. H. It's as plain as the nose on my face you think I've overstepped meself. And there was I, hoping you'd take it as the compliment intended. My house on Herring Street's not a bad place to live, but when it comes to breathing me last, I'd always had me heart set on something classier. Somewhere with a bit of history."

A sob in her voice, Mrs. Malloy laid the gun down, just out of grabbing distance, on the arm of her chair. Opening up the supply bag, she pulled out a black-edged hanky and dabbed her eyes. Daintily. So as not to smudge her mascara. "Mrs. H, we've had our differences, but there's not one of me other ladies I'd want with me at the end."

"Thank you."

The hanky fluttered to the floor. "Is it too much to hope that one day me portrait will hang in the upstairs 'all?"

"I'll have a mural done."

The trick was to stay calm. What good would it do to grab for the weapon and risk blowing off my fingers in the attempt? A mother cannot function with hands turned into boxer's mitts. My best bet was to try to dissuade her from making a fatal mistake.

"Mrs. Malloy, why kill yourself?"

"That will go with me to the grave."

"Well then, how about a nice cup of . . . gin?"

Martyred smile. "One for the road? Better not. Never let it be said I wasn't in me right mind when I handed me earthly treasures into your keeping."

"What?" I sank into a chair that wasn't there and had to grab for the desk.

Rummaging in the supply bag, she produced a china poodle and a brass Aladdin's lamp. "No need to fall over yourself in gratitude, Mrs. H! Earlier, when I was downing the second bottle of tablets, I said to meself, 'Roxie, old chum, there's none will look after your bits and bobs like her at Merlin's Court.' "

"Tablets?" Thank God this was washday! With luck I could use the rubber hose attached to the sink as a makeshift stomach pump.

"Don't get your knickers in a twist." Mrs. Malloy looked miffed enough to take back the statue of David she had fetched from the supply bag. Poor chap, he was missing one of his earthly treasures. "They was me indigestion jobbies."

Oh, what a relief it was! Young David joined the china poodle and Aladdin's lamp on the end table. Should I preach the sanctity of human life or ladle on the guilt? *How can you desert me, Mrs. Malloy, in the middle of spring cleaning?*

"Are things really that bad?" I sidled toward her. "Why, only last week you were on top of the world because your horoscope predicted that the man of your dreams was about to enter your life."

The worst possible thing I could have said. A moan erupted from the depths of Mrs. Malloy's being. Her feather hat trembled.

" 'E came, me Romeo! But ours was a love doomed from the bloody start." Picking up the gun, she nursed it tenderly against her leopard bosom, as if it were the fruit of her loins, born of his love.

"There'll be someone else," I consoled, with all the triteness I could muster.

"When you're on the lying side of fifty, Mrs. H, men aren't thick as flies on damson jam. These last few years, most nights I've gone to bed alone and woke up alone. What kind of life is that for a woman who's had more husbands than you've had hot dinners? In me young days I was never your sort,

Mrs. H—glad to settle for being in a rut, married to the same chappie till kingdom come. But now . . ." A sigh that rattled the collection of inkwells in the glass-fronted cabinet.

My goodness, I thought, remembering Miss Thorn. Romance would seem to be rampant in Chitterton Fells. How I wished Reverend Foxworth were here. "There's that passage from Leviticus," I stammered. "The one about a time for every purpose under heaven. And don't forget the seven years of plenty and seven years of famine. Could this be your time to lie fallow?"

"What?" She drew up her furry shoulders so that she resembled the king of the beasts in his royal ruff. "What the bleeding hell do you take me for—the Virgin Queen? I'm not made of stone, you know. I'm a Woman In Love."

"And he's married . . ."

"In a manner of speaking."

"Horoscopes always leave out the juicy bits."

"The wretch left him years ago. Just upped and walked out one foggy winter's night. My angel still can't talk of it without turning white as a ghost. The old story. He found a note on the mantelpiece. And wasn't one of them Hallmark cards, I can tell you that."

"Didn't care enough to send the very best!" Awful of me to be so flippant, but for the first time since this nightmare started, I was beginning to think this was all a storm in a teacup. So long as no one got shot. Mrs. Malloy gave the gun a buff with her furry cuff and laid it on her lap. Savour the moment. Do not consider the possibility that it might be one of those trigger-happy models ready to go off if she crossed her legs.

"If the wife is out of the picture . . ." I ventured.

"Out of sight don't mean out of mind." Mrs. Malloy's rouged cheeks quivered and her eyes grew misty under the neon lids. "For some reason he can't forget her. I tell you, Mrs. H, I've done me bloody best to shut him out of me heart, but it's no cop. From the moment—a fortnight Tuesday—when our eyes met across the crowded bingo hall, I've known me fate. In all England or out there in the great blue yonder, there's none but Walter Fisher for Roxie Malloy. Life's not worth a salt twist in a packet of crisps without him. When Walter is near, I feel forty again. Me whole body goes snap, crackle, pop."

Jealousy, mingled with a bitter-sweet sadness, flamed within me for a moment, only to be quenched by the name Walter Fisher. Why did it ring a bell? A doleful bell.

"Mrs. H, he's come over two or three nights . . ."

"For dinner?"

"On business. He's been talking to me about . . ."

"Yes?"

"Prepaying me funeral."

"You don't mean . . . ?" But of course she did! Her Mr. Heartbreak was none other than Chitterton Fells's one and only funeral director and embalmer. I'd met the gentleman a few years back when he came to offer his condolences, along with a bill for services rendered, on the occasion of Uncle Merlin's interment. Extraordinary! The man was such a weedy chap. Mr. Walter Fisher seemed as unlikely a sex object as . . . Miss Gladys Thorn.

Lost in thoughts of Walter, Mrs. Malloy ignored my dumbstruck amazement. "Always the perfect gentleman, Mrs. H."

"Darn!"

"Never so much as a hand on my knee. And then last night when I'd unbuttoned me blouse—just the top ones, on the off chance—he started talking about *her*. Mrs. Fisher. To hear him you'd think the woman was a saint. Never a cross word. Always bright and bubbly. Always laughing. Isn't it enough to make you spit?"

"Absolutely. Makes a lot more sense than killing yourself." Torn between sympathy and irritation, I closed in on her, hands locked in prayer. "Come on, Mrs. Malloy, put the gun away. I'll make us a nice cup of tea and we'll try and figure how to reel in Mr. Fisher."

Blast! So far this had been a hellish day. But enough is enough. Already the babies had been left so long they had probably outgrown the clothes they were wearing. Without a "Pardon me," I stepped up to the mat and plucked the gun from Mrs. Malloy's knees in the same way I would have taken a rattle from Abbey or Tam.

If looks could kill, I'd be needing Mr. Fisher's professional attentions myself. "No need to mince words." She huffed onto her four-inch heels. "You don't mind me doing meself in, so long as it's not in your house on your time. A pity them tablets was only for indigestion. Any minute now it could all be over. Me eyes would roll back in me head and me knees would do the limbo bend. Well"—mighty sniff—"beggars can't be choosers. I'm off to throw meself over the cliff."

"Not if I have to pump a few rounds of sense into you."

Shocked to the core, I looked down at my hand, the one pointing the gun at my faithful daily, as if itching to put another notch on my belt. I didn't believe this. What would I say to Ben when he came home tonight and asked what I had done to keep busy? This had to be a bad dream, although it felt more like a bad western. Right on cue, the desk clock struck high noon. When the last note shivered into silence, Mrs. Malloy teetered on her high heels, then slumped back in the leather chair.

"Oh, my God, I've shot her!"

Impossible. There had been no sound, unless . . . could this be what is meant by a deafening blast? And to think how recently I had been sweating the small stuff. All that nonsense about whether or not to keep my one o'clock appointment with Fully Female. I was a murderess. I would spend my children's formative years in Holloway. I put the gun in my apron pocket and approached the corpse. On the count of three, I darted a touch at her dangling arm. Oh, my God! Her feather hat slid sideways, falling on the floor like a bagged bird, and at the same moment . . . the eyes of the corpse opened.

"Promise me," she rasped.

"Anything!" She was alive!

"Make sure I'm buried in me plum taffeta with the sequins and me sealskin stole—you'll have to get it back from the cleaner's. And one more thing . . . Tell Mr. Walter Fisher to eat his heart out when he closes me coffin lid."

What a crazy world. What a crazy day. I hadn't shot Mrs. Malloy, but it said a lot about my state of mind that I thought I had. Apparently Jock Bludgett had been right when he said I needed more than a new pump. Mrs. Malloy certainly needed more help than I could give and there was no time to lose with the clock ticking on like a bomb and the babies to be fed.

"Mrs. Malloy, don't move."

Racing out into the hall, I skated across the flagstones, took a peek into the kitchen, blew Abbey and Tam a kiss, got goo-

goos in reply, dodged back past the gawking suits of armour, and without pausing to regulate my breathing or shuffle my thoughts into a neat pile, picked up the telephone and dialled one of the few numbers I know by heart.

Answered at the third ring.

"St. Anselm's vicarage." The wary voice belonged to Mrs. Pickle, Rowland's daily.

"Emergency!" I shouted. "I must speak with—"

"Just a mo."

Silence, then a clunk as she laid the phone down. Mrs. Pickle takes her own sweet time about everything. She calls it being conscientious. Standing on the dais, treading water like a kiddy locked out of the loo, I pictured her dusting off the receiver and straightening the paper and pens on the table before setting off at a snail's pace, looking back over her shoulder every third step because she didn't like leaving even a telephone caller unattended in the vicarage hall. Might come back to find a couple of church bulletins missing.

Chewing on the telephone cord, I counted out her imagined footsteps going down the hall. The muffled thump of a door closing. Then all was swallowed in deadening silence. Would Mrs. Pickle have quickened her pace had I given my name? Remembering Jonas's idea that she was sweet on him, I could have kicked myself. The minutes dragged on and I began to long for the music that had been piped into my ear during my phone call to Fully Female. But Mantovani was not in my immediate future.

Voices crackled in my ear. Naturally I assumed Mrs. Pickle had unearthed Rowland from his study, but disappointment was only a screech away.

No clue as to the identity of the screecher. But a man—who

wasn't Rowland—spoke, not into the phone, but obviously close by, in one of those whispers that have more carrying power than a shout.

He was answered in screeching accents by a woman who was not Mrs. Pickle. Would Mrs. P have left a divorcing couple cooling their heels, if not their tempers, in the hall? Never! Besides, that scenario didn't work. What I had tapped into sounded more like an untoward meeting than the grand finale.

"This has come as a nasty shock." The man's voice blew in my ear like a rush of chill air through a ventilator. "It won't do at all, you know. For twenty years I've thought myself safe from your wanton ways."

"Does this mean you're not thrilled to see me?" The female voice vibrated on the verge of hysteria.

"Enough! In the name of what we once shared, I ask you to vacate these premises."

"Not until I have spoken to your wife."

"Never. You're not worthy to enter the same room as that saintly woman. If you try, I'll take whatever steps are necessary . . ."

"Gladstone, how can you be such a cad?"

Fade-out, leaving me trapped in the place where fact and fiction merge. I could only suppose I had been listening to a keyhole dramatization of the life and times of the great prime minister. A man carved in stone, before ever death saw his statue installed in Westminster Abbey, but whom modern muckrakers suspect of taking more than a political interest in ladies of the night. It didn't surprise me that Mrs. Pickle toted the wireless around while polishing. Heaven forbid that someone abscond with it while her back was turned.

Had the woman forgotten me? How long would she take

to come back and tell me the vicar was nowhere to be found? Glaring at the receiver, ready to chew on it in frustration, I was clobbered by a chilling thought. What if Mrs. Malloy, encouraged by my absence, made a break from the house by way of the window? At this very moment she might be skittering on her four-inch heels down the gravel drive, bent on hurling herself off the cliff edge. . . .

Dropping the phone—my heart as much a lead weight as the gun in my pocket—I was at the study door before I knew how I got there. Shoving it open, I beheld Mrs. Malloy's fur coat slumped across the desk. No need for heart failure—she wasn't in it. A rhinestone clip glinted in her two-tone hair as she stood stuffing the china poodle and other earthly treasures into the supply bag.

"Won't do to ply me with liquor."

"I wasn't . . ."

"Nor kind words neither." She settled the feather hat on her hat, then took it off and handed it to me. "Here, give this to that bloody cat to remember me by once in a now and then. Well, that's it then, except for this."

Numbly, I took the envelope she handed me.

"Give that to Mr. Fisher. I wrote him a poem."

Somehow I knew it wouldn't be anything like the rhymes of Norman the Doorman.

She pursed her butterfly lips, flung out her chest and with hands clenched to her gut, proclaimed in tones that would have won her an audition in a theatre without microphones:

"Sugar is sweet,

Violets are blue,

Red is the blood,

I shed for you."

Tears burned my eyes. "Mrs. Malloy, it's wonderful! You must live to see it published."

Useless! She was headed for the cliffs.

What followed is branded in my memory as one of those larger-than-life moments of truth. Mrs. M went for her leopard coat in the flash-grab manner of a gunslinger going for his holster. At any cost she must be stopped. Grabbing up the newspaper, which I had brought in here with such high hopes that it would be used for cleaning the windows, I moved to roll it into a cudgel with which to whop her senseless if that was what it took to save the woman from herself . . . and along came déjà vu.

I saw myself standing in the hall a scant few hours since, bent on doing the self-same thing to Jock Bludgett. And in a burst of shining joy I knew that were he to come knocking on the door that minute, washing-machine pump in hand, I would offer him a piece of cherry cake, even if so doing did constitute sexual harrassment. Because thanks to the plumber with the Charlie Chaplin moustache and dodgy eye, I *knew* how to lure Roxie Malloy back to life and love.

Look out, Mr. Walter Fisher, Funeral Director and Embalmer. Your horoscope says you are destined to forget the wife who deserted you. Surely by now you have earned the right to declare her legally dead and fall victim to the charms of a Fully Female woman!

Chapter Three

Humbling as it is to admit, I am not the perfect home-maker. When life-or-death situations intrude, I tend to let the housework slide. Ignore the washing machine still occupying the centre stage in the kitchen. Forget the unmade beds and grandiose plans for repapering the pantry shelves. I would resort to my secret hoard of disposable nappies in the airing cupboard, and Mrs. Malloy and I would be off down the Yellow Brick Road to keep my one o'clock appointment with Fully Female. Hadn't that nice woman on the phone said two for the price of one?

Only one problem. Her Mightiness kept putting obstacles

in the way as fast as I could stick spoonfuls of mashed carrot into the twins, who sat in their feeder chairs on the kitchen table, ready to eat the spoon. My heart went out to mother birds everywhere. How do they cope?

"Load of twaddle, Mrs. H."

"Mr. Bludgett doesn't think so. He came to fix the washing machine this morning, got a call from his wife—who's a member of Fully Female—and rushed home for . . . elevenses, as if someone had lit a firecracker under him."

Mrs. Malloy sniffed. "Jock Bludgett always was a horny devil. Everyone knows he did the hokey-pokey with Gladys Thorn."

Would I never cease to be devoutly shocked by the doings of our revered church organist? The lady had been through more men than there are hymns in the hymnal. But from the bombshell hints she had dropped in the past, Mrs. Malloy was in no position to throw stones. Seems true love makes prudes of us all. As does motherhood. I became aware that the twins were all eyes and ears as they sat chewing on their plastic straps. Possibly they were on the watch for the signs that more din-din was forthcoming, but ever ready to read disapproval in those periwinkle eyes, I steered the conversation away from illicit sex to the wholesome, holistic variety prescribed by Fully Female.

"Mrs. Malloy," I proclaimed, "you are a coward."

"I am not." Standing up tall on her stilt heels, she folded her arms, forcing her taffeta bosom up to her chin. "When it comes to pleasuring a man, there's not much I don't know."

"Doesn't do to rest on our laurels!" If I snapped, it was because I'd tested a spoonful of applesauce for hotness by touching it to my lips. When I licked them, they sizzled and tasted of pork crackling.

"Can't teach an old dog new tricks."

"Rubbish." I'd got my mouth unstuck without tearing it. Swatting Tobias Cat off the table, I wiped my hands on my apron and began dolloping creamed rice and applesauce into the Peter Rabbit dish. "Mrs. Malloy, I'll bet you five pounds that by the end of week one you'll have Mr. Walter Fisher jumping through hoops and woofing at the moon."

"Five quid?" She bridled. "How bloody far do you think that'll go toward paying for this f'ing course?"

"For heaven's sake," I said, popping a spoonful of cooled applesauce into Abbey's rosebud mouth, "they're having a two-for-one special." Out of the corner of my eye I saw Mrs. Malloy plump down on her laurels in the rocking chair.

"Won't cost me a penny?" Her face seemed to waver, as if all sorts of emotions were working their way up to the surface; but that could have been because I was in a tug-of-war with Tam over the spoon. "Thanks ever so, Mrs. H, but I don't see as how I can accept." She was back on her high horse. "Don't get me wrong, it's not me pride. As Mrs. Pickle at the vicarage always says, 'A lady keeps her pride in her pocket. She don't flash it around, no more than she'd flash her bare behind in public.'"

I couldn't imagine Reverend Foxworth's daily saying anything of the sort, but then I hadn't believed Jonas when he claimed she was after him.

"And I know, Mrs. H, as how you feel this is the least you can do, after all me years of loyal service. Never a job too big or too tall." She swept a hand ceilingward.

Remembering my earlier thoughts about Michelangelo, I spooned rice into first one beak, then the other. "So exactly what is the problem?"

"Sounds to me as though this Fully Female is for married women only."

"Rubbish. That would be discrimination. Besides, the number of times you've been married, you make me look a rank amateur."

"Well, since you put it that way . . ."

Time to close in for the kill. "They'll beg you to join. You're a far more interesting candidate than I. Think about it. Mr. Walter Fisher is still a moving target, whilst Ben is already . . ." I broke off, shocked by where my babbling was headed. Was that how I saw myself—as the lady huntress who, having bagged her lion, could sit back and fan herself while watching him prowl the cage?

Bother! I'd slopped applesauce down my apron.

On the bright side, Mrs. Malloy was looking happier than I had seen her in hours. Getting onto her high-heeled feet, she rolled up her leopard cuffs, looked at the clock, which said twelve fifteen, and picked up the toaster—in lieu of a hand mirror—to check that every hair and beauty spot was in place. Satisfied, she wound up the electric cord, stashed the appliance in a cupboard, and signalling time was up, put on her feather hat. Poor Tobias Cat, diddled out of his inheritance.

"Let's get one thing straight from the beginning, Mrs. H. If we're to be partners in this passion pit caper, I won't have you making me late for appointments."

Success can be sweet, or it can come in other flavours. At that moment I, who had vowed never to smack my children, could have smacked my employee. Did she expect me to slip on my coat, wave the twins bye-bye, and tell them to fend for themselves until Mummy got home? I was about to tell Mrs. M that I had old-fashioned ideas on parenting, when the garden door burst open and, with the impact of Norman the Doorman arriving to save the day, in strode my cousin Freddy. Good heavens! Why was he dressed up like a horny Viking?

"Hey, cos!" Kicking the door shut with his booted heel, Freddy dropped down on one knee and flung his arms wide. Rooms, along with people, cower when Frederick Flatts enters. He's a six-foot stick of dynamite waiting to blow. "I come at your command, O radiantly disheveled maiden, to bend your ear with verses sweet from Balda Dead."

"What's he cackling about?" Mrs. Malloy, who has yet to learn respect for her betters, turned on me as if I had invented Freddy for the express purpose of making us late for Fully Female.

"I promised to help him rehearse for a part in the play, *Norsemen of the Gods,* being put on at the village hall." Wiping my hands on my apron, I reached down and lifted Freddy up by his ponytail, dislodging the horns in the process.

"Clumsy," he grumbled, as said appendages bounced into the playpen.

"You do know that you're making a complete goat of yourself? Real Vikings never wore those stupid things." Take that, Freddy, for the crack about my appearance.

Me disheveled? The man should look in a mirror every once in a while. Several weeks previously he had shaved off his beard, but he was still very much the vagabond. A skull and crossbones dangled from one ear and the left sleeve was ripped out of his sweatshirt to reveal the tattoo of two locked hearts (presumably his and that of his girlfriend Jill) on his shoulder.

Aunt Astrid in one of her rare attempts at humour once said that Freddy's parents had tried to donate him to the Salvation Army at birth—without success. Such poisoned arrows never made a dent in my cousin's armour, however. The world would learn the error of its ways when he made famous the family name. At one time he had planned to accomplish this as a rock star, but when Lord Olivier died, Freddy immediately felt there was an opening for him on the stage—sort of like an empty horse stall with his name above the door. Knowing that he really did count on my hearing him practice his lines, which I could see bunching out of his pocket, I thought about broaching Mrs. Malloy with the possibility of changing our appointment until tomorrow. But she read my mind and wasn't having any.

"Ready, Mrs. H, or do I return to Plan A?"

Family discord is bread and butter to Freddy. And being a matey soul, he considers Mrs. M a member of our tribe. Eyeing us both, he practically smacked his lips at the prospect of digging into some dirt.

"Ladies, please!" He leaned against the pantry door next to the broom—and really, the resemblance was amazingly strong. "The two of you are obviously up to something. The twins are absolutely agog, on the edge of their seats . . ." He paused to tuck his thumbs in his ears and wiggle his fingers at the twins, who squealed for an encore. "Tell Uncle Freddy. What's this Plan A?"

"Nothing important." Now was not the time to remember that Mrs. M's gun was still in my apron pocket.

"What?" She scorched me with her eyes. "*Not* important when I'm all gung-ho to kill meself over the man of me dreams and you talk me out of it—"

"With Plan B!" Freddy was beaming from ear to ear. "Gosh

darn, Ellie. This is the most fun I've had since I came off my motorbike last week and went floating halfway down the cliff. Come on, tell all to Papa Confessor."

Lifting Tam from his chair and pressing his sticky face to mine, I snapped, "What makes you think—"

"Cousin, dear, I always know when you're up to something. You get that priggish look on your face."

"Bloody hell! Tell him and be done with it."

"Yes, Mrs. Malloy." I handed her Tam and squared off to face Freddy. "For your information, Mr. Nosy Parker, we have an appointment at one o'clock, barely fifteen minutes from now, with—don't you dare laugh—Fully Female."

Freddy's eyebrows shot up like a nosy neighbour's windows. "That place? For state-of-the-art sex? Girls, you can't! They'll be steeping your minds in all sorts of bosh. Lesson one, students dear"—he mimicked a tutorial female voice—"an orgasm is not something nasty growing in your refrigerator." Freddy's grin now threatened to split his face in two. Good, it would save me the trouble! "Does Ben know?"

"Not unless he has ESP."

Freddy took Tam from Mrs. Malloy as if we were playing a game of Pass the Parcel. His face sobered. "You and the boss aren't having problems? You haven't joined the ranks of newlyweds who become the newly deads, have you?"

"Certainly not." Avoiding his eyes, I watched Tam jiggle Freddy's ponytail. "Mrs. Malloy and I thought it might be interesting to do some in-depth study into the marital arts, that's all. We were on the verge of heading out the door when you walked in."

"Right. You were going to toss your pinny in the air, tuck a baby under each arm and go gamboling off—"

"Enough!" I swallowed a mouthful of humble pie. "I had thought of asking you to watch Tam and Abbey, but by the time I got round to it . . ."

"Here I was."

"Freddy, I am sorry about play practice." I finished washing my hands at the sink and dried them on the last of the clean nappies.

"And I'm sorry we're going to be late." Mrs. Malloy rolled down her leopard cuffs, gave her feather hat a twitch, and supply bag in hand, headed for the garden door.

"Freddy, would you really mind awfully?" I gestured to Tam, whom he was still holding, and Abbey still in her chair. Oh, my goodness! My daughter, a fastidious little mite, was making known by a reddening face and puffer train noises that she desired a nappy change. Spit spot.

"Give her here," said our very own Mary Poppins. "Go on, I'll top and tail the pair of them while you doll yourself up for your interview. Can't have the lady of the manor showing up at headquarters looking like Mrs. Muck, can we?"

Stowing Abbey in his arms, I said, "There isn't time. You know where everything is, don't you? Disposable nappies in the airing cupboard and plenty of formula in the pantry, but I should be back way before their next feed." I had unhooked my raincoat from its peg in the alcove by the door and slipped it on as I spoke. "If you should be the least bit worried about either of them, phone Dr. Melrose. And another thing . . ." Bother! Mrs. Malloy was toting me outside by the belt.

"Wave bye-bye to Mummy!" Freddy jostled the babies higher in his arms and flapped one of Tam's tiny paws. "Don't worry about a thing. I'll get them down for their naps, put on my Viking headdress, and read to them about wicked Loki and the lethal mistletoe."

Stumbling backward down the steps, I cried, "What's wrong with a nice fairy tale?"

"Sure! How about Cinderella and the Ugly Sisters hacking off their feet to fit the glass slipper?" Freddy edged the door closed with his elbow.

"Roger," I said and raced after Mrs. Malloy, who was teetering across the courtyard at a breakneck pace. We collided under the archway that leads to the stables where we house the cars—Ben's Heinz 57 crock and the estate car we bought when the twins were born.

"That Freddy!" Mrs. M climbed in the passenger side. "Looks like something the cat coughed up, but he's no fuzz brain, I'll say that for him. I never heard mistletoe was poisonous. Now yew leaves, that's a different matter. Mrs. Pickle's been telling me how some bunch of safety-conscious perverts has been after the vicar to take down the trees in the churchyard. Now that's what I call putting nasty ideas in people's heads."

With Mrs. Malloy rattling away, I drove the estate car at an unlawful pace down the gravel drive, past Freddy's cottage, through the iron gates, and out onto Cliff Road. The sky was the colour of damp blotting paper. It wasn't so much raining as misting, so that the windscreen appeared to be perspiring heavily—as was yours truly. Definitely one of those times when one's deodorant is all set to play either the hero or the villain of the hour. The thought of trying to shake hands with the interviewer at Fully Female with my arms locked to my sides sent me into a spin that brought a breathtaking view of the sea surging up the beach and cascading onto the crags at the base of the cliffs.

"It was an arrow," I babbled.

"What?"

"In the story. Balda Dead, he was killed with an arrow made out of mistletoe."

"Don't break me heart, we all have to go somehow." Mrs. Malloy bounced up in her seat when I hit a rock in attempting to get over to the middle of the road. With her window open, we were within grabbing distance of the hawthorn and honeysuckle bushes which rambled along the right-hand verge of rocky incline, which gave way above to meadows ripe with buttercups and clover. "The way I look at it, Mrs. H, dying is big business worldwide. No one has a monopoly on it, not even the bloody Yanks. And good thing, too, or my Walter would be out of business."

Her Walter? From the sound of it she had high hopes of Fully Female, while I was growing more certain with every flash of road that disappeared under the wheels of the car that I had made the mistake of my life. For starters, I should never have left the twins with Freddy. Remembering his good-bye wave, I was sure there had been something suspicious in his manner, a glint of mischief in his eyes. Surely he wouldn't phone Ben and inform on me? No, whatever his faults, Freddy was not a sneak. But something was brewing. I would swear to it.

"Mrs. H, we are already two minutes late."

"Oh, dear! And if your watch is slow, it could be worse than that. Perhaps we should turn back and reschedule—"

"Not on your Nellie."

Blast! But hope—if it does not spring eternal—does tend to

bubble up like a blocked drain. We could always develop a flat tire, or better yet, realize we had not brought the address of Fully Female with us.

"WELL, HERE we are!" Glowering, I parked the car under a canopy of boughs provided by the copper beach, which rose up from a grassy island in the middle of a ritzy pink drive. My word! Fountains galore and flower beds in the shape of figure-eights, all bordered by mosaics of multicoloured tile. And behind a mesh enclosure a peacock spread his majestic fan and did the royal strut, trailed by a couple of watchful hens in governess garb.

"Don't take much imagination to see why the place is named Hollywood. Built by some hotsy-totsy American in the sixties. Bloody Yanks." Mrs. Malloy's voice held a note of grudging admiration.

Being immeasurably grateful to her for having remembered the address of Fully Female, I didn't burst her bubble by saying the house looked too much like a sacrificial temple for unsuspecting virgins for my taste.

"Can't sit here gawking, Mrs. H, not when someone has already made us fifteen minutes late." She cocked a leg out of the car and I followed her across a mosaic piazza with a dragon-headed seahorse at its center and up the broad flight of marble steps. The wind batted against my legs, giving me the uncomfortable feeling that the hem of my raincoat had come down. I was straining over my shoulder to make sure that such wasn't the case when Mrs. Malloy buzzed the bell. The door opened with such immediacy that we clutched each other like a pair of children caught sneaking downstairs in the middle of the night with Nanny's body.

Most peculiar. No one stood in the doorway to greet us. We stepped into a blaze of white foyer, rising to a sloping ceiling of glass panels separated by stone beams. Directly ahead and two steps down was a living room the size of a football field, decorated in stark modernism with Egyptian overtones. Nubby white couches. Steel tables and free-form sculptures on block pedestals. One wall hanging in particular caught my eye—a floor-to-ceiling sheet of blocked canvas with hundreds of nails punched in between globs of bronze. The sort of artwork nobody expects you to like so long as you appreciate it. The one homey touch was the grand piano standing in a sort of orchestra pit by the glass wall overlooking the terrace, but it looked lost without the rest of the orchestra.

"Must be the right place." Mrs. Malloy looked ready to thump me with her supply bag if I said otherwise.

"You couldn't have made a mistake," I said, my eyes slinking left to a glimpse of kitchen with white laminated cabinets, then right to a wide hall with lots of very tall, very closed doors. "How about . . . ?" I took a step toward Mrs. M, with the unnerving impact of having trodden on the button of a loudspeaker. Instantaneously, a voice vibrated up through the floor to fill the entire foyer.

"Welcome to Fully Female! Kindly take the stairs down to the lower level and enter the waiting room. Please excuse any delay. I'll be with you as soon as possible."

"Well, I never!" Far from being affronted by this disembodied reception, Mrs. Malloy's damson lips curved into a smile. "Must've have used one of the remote control contraptions to open the door."

"Excuse me, where are the stairs?" Pumping my foot, I

spoke to the floor, but got no reply; obviously a bad connection.

"Not standing here looking at us, are they, Mrs. H? But seems to me—what with you being a home decorator by trade—you'd know by the feel of the place where they stashed the stairs."

Thus put on my mettle, like a pointer who's been told not to come home without at least one dead duck, I took three giant steps toward the hall, pressed my fingers to my forehead, turned a half-swivel to my right, and there, tucked behind the foyer wall, was a spiral staircase, its bars intertwined with grapes and leaves, its steps comprised of pie-shaped wedges cut in extremely stingy portions. "Who wants to play Let's Break an Ankle?"

Much to my surprise, Mrs. Malloy and I made the descent without tripping each other up, or rather, down. Upon reaching the spacious lower hall we spared a moment to admire the waterfall splashing down from the inside base of the stairs into a pebbled pool where a nymph sat on a rock catching the cascade in her cupped hands. Everywhere else—to the right, the left, the front, and the back of us—were closed doors. Hark! Music was creeping out from one as if desperate to escape the thumping and stumping that accompanied it. "Aerobics," I whispered to Mrs. Malloy. Far from paling under her rouge, she went into a stomp-and-grind then and there, her leopard coat gyrating so fast the spots blurred.

"Believe it or not, Mrs. H, I was Miss Teenage Twist."

"My word."

"And me gone forty at the time."

"Mustn't loiter," I admonished, and with what I was beginning to consider genuine ESP, I chose the door labelled Waiting Room and ushered Mrs. M in ahead of me.

Splendid! We found ourselves in a white box where a brisk row of chairs lined the wall under the narrow window. A coffee table stacked with magazines stood in the middle and a second door (to the inner sanctum) stared us in the face. After debating about knocking and deciding we wouldn't—or shouldn't, for fear of horning in on someone else's interview— we perched on neighbouring chairs, feet together, hands neatly folded on our handbags. Mrs M looked so smart in her feather hat, her open coat revealing the crisp taffeta of her frock, that I felt like a real dowd.

"Like bloody waiting to go in the confessional." Mrs. Malloy crossed herself, a habit she had picked up from my Roman Catholic mother-in-law, but whether for good luck or in hopes of absolution for swearing, I hadn't the foggiest. I was busy replaiting my hair and licking my lips to give them a little gloss.

"We're waiting as fast as we can."

"Easy for you to talk, Mrs. H. You don't have to go home and cook dinner."

"Wrong. Ben recently got this bee in his bonnet that he was undermining my femininity by bringing meals home from the restaurant."

"Men," Mrs. Malloy said, and we sat in companionable silence for a moment, until I got a bird's eye view—we'd left the door open a crack—of a troop of leotards heading up the spiral stairs. Good heavens! I recognized two of the rumps. There went Dr. Melrose's wife and . . . Mrs. Pickle from the vicarage. Some heavy panting reminiscent of a northeast gale came our way and I knew—with the swift certainty of opening a cupboard door and having a heavy object land on my head—that I had made a ghastly mistake. I didn't have the time, the interest, or the fortitude to rebuild my body from the ground up. This wasn't the place for blushing violets. They would make you take communal showers with your clothes off. And I hardly ever let me see me naked. One makes exceptions for a husband. But a bunch of women, all of them with smaller waists and bigger . . . Already I was breaking out in a cold sweat.

"Mrs. Malloy, I can't go through with this!"

The supply bag trembled on her knees. She was looking up at me like a wounded animal, but I was the one caught in the trap. For how could I balk at sacrificing myself on the altar of her survival? If we walked out of here, Mrs. Malloy would be back to Plan A. Clenching my hands, I sent up a prayer for guidance. A bit of cheek really. Sometimes I worry that I treat God like a distant cousin many times removed, to be remembered at Christmas and Easter, with the occasional reversed-charge call in between.

"Well?" The beauty spot on Mrs. Malloy's cheek quivered and indeed seemed to buzz like a bee about to launch into the air. But before I could respond, the door from the hall opened and in walked a woman all in black, from the draped scarf around her head to her coat, gloves, and sunglasses.

I had been sent my sign. I could hardly go fleeing past this person without causing serious alarm. Sinking back in my chair, I whispered to Mrs. M, "Sorry, the wait was getting to me. This is worse than the dentist."

The woman in black took a chair across from us, and the three of us sat in uncompanionable silence. A couple of times I cleared my throat in an attempt at conversation, but I couldn't get out so much as a "Good afternoon." Those sunglasses spoke loud and clear. Unfortunately, Mrs. Malloy can be in some ways remarkably deaf. She was almost falling off her chair gawking; I wouldn't have been a bit surprised if she had produced an autograph album from the supply bag and gone groveling across the room. The woman is a confirmed celebrity-hound.

"That's not the late great Greta Garbo," I whispered.

"Tell me something I don't know." Her hoarse whisper would have filled a stadium. "That there is Mrs. Norman the Doorman."

"No!" Now I was the one with eyes as big as Frisbees. What an incredible experience: to be in the same room as the wife of my children's favourite TV personality. I had known he was local, of course, but I had never dreamed, never dared hope that I would come this close to touching the cape of the Noble Defender of Tinseltown Toys. "Quick!" I jogged Mrs. Malloy's furry arm. "Pencil . . . paper!"

"Hold your horses." Opening up the supply bag, she produced a toilet roll. "Here, I can spare this. I took a couple from your airing cupboard this morning when I got all teary."

She expected me to beg Mrs. Norman for a signature on toilet paper? Not even a pencil? A lipstick was the best she could produce. Still, beggars can't be choosers. I was stumbling up from my seat, when the door to the inner sanctum opened and out came Mrs. Huffnagle, unquestionably the snootiest person in Chitterton Fells, one of those well-corseted women whose own hair never dares to come unpermed or stir in the wind. Amazing to find her here, cradling an armload of plastic containers and pamphlets as she stalked past without deigning to recognize any presence but her own.

"Barracuda."

I dropped the toilet paper. The words fitted Mrs. Malloy's style of commentary, but the voice . . . Mesmerized, I watched the woman in black slide back her head scarf and unpeel her sunglasses. "Relax, girls. If hoity-toity Huffnagel isn't afraid to show her chassis here, why should we worry?" Raising a well-groomed eyebrow, she smoothed back her ash-blonde hair. Not a beauty exactly, but she possessed a ropy thin chic. Those sleepy eyes had a downward tilt and her mouth an amused twist. "Did either of you bring an extra toothbrush? We are planning on being here overnight, aren't we?"

"It looks that way," I managed.

"Indeed it do!" Mrs. Malloy contributed in her poshest voice. "It has been a frightful long wait. I were just saying to Mrs. H here that it don't make a speck of difference to us. We're nobodies. But a lady such as yourself, well, it do seem wrong, it do indeed."

"We guessed who you were." I leaned forward in my chair. "The glasses didn't fool us at all, Mrs. . . . ?"

"Diamond. Mrs. Norman Diamond."

It suited her. In removing her gloves she revealed enough rings on her fingers to light up a room. "But feel free to call me Jacqueline."

"And I'm Ellie Haskell."

"Roxie Malloy." Snap went the catch of the supply bag. "If I may present me card—all household services provided and I do mean all. Ceilings, gutters, chimneys—you name it!"

I bent to retrieve the toilet paper, but it got away from me and went unravelling its way across the room.

Mrs. Diamond . . . Jacqueline . . . put out a foot to stop it going under her chair and sent it rolling back to me. "You sure came prepared."

Encouraged by this small jest, I babbled, "You can't know what a privilege it is to be in the same room with you . . . I wish I could express . . . But there are no words . . . except to say that my children and I are your husband's biggest, most devoted fans. We hate to miss a program."

"Aren't you sweet! You see more of him than I do."

"Our all-time favourite segment was when he returned the broken toys to Santa's workshop."

"The one where he hung suspended from Rudolph's sleigh fifty thousand feet up? I'll let you in on a secret."

"Such a thrill!" The cutie-pie was Mrs. Malloy.

"At home, Normie is afraid to stand on a chair."

"Would it be imposing dreadfully to ask for your autograph? And if you would be so kind as to sign it Mrs. Norman The Doorman." I bent down after the toilet paper, but didn't get to pick it up. My eyes fixed on the gap in my raincoat and I became totally paralysed. My heart did a flip flop to join the lead weight in my apron pocket. How unutterably ghastly! In rushing to leave the house, petrified of being late for the appointment, I had forgotten to remove my apron. What must the impeccably groomed Mrs. Diamond think of me? And she didn't know the half. The gun! Fool that I was, I could have blown off my knees just bending down to pick up that damned T.P. But thank God for small reprieves. Mrs. Malloy was making a great business of scooping up the toilet paper and putting it away. By the time she had produced a couple more of her cards and presented them, along with an eyeliner pencil, for the coveted signature, I had regained my composure.

"Excuse me, I have to find a loo." So saying, I scuttled from the room, closed the door, unbuttoned my raincoat, whipped off the apron and tried to shove it into my raincoat pocket. No go. I'd have to stash it somewhere until I was through with this cursed interview—should it ever come to pass this side of the grave. The splash of the waterfall beckoned me to the pebbled pool under the spiral staircase. Standing next to the drippy-faced nymph on her rock among the water lilies stood a terra-cotta urn. Neptune be praised! Not so fast—I looked up the well that formed the inside of the staircase and saw a dark scurry of leotards. How embarrassing if anyone should look down and see me cowering here clutching a suspicious-looking bundle! But time was awasting. And life is a game of chance.

I had just dropped in my bundle, getting spattered in the process, and was wishing I were home doing something meaningful like scrubbing the kitchen floor when the waiting room door smacked open. There stood Mrs. Malloy, hands on her leopard hips.

"Couldn't find the lav?"

Blushing a deep terra-cotta, I assured Her Mightiness I had not used the pot for the purpose she suspected.

"Neither here nor there to me, Mrs. H, where you go. Didn't you hear the buzzer? We're being summoned for our interview. I did offer to let Mrs. Diamond go in ahead of us but being a proper lady she wouldn't hear of it. That's how you can tell real class, you know—by how they treat the little people. Cat got your tongue? You look like you've come over queer."

"I'm nervous."

"Piddle. You've got *me*."

"But Mrs. Malloy," I said, as she took hold of my arm and marched me back into the waiting room. "I had thought it might be better if we went in separately. After all, we will both have things of a personal nature to discuss."

"Any secrets I had from you, Mrs. H, went out the window this morning. When I bared me soul, I hoped it went both ways. *Pardonnez-moi* for forgetting the difference in our stations. Seems I'm good enough to scrub your toilets but not good enough to know the ins and outs of your married life."

Couldn't she have phrased it some other way?

Realizing Mrs. Diamond was lapping up every word, Mrs. M lowered her voice a boom or two. "I'm not saying you haven't hurt me feelings something cruel, but never let it be said I don't know me place—in the back of the bus."

"Oh, don't be such a ninny." My hand on the doorknob of the inner sanctum, I turned to flash a smile at Mrs. Diamond, got a thumbs-up sign in return, and pushed Suffering Sarah in ahead of me. Not so fast. She backed up, treading on my feet.

"When she asks for me married name, I'll say Mrs. Alvin Vincent-Malloy. Me first husband was Albert and the second Vincent so it's a bit of sentiment like."

"Got you," I whispered back.

The *she* who would do the asking was a bubble-haired blonde wearing a black leather mini-dress. Talk about posed for success! She was perched cross-legged on the edge of the enormous desk in a room that looked like a glass house transported there from Kew Gardens with tropical plants intact.

"Good afternoon, Mrs. Hapskill." Ms. Fully Female looked up from the date book she was examining. Her big eyes sparkling, her glossy mouth stretching into a wide smile, she threw out her arms, dropping the date book in the process.

"Ellie!"

"Bunty!" My delight was not unmixed with horror. I had been braced for a stranger. The anonymity of the impersonal. Bunty Wiseman—ex–chorus girl and wife of Chitterton Fells's most prominent solicitor—and I had seen quite a bit of each other for a while. Illegal activities on the part of a white gloves ladies' club had brought us together and we'd had some chummy times. But after said excitement died down, we lost touch. Bunty was busy at the health club and I was busy being pregnant. She and husband Lionel had sent a gift when the babies were born; I'd sent a thank-you note and had really meant to have them over for dinner. But you know how it is.

"That stupid secretary! She wrote down Ellen Hapskill and I never dreamed it was you! For starters I know your name isn't Ellen and . . ." Bunty stopped hugging and held me at arm's length by the shoulders. "To be straight with you, ducky, you are the *last* person I'd have expected to be in need of my services. My clients aren't usually married to dreamboats like Ben!"

I stared back at her, not knowing what to say.

Bless Mrs. Malloy; she could always be counted on to get things back on an even keel.

"Excuse me, am I expected to stand here like a doorstop, or can we get down to business?"

I explained that we were taking advantage of the two-for-the-price-of-one offer.

"Right you are, ducks, let's all get comfy." Long-legged in heels that were even higher than Mrs. M's, Bunty dragged forward a couple of chairs, waved us into them, and perched back on the desk. "There, loves! I'll take it from the top. You want to know how come I founded Fully Female? Well, here goes. You know how people always talked about Lionel and me—what with him being a good twenty years older and me not being up to scratch class-wise. We used to have some good laughs about it. I'd look at those women in their pearls and tweed skirts and think, you poor dopes, you don't know the half of how to keep your men happy. Li didn't give a bloody hoot when I'd flub at cocktail parties. You should have heard him laugh the time I told some bigwig I didn't care for ballet because it wasn't in English. Li said the old fart would trade places in a minute, to slip between the sheets with me. But after a while of living here in Chitterton Fells . . ."

"Spit it out," urged Mrs. Malloy.

Bunty picked up a pencil and twirled it between her manicured fingernails. "After a while I got to know some of those tweedy dames . . . and there was you, Ellie . . ."

"Thanks awfully."

"You get what I'm saying?" A flash of her pearl-pink smile. "I began to see that under their toffee-nosed exteriors and my cockney ways we were sisters after all."

"Anyone got a harp?" asked Mrs. Malloy.

Bunty went on as if there had been no interruption. "It was just that some women never let themselves be *women*. I'd been thinking for some time that it might be fun to go back on the stage and work summers. There's a bloke runs the theatre on the Shipston pier who'd been after me—in more ways than one. Then my hairdresser suggested I teach aerobics and it came to me like a stroke of genius. I'd teach the works. I'd offer a program for women wanting to be Fully Female. Li saw the possibilities right off. We sold The Laurels . . ."

Mrs. Malloy's brow darkened. "Sold it out from under me without so much as a do-you-mind—after all me years of loyal service. That's when I walked out their door, Mrs. H, for the last time."

"Worst day of my life," Bunty said. "I haven't been able to smell Johnson's Lavender Wax since without bursting into tears." Her wink surprisingly wiped the cross look off Mrs. M's face.

"Now where was I? Oh, yes . . . Li was all for my becoming an entrepreneur. He sent me to spas all over Europe and to the States. I studied aroma therapy, vita-nutrition, aphrodisia, you name it, and . . . Bob's your uncle."

My eyes followed Bunty's to a cabinet lined with clear plastic jars such as Mrs. Huffnagle had carried out earlier. "Everyone who signs up for Fully Female uses our diet supplement and herbal beauty aids prepared for us by a clinic in Switzerland. And things are going great, despite the occasional bugaboo. Can't get good secretarial help, as you can tell, Mrs. Hapskill." Wrinkling her cute little nose, Bunty tossed down the pencil she had been twirling, raised her arms above her head, clasped her hands palms upward and stretched. "One of the things we teach, duckies, is to always take time out to remobilize after you've been sitting for a while—no matter where you are, even in church."

"I'd like to see the vicar's face." Mrs. Malloy gave a heathen chuckle.

"Bit of an old stick, is he?" Bunty arched her neck, so that her blonde curls shone golden in the full beam of electric light. "Must be why he's being put out to pasture."

"Oh, but he isn't!" I cried, aghast. "He's a healthy young man." Church would never be the same without Reverend Rowland Foxworth. "Where could you have heard such a thing?"

"From Gladys Thorn, I suppose. You know, the church organist. Which brings us back to what I was saying about office help. Li even suggested I offer her a secretarial job. She's been pitching in at his office since his secretary left. You remember Teddy Peerless? She finally tied the knot with Edwin Digby, the mystery writer. From what Li says, old Glad Bag is a whiz at the typewriter but to be frankly bitchy, she isn't exactly front desk material. I ask you! A woman whose hobbies are bird-watching and collecting telephone directories! Everyone clucks about the mystery of her sex appeal, but if you ask me, it's the con of the century. Even my miracle products couldn't help—"

Bunty was rudely interrupted by the telephone. "Won't be a sec." Reaching out a manicured hand, she held the receiver to her ear. "Li, darling! You've got it, sugar, this isn't a good time but . . . oh, no, don't change things around and come home for dinner. I'm up to my belly button in work. At this very moment I have two women in my office who are considering signing up." She placed a hand over the receiver, eyes dancing, and mouthed, "You are going to join? Pretty please!"

"What do you think, Mrs. Alvin Vincent-Malloy?" I asked.

Chapter Four

In the days of my spinsterhood I fantasized about the Halcyon Hour, that moment gentled by twilight when on the last stroke of six, the front door would open and that sweet serenade would be heard: "Darling, I'm home." Fantasy always found me marinating in a bubble bath, one tempting knee rising from the foam, my Grecian curls spilling from a satin ribbon. Hubby would stride into the bathroom, lay a bottle of champagne in the heart-shaped basin and stand transfixed. "My God, woman, you're lovely! Don't move an eyelash, my sweet. Let me imprint this vision upon my soul for all eternity."

Ben, entering by the back door, found me in the kitchen, up to my elbows in nappy suds.

"Don't tell me you're home!" Accusing eyes on the clock. "You just left." All four walls got splattered as I wrung my hands.

"Glad I took the evening off." Eyes darkening, he looked for a vacant space to toss his coat, but the table was cluttered with remnants of the babies' five o'clock feed and every chair was up to its kobs with folded clothes or bags of groceries. Tossing the coat over his shoulder, he stood, hands on his hips, looking the place up and down. Nelson on his column surveying the pigeon poop in Trafalgar Square. The man had me with my back to the sink.

Swatting soap suds off my forehead, I said, "So, it's a jungle in here."

"Babies cranky?"

Only a coward hides behind her children. "Good as gold and already in bed."

"Didn't Mrs. Malloy show?"

"Yes, but she was feeling poorly . . . and had to leave early." I was bracing myself to tell him that I had gone with her to Fully Female when he began loading the dishwasher. I knew how he hated having his concentration broken during said procedure. Heaven forbid that a cereal bowl might end up in the wrong slot.

"Ellie, don't think I'm criticizing—"

"Perish the thought!"

"—But you might try making lists."

I continued wringing nappies as if they were chicken necks. "I suppose your mother . . ."

"Well, you know Mum—a perfectionist."

"To the death!"

Yanking the plug out of the sink, I listened to the gur-glings—so reminiscent of a person, preferably male, being choked to death. And to think I had been ready to rebuild myself from the ground up in the interests of making this marriage work. Well, no dice. Mrs. Malloy would have to be a big girl and go to her first Fully Female meeting alone. To-morrow morning I would telephone Bunty and . . .

My thoughts came to a screeching halt. I'd gone to wipe my hands on my apron and found I wasn't wearing one. It was back at Bunty's house, wadded up in the clay urn by the waterfall—with Mrs. Malloy's gun in the pocket.

"What's up, Ellie?"

"Nothing."

Dumping the nappies in the wash basket, I looked around the kitchen. What a transformation! In five minutes flat, Ben had rendered order from chaos. Every surface was wiped clean. Foodstuffs were returned to the pantry and the ironing board banished to its cupboard. Not by a grease spot on a shirt cuff did the man betray that he was reduced to being a skivvy in his own home; in his elegant grasp the broom might have been a silver-topped cane.

The smile Ben bestowed upon me would have once turned my heart to pâté. "Why don't I pour us both a glass of white wine before dinner?" His eyes strayed to the cooker, standing wantonly idle.

"Frozen dinners all right?" Crossing to the freezer, I re-moved a tinfoil package. "How do you like your meat thawed, dear?"

It was a moment of such exquisite fragility that it took only a whimper filtering through the intercom from one of the babies to shatter the mood.

"I'll go up to them," he said.

"The steak tartare will be ready when you are." My smile stuck to my face the way the frozen package stuck to my palms.

"Forget it. We'll pig out on cheese and crackers at the Hearthside Guild."

Blast! Ben was out the door before I could explain that the stupid meeting had completely slipped my mind. Surely he could understand there was no way on God's green earth that I could be at the vicarage by seven. Even if Freddy could be cajoled into watching the twins for the second time in one day, I wasn't up to the rigors of making myself presentable for the Reverend Rowland Foxworth. No way could I lose two stone in an hour's time. Ben would have to go on his own, that was all there was to it. As program chairman for the Doting Dads Committee, he'd undoubtedly have such a thumping good time he'd never miss me.

Putting the meat back in the freezer compartment, I spied the Fully Female manual on top of the fridge where I had stashed it on coming home. All the while I'd had it in my handbag I'd felt . . . undressed. Now here it lay, flaunting its black-and-white cover while I went hot and cold thinking that Ben might have seen it and leaped to the idea that I was some sort of pervert. The last thing I needed with the nappies still to hang out was to have him flat on his back moaning "Take me."

But even as I was having these unwifely thoughts, I was flipping the Fully Female manual to Chapter One.

THE MATING GAME

Ladies, are we sitting comfortably on the edge of our seats? Then we'll begin with a little story based on the life of yours truly—Bunty Wiseman. And don't any of you fellow females go getting ideas that this publication was ghostwritten by the chappie who writes those pork belly ads for Hoskins the butcher. These words of wifely wisdom are all straight from the horse's mouth. Now, as I was about to say before I rudely interrupted myself, Lionel Wiseman of Bragg, Wiseman & Smith, Solicitors at Law, married me—a blond bombshell, young enough to be his daughter—while the town's back was turned.

Talk about a modern-day fairy tale! You bet your brassieres it was! I began my stage career as a kiddy dancing on the bar of my Aunt Et's pub, The Pig & Whistle, in Luton. At twenty-something, there I was, kicking up my heels in a dinner theatre production of Tin Can Alley at Gravesend, when one night in strides this bloke who looks like Cary Grant, talks like the BBC, and wears custom-made socks. After the show he comes knocking on the dressing room door. Would I care to join him for a spot of supper? His Jag awaits outside and he names a nightclub where a glass of water costs more than a four-course dinner.

They said it wouldn't work. But we had the last laugh, Li and me. Everywhere we looked someone was getting divorced, while we kept right on living the Arabian Nights fantasy. Then came the day when the gal with the X-rated smile became a woman with a mission.

An acquaintance of mine—we'll call her Mrs. A—cornered me at the check-out lane at Tesco's and poured out her heart. Seems her marriage was in big trouble. Other Woman trouble. And it didn't take a degree from Oxford to see why. Mrs. A hadn't a clue how keep her man's hormones hopping. She'd never owned a black garter belt or peekaboo undies. Sex was something a man needed, sort of like a dose of salts to be dished out once a week on Fridays along with a bath and a clean set of underwear. Poor Mrs. A. She used "those times" to plan her meals for the following week.

Trust me, I was shocked! I hadn't known there were women still living in the Dark Ages, women who still did their big nude scene in the dark. I gave Mrs. A some little tips, one being not to throw away that old electric toothbrush, and she was so well satisfied that she mentioned me to Mrs. B, and before I knew it, I was swamped by women all yearning to be the Happy Housewife.

So what do you think, Fellow Female? Are you ready to trade in that old body for a new one? Are you willing to become the woman he always wanted? Do I hear a resounding yes? Hurrah! Then we begin. Now. At once.

Before you can do nice things for your husband, you have to do nice things for yourself. First, mix yourself a drink. Two tablespoons of Fully Female Formula combined with eight ounces of water or fruit juice . . .

"Ellie?" Ben's voice exploded around me.

"What?" Clapping the book shut, I tried to stuff it under my waistband—completely futile and unnecessary because my spouse hadn't joined me in the kitchen. From the acoustical reverberations, he was yelling over the banister rail.

"I phoned Freddy and he'll be over in half an hour to watch the twins. Isn't it time you were getting ready?"

Something had changed for me in the last few moments. I wasn't suddenly afire with renewed passion. What I felt was a stirring of sweet memory—of the days when the mere touch of his hand was enough to make me long to toss my smalls in the air. I couldn't stand there with the Fully Female manual in my hands and tell him I wasn't going to the Hearthside Guild meeting. It would have been tantamount to saying I was too busy to go to church while clutching a Bible.

"I'll be up to change in a minute," I called, before heading into the pantry. There I shifted aside the flour bin and biscuit barrel as if they were the secret panel to a priest hole and brought out my lifetime supply of packets of Healthy Harvest Herbs and jars of Fully Female Formula purchased during my interview with Bunty Wiseman. With what I had paid for me and Mrs. Malloy, I could have purchased a new body for each of us, but she had said she was sentimental about hers. I rehid the herbs, along with all but one jar of Formula. I mixed my two tablespoons (vigorously, as instructed) until the grainy texture turned glutinous. Ah, fibre! With book and glass in hand I mounted the stairs to the bathroom.

Lesson One, Fellow Female. I want you to think of your bath as a lagoon that you are going to bask in—not a place to boil like a ruddy lobster. That's the ticket, lots of lovely warm water. Now pour in a good slosh of Fully Female Fantasy . . .

By the time I had unearthed bottle of same from the towel cupboard and turned off the taps, my glass of Fully Female Formula had set solid. Should I unmold it on the soap dish and pretend it was a mousse? A finger-dunk taste settled the matter. Toss this one down the toilet and start fresh tomorrow. Sliding into the scented water, I experienced a moment of pure peace as it lapped over my chest. My hair had come down and was floating on the surface. I felt like a water nymph fated to dwell here until Prince Charming came riding around destiny's corner. Was it possible that Ben and I could rediscover the old magic?

Reaching out a soggy hand, I picked up the manual and continued reading where I had left off.

Submerge, mermaid. Feel the movement of the water as you shift beneath its warm weight. Let it roll with you. Let it mold itself to your body until the ripples become his hands caressing your moist flesh . . .

"Ellie?" Plaintive voice at the bathroom door.

The mood was broken. My hand came sloshing down on the groping bathwater, sending a six-foot spray hurtling toward the ceiling. *Plonk* went the book to the floor.

"What now, Bentley?"

"Where are my good socks?"

"Your what?"

"The ones Mum knitted for my birthday." The door cracked open, then closed again as if he feared the worst—a flannel in the face or the news that I had put the socks in the drier and something bigger and woolier had gobbled them up.

"In the usual drawer."

"And what about my taupe striped shirt?"

"In the ironing basket."

"Ellie, I have begged you—*pleaded* with you—not to put my shirts in the basket! Is it too much to expect you to hang them up?" Footsteps stomping down the stairs.

Emerging from the bath as wrinkled as the damned shirt, I faced facts. I had a lot of chapters to go in this Marriage Makeover and—if my watch wasn't telling bald-faced lies—about fifteen minutes in which to ready myself for the evening soiree. Decisions, decisions! Should I French braid my hair or make do with a quickie knot? Could I spend the entire evening with my cheeks sucked in, while maintaining a flow of social repartee?

Rap rap on the bathroom door, but thank heaven for small

mercies. It was only that *homme horrible,* Cousin Freddy, whose voice filled the silence left humming when I unplugged the hair dryer.

"Mary Poppins reporting for duty."

Hands trapped in my hair, which fell down faster than I could put it back up, I pictured him leaning against the door, perhaps wearing his Viking horns, a gleam in his eye, and a gloat to his lips.

"Favour for a favour, Ellie, old chum. Understand you were rushed when you got back this afternoon, but do spill the beans. How was your session at the sex clinic? Anything deliciously ribald to report?"

"Shut up, Freddy," I said, wrapping myself up in a beach towel, "I have no intention of discussing any of this with you, except to say that . . . should you happen upon any jars of Formula in the pantry, they are not for the twins."

"An aphrodisiac, eh?" His voice, thrilling to every syllable, crept up behind me as I was hiding the Fully Female manual behind the toilet tank. "Word from the wise, old dear, they can be kind of dangerous."

"What could be dangerous"—I glowered at the door— "would be your saying anything about this to Ben."

"He hasn't suggested you sign up? The whole town is buzzing about this thing."

"Not a word." Removing a hair clip from my mouth, I paused for a moment, wondering why Ben hadn't said boo.

BEN AND I motored in his car, a vehicle of uncertain parentage, along the ridiculously short distance of Cliff Road to the vicarage. Wheels spitting up gravel, we roared into the churchyard, sending a scurry of birds into twittering flight among the cowering tombstones. St. Anselm's church came at us in a rush of bell tower and stained glass. The interior was lit up like a Christmas tree.

"Ben, do you think we're to meet in the church hall instead of the vicarage?"

He didn't answer. An instant before hitting either of the cars already parked on the narrow path that looked as though it belonged inside a maze, he swung the Heinz 57 left, through a two-inch gap in the shrubbery. We ground to a halt on a stretch of crazy paving, with a birdbath hunched in one corner.

Ben's hand went to his throat.

My sentiments exactly.

"Damn tie! Makes me look as though I've gained ten pounds."

Of all the insensitive clods! I froze him with the sort of stare my Aunt Astrid bestows on anyone who laughs at her jokes before she gives the nod. "Have no fear, Bentley, my darling! You look radiant as always."

Switching off the ignition, he clenched his manly jaw. "I worry that I have bitten off more than I can chew, in agreeing to be program chairman. You're sure this tie strikes the right balance between responsible leadership and fellowship?"

"Perfectly." With all due duplicity I hadn't the foggiest idea whether he was wearing paisley or stripes. While I had fought my way into my clothes, Ben had blocked the mirror, looking for all the world like a Regency dandy left to tie his own cravat because his valet was smitten with the pox.

"Ellie, I'm also having second thoughts about the speaker. Have I violated the ethics of my position in making a unilateral decision on tonight's topic?"

"Perhaps if I knew the identity . . ."

"Of the speaker?" My trusty program chairman gripped the wheel and shot up in his seat. "I am not at liberty to tell you that! Not ahead of the other members. To do so would be to indulge in as nasty a bit of nepotism . . ."

And for this I had abandoned my darling babies? Disembarking, I slammed the door and was brought up short by my raincoat belt . . . and the sight of a figure bolting down the steps of the church, which was now—as befitted a Monday night—steeped in darkness. A hurry-scurry of footsteps coupled with noisy sobs. And in the flare of light from the open car door I beheld the gaunt figure of Miss Gladys Thorn. Her arms embraced a shuffle of papers, some of which had been caught by the wind and whirled about her head like disembodied white-gloved hands, biffing and bobbing. Pathetic creature! Her lank hair broke free from its clips. Her spectacles were askew. Behind the thick lenses her eyes bulged like mushrooms.

"Why, Miss Thorn, whatever is the matter?"

She heard me not. Blind to my presence, the imperiled one threw back her head and howled at the moon, then cast herself upon Ben, who was hovering a few feet to my right.

"Mr. Bentley Haskell! Thank God you're here."

"Pleasure, I'm sure." Sounding uncannily like my Uncle Maurice when asked to vacate the Ladies Room at Harrods, Ben made a masterly attempt to unbuckle his knees and stand up straight. Not easy. Miss Thorn, being the taller by many inches, hung over him like a felled tree.

Loud sobbing. More papers escaped from the hatches of her elbows to fly in the wind.

"Oh, hapless me, Mr. Haskell. Never in the sweet years of my youth did I dream so grievous a misfortune should befall me."

"Surely this is a matter for the vicar?" Arms pinned to his sides, Ben sounded in desperate need of an immediate tracheotomy. Was he, like me, suspecting that the lady was with child, courtesy of one of her many swains?

Miss Thorn released him with such force that he slammed into me, almost sending us both into the herbaceous border.

"*Speak* to the vicar!" Her face stretched the length of a tombstone, etched with mournful sentiment. "Be advised, Mr. Haskell, I shall never again speak to that creature! That monster in clerical duds! Let me go unshriven to my grave! It matters not!" Here Miss Thorn clasped her knobby hands to her breast and let loose a throbbing moan.

"By Jupiter!" Ben, who had given up taking the Lord's name in vain when the twins were born, evinced profound shock, tempered with glee. "Are you telling us, Madam, that the Reverend made unseemly overtures?"

Intriguingly, Miss Thorn looked quite shocked by this suggestion. "I should hope not! Never let it be said I am that sort! No indeed. The upstart informed me about fifteen minutes ago that my services as church organist are no longer required. Can you believe that, Mr. Haskell? After all these years of bashing out hymns on that worm-eaten instrument, I am cast off, or—to use the vulgar parlance—sacked!"

"Oh, Miss Thorn," I whispered, "I'm so sorry."

"Too . . . too kind." Wrenching a handkerchief from her coat pocket she buried her twitching face in it. "I come from the choir loft. None shall accuse me of theft, I trust, when all

I took were my own sheets of music. Dear Mr. Haskell, how gripping the compulsion to cast myself o'er the parapet! But, alack, I do not have a head for heights and could not mount the steps to the bell tower."

"Did the vicar offer a reason?" To avoid sneaking a second glance at his watch, Ben placed his hands behind his back, out of temptation's way.

She raised her fogged glasses to his face. "Some trumped-up story about my being seen frequenting one . . . of . . . those places."

"The Dark Horse?" I ventured.

"No, not a pub." Miss Thorn shook her mousy head, sending a spray of Kirby grips to the four winds. "The Methodist Church. As if I am capable of such a defection, having seen my sister banished from the familial home for entertaining Wesleyan sympathies. A hedonist, my Daddy called her."

"Meaning, perhaps, a heathen?" Ben suggested.

"Oh, deary me, no!" Miss Thorn sighed gustily. "Daddy invariably said what he meant and meant what he said. He used to call me his rose without a thorn. You get the humour, Mr. Haskell?"

"Indeed."

"And he called my brother a 'skirt,' because he liked to cook."

Ben winced. But this harkening back to the good old days proved too much for Miss Thorn. She collapsed once more against Ben, who in slow motion brought round his hands to support her. Above us the moon nosed out from behind the clouds like a bloodless Peeping Tom. In the groping dusk the vicarage shifted a few paces closer to us, as if eavesdropping too. From every corner of the churchyard came the dark rustling of the trees, and from far off came the sly murmur of the sea.

"Miss Thorn, is there anything my husband and I can do?" I reached into my coat pocket, thinking to lend her my hanky, but pulled out a nappy instead.

"How sweet; industrial size." Taking it, she mustered a heroic titter. "You are too, too kind, but only I can pick up the shattered pieces of my life. The Lord be praised, I do have my bird-watching and my collection of telephone directories to occupy my time . . . and the affection of a certain gentleman. His name, not to make a mystery of it"—a demure lowering of the eyelids and a coy lift to the lips—"his name begins with W."

Oh, knickers! Instantly, my eyes became glued to her face, as if by some force of will I could draw the *nom de l'homme* from her lips the way a snake charmer lures the serpent out of hiding. Surely Miss Thorn's swain wasn't . . . couldn't be . . . Mr. Walter Fisher, undertaker extraordinaire, he who had stolen Mrs. Malloy's heart?

BEFORE MISS Thorn was halfway down the drive on her way to catch her bus, Ben had managed to make our being a good ten minutes late for the meeting entirely my fault. He thumbed the vicarage doorbell; its gentle chimes added disharmony to discord.

"Ellie, if we had left home on time, we would never have collided with that woman, and if you hadn't been so damned sympathetic—"

"Me?" I screeched like an owl. "Almost every remark she made was addressed to you—*dear* Mr. Haskell."

Hush! At the sound of stirrings within the vicarage, we

wiped the scowls off our faces and clapped on a pair of the phoniest smiles you would ever wish to see. Precipitously, as it turned out. When the door didn't open, Ben punched the bell again.

"Jealousy ill becomes you, wife."

I started to say that he was talking utter rubbish. Me, jealous of Miss Thorn? That would be the day! But a little voice deep inside whispered that he just might be right. And far from feeling horribly cornered, I felt a stirring of excitement. Was it possible that I was already feeling the effects . . . reaping the rewards of my Fully Female novitiate? Could it be that I was destined to fall in love all over again? And even supposing the wonderful happened, would my feelings be reciprocated? Staring straight ahead, I prinked in the door's glass panel. My French-braided hair looked nice and the chilly night air lent a flush to my cheeks and darkened my rainwater eyes. But I mustn't get cocky. Easy enough for a headshot to pass muster. The full-length version is another matter. Bother! Why hadn't I brought a bigger handbag? This stupid thing wouldn't cover my belt buckle, let alone anything else.

"Damn!" Ben lifted a fist to pound on the door, but managed to control himself. "I should have brought along a book to read."

The words were scarcely out of his mouth when a face blurred the glass a split second before the door opened, rocking me back on my heels. A sense of unworthiness came at me in a rush, like a dog who had been lurking in the twilit hall. What would Reverend Foxworth have to say about my missing Sunday service these last few weeks? Would he buy my explanation about God preferring quality time?

"Good evening, Mrs. Pickle." I spoke without thinking,

without seeing, programmed by other visits to expect the vicarage daily to do the honours of admission.

"Sweetheart"—Ben resumed his pose of devoted spouse—"I know I'm not wearing my glasses but . . ."

Say no more. The woman eyeing us from under neon-painted lids was not Mrs. Pickle, but our very own Mrs. Roxie Malloy. A scarlet organdy apron added a splash of colour to her black taffeta ensemble with its rat fur collar.

"Mr. and Mrs. H, what a treat!"

This was tantamount to going to get my teeth checked and finding the dentist in the chair. Following Ben into the hall with its twisty turny staircase, porridge wallpaper, and chocolate-brown radiators, I said, "Mrs. Malloy, I had no idea you worked here. What happened to Mrs. Pickle?"

"Don't tell me you haven't heard!" Her voice rich with reproof, Mrs. Malloy bumped the door shut with her rump.

"Dead?" Ben had given up euphemisms, along with saturated fats, when the twins were born.

"Now you know me, Mr. H, I don't do drains, I don't do chimneys, and I don't gossip." The butterfly lips were sealed.

"She's . . . pregnant?" I backed into a portrait of the Archbishop of Canterbury. "At her age? Why, she must be close to seventy!" The absurdity of the accusation dawned, but then again we are forever reading about such things in the scandal sheets . . . and the Bible. Just look at Sarah! All those chaps patting Abraham on the back and telling him he'd never be bested in the Guinness Book of Records, while his poor wife was coping with night feedings at ninety.

Mrs. Malloy scoffed a laugh. "What, Edna in the family way? You must be joking. Her Albert's been gone thirty years. And if a man so much as put his hand where he shouldn't, he'd be singing soprano in the boy's choir. Anyone but old Jonas that is; Mrs. P's had a crush on him since she was a young chick of fifty. Ah well," she said, checking herself out in the hall tree mirror, "since you've twisted me bra strap, I'll tell you . . ."

"Yes?" I prodded. Ben was eyeing the closed door across the hall. From the murmurings wafted our way, the meeting of the Hearthside Guild was in full swing.

"At six-thirty-seven this evening, Edna Pickle threw down her apron and walked out."

"Left Reverend Foxworth?" I couldn't take this in. "There must be some mistake. She was devoted to him; no polish was ever good enough for his floors, no starch ever crisp enough for his collars."

"Where've you been living? In an igloo?" Mrs. Malloy folded her arms, forcing her bosoms upward, so that they resembled a pair of balloons bound to pop at any moment. "The Reverend Mr. F moved on to greener pastures yesterday afternoon."

"Gone, without so much as a good-bye?" The picture of the Archbishop of Canterbury was tilting at a crazy angle.

"You got it, Mrs. H: a parish in Kent, from what I could make out from Edna. Horribly sudden it was. But that's bishops for you. Always getting too big for their mitres."

The ground had gone out from under me. I had to clutch at Ben to keep myself steady. No more Rowland. Surely there was something sacrilegious in the concept. The St. Anselm's pulpit would never be the same. Was this God's way of punishing me for poor attendance?

"What brought this on?" Pacing the frayed strip of carpet, Ben did the asking.

Mrs. Malloy patted her two-tone hair and assumed a repressive mien. "I keep me suspicions to meself."

"Not," I quaked, "money missing from the collection plate?"

"Ellie, get a grip on yourself." My husband proceeded to unbutton my coat as though I were a rag doll. "The chap was integrity itself. Remember how he tried to ban the pool some of the parishioners got up before the twins were born?"

"Yes," I whispered, dizzy from being spun around for the removal of my scarf. "Dear Rowland gave that wonderful sermon—the one about the money lenders in the temple, but to no avail. They still laid bets on the sex of the babies. And now the bishop has found out about the gambling and in a fit of ecclesiastical fury banished that saintly man to the wilds of Kent. Ben, this is all my fault, and I quite see why Rowland could not bring himself to say good-bye."

"There, there ducky," Mrs. Malloy said with unwonted gentleness. "Why don't you go in and have a nice chat about all this with the new vicar?"

Replaced so soon! I was lost in a whirlpool of remembrance . . . my wedding day, the twin's christenings, and those many other luminous occasions enriched by Rowland's presence. Would I ever again smell pipe tobacco without recalling how his cassock breathed that sweetest of all incense?

"Change is the name of the game." Ben hung our coats on the hall tree.

"You've said it, Mr. H." Mrs. Malloy tugged at the bodice of her frock so that the requisite amount of cleavage showed. "First Mrs. Pickle gone and me playing understudy. Then Miss Thorn—she gets her marching orders! Better than a box at the opera it was. Such a caterwauling she made! And while I've never been overly keen on Miss Thorn, I don't mind saying that new vicar has made one bloody big mistake. There won't be a man in church next Sunday, they'll all be outside picketing."

Entirely possible.

"No time for tears. Duty calls." Giving her cranberry apron a flounce, Mrs. Malloy headed for the kitchen while I followed my husband across the hall to the sitting room. So many memories behind that closed door. Rowland had been my first friend in Chitterton Fells and now I must face the new vicar. Truth be told, the word *usurper* sprang to mind.

I barely had time to hitch up my smile before entering that book-lined room. All was the same, from the monk brown sofas and striped wallpaper to the towering grandfather clock, the worn rugs and picture of Rippon Cathedral above the fireplace. No, not quite the same. Silk poppies sprouted from the vase on the bureau and the odds and sods in the curio cabinet had been replaced with what looked like Waterford crystal.

Ben, in his role as program chairman, was not focusing on the furnishings. Instead, he was toting up the members of the Hearthside Guild present and reaching the inevitable conclusion that whichever way he counted, they still numbered only four. Dr. and Mrs. Melrose and, yes, over by the window sat Jock Bludgett, the shifty-eyed plumber, and his better half, the siren who lured him home from work, leaving my washing machine high and dry. I could see Ben was taking the poor attendance hard. As for me, the sparsity of the group was a dubious bonus. It made it impossible to miss the most obvious disruption of the old order.

Standing before the fireplace, a teacup poised on his palm,

was your stereotypical vicar. A balding man, slight of build, stooped of shoulder, whose nearsighted eyes peered wistfully upon the vagaries of this world through a pair of wire-rimmed spectacles. Beside him stood your made-to-measure vicar's wife. A pillar of the church. Her iron-grey hair of the sort that does double duty as a hat. Her beige twin set and houndstooth skirt made clear she would do a masterly job of organizing the summer fête and the Christmas bazaar. She would introduce weekly altar cloth bees and . . . she had seen Ben and me.

She touched her husband's arm. "We have some new arrivals, Gladstone, dear."

"Ah, lovely." He smiled his blessing upon us from the hearthrug, while I felt the floor shift under my feet. Gladstone! Why, this had to mean that when I phoned the vicarage this morning to seek counseling for Mrs. Malloy and overheard what I thought was a radio program about the great prime minister, I had been sadly mistaken . . .

"Good evening, Vicar," Ben gushed. "I'm Bentley Haskell, Program Chairman, and this is my wife Ellie." Normally I would have given him a discreet kick in the shin for ignoring the vicar's wife, but I was only vaguely aware of the startled look on her face. My mind had gone gallivanting back to Gladstone's words to the woman I had pictured as bonnetted and shawled, with a scarlet letter on her brow:

"In the name of what we once shared, I ask you to vacate these premises."

And her reply:

"Not until I have spoken to your wife."

I was brought back to the moment by the vicar's eyes on my face. His gentle smile had dimmed.

"I am not the vicar."

"You're not?"

"*I* am," said the wife.

Unable to meet her husband's eyes, mine flickered downward, and I saw that what I had taken for a clerical collar was but a white polo neck worn under the grey cardigan. Futile to blame the vicar for wearing civvies.

Good heavens! This was akin to being pushed onto a darkened stage and finding oneself an actor in a Victorian melodrama. From the audience—I mean, the other members of the Hearthside Guild—came chortles at my bumble. But who in this quiet hamlet could have suspected? A female clergyman! St. Paul would turn in his grave. The congregation would go on strike over this, even if they did not take up their picket signs on Miss Thorn's behalf. My brain stopped whirling and took a couple of steps forward and three back. Miss Thorn! Was she the woman from The Past? Was the vicar's husband another notch on Miss Thorn's black lace garter belt? Were old secrets and old sins about to take up residence in this house which heretofore had known no worse than an occasional puff of tobacco smoke and discreet glass of sherry? And which of them— the vicar or her husband—had dismissed the church organist on the trumped-up charge of being a back-door Methodist?

"I am afraid I have been teasing you," the reverend lady smiled. "I am not a fully fledged vicar. I'm a lowly deacon sent here until a permanent *male* replacement can be found for Reverend Foxworth."

"You don't know St. Aselm's," I replied. "To us you will be the vicar in thought and probably name."

"Something to drink?" asked Mr. Gladstone Spike.

Suspicion reared its serpent head. Rowland had not frowned

on the occasional glass of Oh Be Joyful, but the new incumbent might have more exacting standards of sobriety. The Melroses gave nothing away. Neither was partaking of liquid refreshment. They stood by the harvest table holding hands—or, I should say, Mrs. Melrose, tonight wearing a sack dress that made her look more than ever like a female Friar Tuck, was holding the doctor's hand. Hmmmm! What had we here? Far from appearing his usual sanguine self, Dr. M's expression was reminiscent of mine when greeting him from a supine position with my feet in the stirrups. Neither of the Bludgetts was holding a glass. They were standing so close it was hard to tell which was wearing the Charlie Chaplin moustache. While I stood gawking, Ben asked for a glass of wine.

"Whatever you have in the cellar." He exuded affability until I spoke up, having determined better safe than sorry.

"Have you forgotten, Bentley, that we've given it up except at Communion?"

He kept a grip on his smile.

"We'll take tea," I informed our hosts.

"Milk, no sugar, if you please." My husband measured out the words as if they were ground glass to be stirred into my cup.

As for the vicar, I had no idea whether I had scored points with her or not. Her smile was as neutral as her mode of dress. Would even the advent of a rival for her husband's affections ruffle her finger-waved hair?

"Mind doing the honours, dear?" she said, addressing her spouse. "And how about the cake? Our new brethren will find they haven't lived before sampling your chocolate madeira."

See the nice man blush.

"Gladstone's cakes always took First Place at the summer fête when we were at St. Peter's in the Wode. Let St. Anselm's cooks beware." Now the vicar's smile embraced all present, especially, it seemed to me, the Bludgetts, who bashfully emerged from their own little world. Even so, my Aunt Astrid would have ordered their immediate excommunication, public flogging having been abolished.

Woe to he who lusts after another man's culinary success. With elaborate indifference, Ben prowled over to the table where Gladstone Spike now had the silver teapot well in hand. Black brows fused, my husband subtly sized up the competition posed by the chocolate madeira cake. Joined by Dr. Melrose, he accepted a floral cup and saucer and stood watching the wistful drift of steam go spiralling upward.

"The smallest sliver of cake, if you please," I heard him say, adding that the evening's speaker was due to arrive at any moment. The inference was that the concentration required by a big piece of cake might cause him to miss the grand arrival, thus putting the kiss of death on the evening's proceedings.

What did one talk about to a lady cleric? I hovered in her shadow, pleating my bag strap until she made things easy for me.

"Please call me Eudora."

"And I'm Ellie."

"I understand we are neighbours." She had large, slightly protruding hazel eyes and I caught in them a flicker of the same surprise she had shown when I first entered the room.

"Yes!" I put my bag down on a chair and tried not to notice

when it fell with a plop to the floor. "We live at Merlin's Court. You can see the house from this window, which of course makes it absolutely dreadful that I missed church the last three Sundays, and I am not nearly dedicated enough to the Sewing Circle or the Friends of St. Anselm . . ." I paused, drew a shaky breath, and was amazed to find how much better I felt.

Correctly interpreting my smile, she said, "Helps to make a clean breast of things, doesn't it?"

"It certainly does."

"Which is why I hope to reopen the confessionals here at St. Anselm's. There will be objections, I am sure, and cries of popery, but I intend to make waves."

As Miss Thorn had found to her cost? But I couldn't worry about that lady or lament that dear Reverend Foxworth was gone from my life. This room was aglow with the breath of life, the promise of new beginnings. For the first time in months I felt the stirrings of my old vitality. If Mrs. Eudora Spike could take on the male-dominated Church, then surely I could work at one marriage. What was it the Fully Female manual had said? *Light his candle and make love till you feel the burn.*

I turned my eyes to Ben, ready to begin now to feast upon his maleness, to caress his dark good looks with my eyes, my hungry breath . . . but Mrs. Melrose chose that moment to put a cup of tea in my hands. And I couldn't say I was sorry for the intrusion. I had forgotten how exhausting desire can be.

"You two ladies have a nice chat." Eudora left us to catch up with the rest of her flock, who had wandered away to the other side of the paddock . . . I mean, the room.

From a distance I hadn't noticed anything particularly different about Flo Melrose—other than the way she was cosying up to her husband. But standing next to her, I was startled by the new woman. The Friar Tuck hair had a bounce to it and the once doughy cheeks possessed a peachy blush. Even more startling was that the doctor's wife wasn't wearing a stitch under her sack dress . . . not so much as a fig leaf. You could tell from the flounce of her bosoms and the way the material grooved to her generous proportions.

"Gained weight by the looks of it." Flo roared the whisper in my ear.

Heretofore I had quite liked the woman. Flo Melrose was the least snobbish person I knew. She would take a blind person across the road whether he wanted to go or not, and she had been there for me when I failed my Lamaze course. But I wasn't about to take her comment with a simper.

"Wrong, Flo. I have not put on weight. I am one of those unfortunates who can never gain an ounce." That was no lie, for I always go up in increments of five pounds. Deep sigh. "If you only knew how sick I get of chugging down those milkshakes."

Her hearty laughter joggled my teacup. "Get off your high horse, Ellie. I wasn't talking about you. I meant Ben. Those extra pounds look good on him. They've turned him from a yearling into a full-grown buck who's earned his antlers."

I stared from Flo Melrose to my husband in disbelief. Certainly he was forever standing before the mirror, sucking in his navel so that it touched his spine and bemoaning that his belly was going to pot. But who could take him seriously? Perhaps he had gained some muscle, but what man worth his steroids could complain about that?

"Ellie, I would like your Ben to model for me."

"What?"

"I've taken up painting again."

"Wonderful."

"Nudes." Mrs. Melrose stood there, blatantly shaping the air with her hands while she stripped Ben down to the bare bones of light and shadow. "Ellie, three weeks ago a splendid thing happened to me. I joined Fully Female. Now, for the first time in my life, I am in touch with my own sexuality. At age fifty-two I finally see beauty in buttocks. I want to emblazon them upon canvas . . ."

At that propitious moment the door opened and Mrs. Malloy, with the glow of the evening star in her eyes, ushered in our speaker for the evening. Good grief. I didn't know whether to laugh or ram Ben's piece of chocolate madeira down his throat. This weedy chap with the face of a haddock was Mr. Walter Fisher, the undertaker!

"My most abject apologies, ladies and gentlemen." He bowed, folding in two over the briefcase he clutched to his pin-striped middle. "Just as I was leaving the house I was called out on a job. A Mrs. Huffnagle, taken from us while in the bath. Another case of the accidental immersion of an electrical appliance."

Oh, my heavens! That haughty matriarch who had swept past me in the waiting room of Fully Female this very afternoon! It seemed such an impertinent death—to be frizzled by a hairdryer or . . .

My eyes met those of Flo Melrose and Mrs. Bludgett with whom I had not yet shared a word. Some words don't need to be spoken. They hum in the air. They vibrate. From the way Mr. Fisher said electrical appliance, I knew the ghastly truth.

Through a gap in the chocolate-brown curtains I glimpsed the moonwashed tombstones growing wild in that garden of death. What would be the epitaph on the imperious Mrs. Huffnagle's stone?

An alligator didn't ate her.
She was done in by a vibrator.

Chapter Five

W hat an evening, Mrs. H!"

"All right for you to talk, Mrs. Malloy," I rounded on her as she pranced into the kitchen on the morning after the Hearthside Guild meeting. Lifting Tam from the high chair, I pressed his sticky face to mine. "My whole life is a lie!"

"If this is one of them born-again confessions, I say wait until the new vicar cuts the ribbon and officially opens the box."

I ignored Tam's tugs on my hair. "Contrary to public opinion, I am not Ellie Haskell, success story. I'm a woman drowning in tears and ... sweat. My deodorant doesn't work, my hair's falling out, my clothes don't fit, and worst of all, I may be going to prison."

Eyeing me as though I were Jack the Ripper in drag, Mrs. Malloy removed Tam from my arms.

"Last week in the village square," I cried wildly, "I was stopped by a woman doing a survey on frozen yogurt. And I lied about my weight. Afterward I nearly phoned our solicitor, Lionel Wiseman, to ask him the penalty for falsification of a legal document, but I was afraid he would tell me I'd get six months, meaning I'd never get caught up with the spring cleaning."

"Mrs. H, are you trying to make a point?"

"Yes." I leaned against the washing machine that was still in the middle of the room. "I am admitting defeat as a human being. Even Fully Female can't help me."

"Rubbish!" Mrs. Malloy finished wiping my sonny boy's face and stowed him in the playpen with his sister who was deep in gurgling conversation with the Peter Rabbit mobile. "What I rushed over to tell you was that you did right, Mrs. H, to drag me along to that place. When I got home afterwards, I did me homework. I read Chapter One of the manual, and believe you me, it opened up whole new vistas. As I was lying back in me bubble bath, sipping me Fully Female Formula, it come to me that Walter Fisher wasn't mine for the taking. I'd have to earn his affections. I'd have to become the docile dove if ever I was to win his heart."

Love truly is blind.

"I've given up the bottle, Mrs. H."

"What? Turned teetotaler?" I could hardly believe it.

"Never!" Mrs. Malloy looked deeply affronted. "That wouldn't do at all—would be against me religion."

"But you said . . ."

"That I'd given up the bottle of indigestion mixture Dr. Melrose prescribed. From now on I'll rely on me Fully Female Formula to keep me insides from corroding." Having finished drying her hands on one of the nappies I had just brought in from the line, Mrs. Malloy's lips curved in a dreamy damson smile. "Wasn't Walter a living doll last night? I tell you, Mrs. H, I stayed up half the night going over them lovely little verses he told us:

" 'Some have children,

Some have none,

But here lies a woman

Who had twenty-one.' "

To each his own. Mr. Fisher continued to remind me of sushi. But, to be fair, I had been so furious with Ben for inviting the man to be the Hearthside Guild speaker, I had done nothing but carp . . . sorry about that . . . from the moment Mr. Fisher opened his briefcase and produced samples of coffin linings.

"Madam Vicar, ladies and gentlemen." He had folded a swatch of white over his arm in the manner of a waiter about to pour the wine. "The ever popular virgin silk."

"My favourite every time. So elegant and yet snuggly soft!" That comment had come from the vivacious Mrs. Bludgett, and it seemed to me that Mr. Fisher had looked coldly upon her.

"Not my first choice, if you will forgive the intrusion of personal taste." Mr. Fisher's mouth had stretched into a frayed smile. "I particularly like a rich look of paisley when we are catering to a gentleman who likes to make an understated . . . statement. And paisley works so well if you want to match the client's tie. Superb with a mahogany cabinet. Then again, for the sportier gentlemen, a Harris tweed lining with matching traveling rug does seem the way to go." Mr. Fisher continued to fold lengths of material over his arm. "We offer either knotted pine or bleached oak with the tweed."

To my annoyance, Ben chose that moment to announce to the room at large and Mr. Fisher in particular that the program was of special interest to me.

"My wife is an interior designer. You find this fascinating, don't you, Ellie?"

"Oh, yes." Before I could stop myself I had blurted out, "What about Victorian tea caddies, Mr. Fisher? I would think they'd make charming cremation boxes." My tongue got all tangled up when I met his cold fishy eyes. But instead of subsiding into wise silence, I blundered on to make matters worse. "Awfully embarrassing if you went to add one for the pot and realized you had spooned in Grandma . . ."

A suffocating silence ensued, during which lifetime I plotted what I would do to Ben when I got him home. This was all his fault. Agreed, it made sense to plan for the possibility . . . the *certainty* of death, but did he have to make a Tupperware party out of the event? Any minute now we'd be playing pencil games for prizes—black-edged notepaper and monogrammed arm bands.

Mr. Fisher gave me a look that dripped embalming fluid into my veins. Tut, tut! Bad for business. He adjusted his rimless glasses to bring me back into focus as a prospective customer. Stretching a smile, he cleared his throat and fetched forth another swatch of white silk, this one patterned with tiny blue flowers.

"Our forget-me-not *peau de soie* is ever the perfect compliment to our Vintage Champagne cabinet. Not for everyone, of course, but lovely for brides and virgins of any age. Our deluxe model has the added feature that when the lid is raised it plays 'We'll Meet Again.' "

A chill fingered my throat. Several heart-pounding moments passed before I realized the culprit was my own hand, not some ghost from the graveyard. Everything and everyone around me from the grandfather clock to the others in the room—the vicar and her husband, the Melroses, the Bludgetts, and Ben—had flattened to silhouettes upon the wall. Only Mr. Fisher was real . . . and yes, Mrs. Malloy standing in the doorway, her face flushed the colour of her cranberry apron, her eyes shining with adoration!

"MY WALTER, what a dream!"

She brought us both back to the present moment, in the kitchen at Merlin's Court, on the morning after. Unbuttoning her purple crushed-velvet coat, she pushed up the sleeves and shocked me by filling the kettle. Tradition had always dictated that I make her a cup of tea. Even Tam and Abbey were amazed. They stopped their rattle wrestle to stare at her with their little mouths open. Mornings generally find me slow on the uptake, but it finally dawned that there were a couple of other incongruities to Mrs. M's arrival. The supply bag had not accompanied her and . . .

Plonking the kettle down on the cooker, she shot the gas flame under it as if trying to heat the house in a hurry. She turned to face me, hands on her purple hips. "Don't fall all over yourself, Mrs. H, thanking me for coming on me day off. I'm a woman who likes to clear her debts and I do owe you for yesterday. You saved me life and that's a fact."

"Why, Roxie!" I was moved almost to tears.

"Yes, well, we don't want to make a Gilbert and Sullivan production out of it, do we?" Switching off the kettle, she made the tea in a cloud of steam and came rattling across the room with cups and saucers. "Now then, Mrs. H"—she hooked a chair away from the table with her foot—"take a load off while I tell you about me night of sin."

"You don't mean . . . ?

"I bloody well do. Mr. Walter Fisher escorted me 'ome from the vicarage."

"No!"

True to form in the shock process, Mrs. Malloy and I reversed roles. I was the one pouring the tea while she settled down in the chair and took off her coat to reveal an outfit stolen from the wardrobe of the lead biker of Hell's Angels. "Now, before your blood pressure goes up, Mrs. H, I'll confess that me sin were letting the man out of me clutches without so much as a good-night kiss."

"But you did invite him in?" I squeezed around the washing machine to shift the playpen away from the glare of the sun striking through the greenhouse window above the sink and rejoined Mrs. M at the table.

"You bet your bloomers I asked him in for a drinky-poo, and you know what the angel man said?"

"What?"

"He'd take a cup of cocoa."

"Enough to warm the cockles of your heart."

Mrs. Malloy leaned back in her chair, folded her ring-encrusted hands on her black sateen middle, and exhaled a blissful sigh. "I tell you, Mrs. H, the sight of Walter sitting on me calf-skin sofa, why it gave me palpitations—someplace other than me heart, if you get my meaning?"

"Quite." I cast an anxious look at the twins. They appeared to be listening to every word, but perhaps that was because they hadn't yet grown into their ears.

"I was that pleased, Mrs. H . . ."

"Yes?" I turned back to her, realizing I had missed something.

"I'd put an orange bulb in me Venus lamp. Such a lovely glow it cast over him. You should have seen his spectacles, Mrs. H, they was like rainbows. Believe you me, I had to remove meself from temptation's way and sit in the easy chair."

"It must have been torment."

"True, Mrs. H, but if you can understand me, it was a blessed pain—a religious experience, to put it bluntly, and I've never been one for bobbing up and down in church." She raised a hand to her black hair with the two inches of white roots as if expecting to find a halo nestling there. "I felt like a virgin again, although truth be told, if I ever was one, I've forgot. Always before the blighter only had to say, 'How about it, Roxie old girl?' And I'd think 'What the hell, if he brings in the coal, why not?' But last night . . ."

"Yes?" I poured her a fresh cup of tea.

"Last night I wanted to do things by the book."

"The Fully Female manual?"

"After I gave Walter his cocoa, I excused meself and nipped in the back room for a peek at Chapter Two. Here"—she produced the book from her coat pocket—"I've found the place:

" 'When a man comes home from the hustle and bustle of his job he doesn't want to be romped over by his wife like she's Rover the dog barking the bad news at him that the cooker doesn't work and the washing line came down in the mud. Come on, Fellow Female, unbutton his coat for him, hang it up, and lead him gently by the hand into the sitting room, which you have turned into his private oasis. The Fully Female woman has arranged fresh flowers in vases, sprayed her best perfume on the cushions, decanted a bottle of wine, lit her prettiest candles, and replaced her hundred-watt bulbs with softly coloured ones . . .'

"Hear that, Mrs. H?"

"Your orange light was preordained."

Mrs. Malloy flipped over a few more pages. "Here's where we get to the meaty part:

" 'According to Dr. Tensel Reubenoff, a quiet woman is like still water. At the end of a long day she awaits her hot and dusty traveller from the workplace. She invites him to immerse in her calm, float in the comfort of her arms, and when the last candle dips below the horizon, she draws him down to those hidden depths . . .' "

"Lovely." I began clattering up the teacups with one eye on the twins. Was my darling Abigail blushing?

"Mrs. H, you know me! I'm not the quiet sort. Not one to tiptoe through the tulips, so to speak. And where did all me feisty charm get me? Buggering nowhere with Walter, until last night when I took a leaf out of the Fully Female manual. There he sat on me sofa sipping his cocoa, and he says to me, "Mrs. Malloy, I *like* this room; it has a restful atmosphere that I rarely find away from the business premises."

"High praise." Gathering both babies up in my arms, I brought them over to the table.

"Walter said I was very different from that Mrs. Bludgett." A demure lowering of the neon lids put me forcibly in mind of Miss Gladys Thorn, former church organist.

"Really?"

"Seems Walter had some business dealings with Mrs. B; not to talk out of school, she and the mister bought a plot on the never-never. And between you, me, and the clothes horse, my Walter didn't take to the woman, called her a jack in the box. A bloody good tip-off, wouldn't you say, that what he has in mind is the blushing-violet type?"

With the twins ganging up to strangle me I could only signal assent with my eyes. But truth be told, I would have thought any woman alive too noisy for Mr. Fisher.

"Chapter one of my love story." Mrs. Malloy rose majestically to her feet. "What about you, Mrs. H? Any progress to report? Did you and Father Bear"—she squinted at the twins—"set the sheets on fire when you got home from the Hearthside Guild meeting?"

"The mood wasn't right." I could feel my face setting in priggish lines. "For starters, we couldn't get rid of Freddy. He was agog to hear all about Mrs. Vicar. And the moment Ben and I did get into bed, Abbey woke up."

"And I don't suppose," she said with a self-righteous smirk, "you've drunk your Formula neither?"

"Not this morning."

"A bloody drop-out, that'll be you, Mrs. H, if I don't put me foot down. You hand over them kiddies and go put your coat on. We'll arrange things so as you do the morning sessions at Fully Female and I go afternoons." A baby tucked under each arm, Mrs. Malloy hustled me toward the door. "Off with you now, and don't disgrace me. I intend to get me cap and gown from Fully Female if it kills me."

"EVER THOUGHT you'd sink this low, ladies?" Bunty Wiseman's voice gurgled overhead as I went down into a deep knee bend ... and decided to stay there. I liked being this short. But I found it wasn't safe. Talk about lethal leotards. The rest of the Fully Female aerobics class had finished warming up and were stomping and bomping to piano music that I recognized as "Old MacDonald" with overtones of "Abide With Me." I had fought my way back to daylight again, when Bunty called a halt.

"Relax those neck muscles, ladies! Loll your shoulders, let your arms go floppety flop at your sides."

The class was being held in the large room on the lower level of Bunty's house, the one from which I had heard gasps and rasps on my interview visit. At the front of the room across from the door was a small platform. There Bunty, a mike in her hand, was stationed, marshalling the troops. To her right, back to the window wall, sat the ubiquitous Miss Gladys Thorn at the piano. And hemming me on all sides were my fellow females. Damsels and dowagers. I counted three octogenarians—all sporting Roman noses and feather-duster hats along with their leotards. How unutterably depressing. I had always counted on old age being the great equalizer. At some point in the dim and distant future, the loveliest and the plainest of us all become much of a muchness. How many breathtakingly lovely eighty-year-old women enter rooms to masculine gasps and the clatter of dropped wineglasses? Trust me to be out of step with the times—as well as my aerobic steps. Kicking out a foot to the left when it should have been right, I got a woman in a cerise-and-silver ensemble in the rump.

"So sorry."

"Don't"—shake, shimmy, lunge—"worry!"

My leotard was too short in the leg and so tight in the top I felt as though I was wearing one of those breast depressors nuns used to wear. But beggars can't be choosers. I had appropriated the togs from the lost-and-found box in the changing room, and the fear of some furious female opening the door and screaming "Who's the thief?" finally got me moving in what I hoped was a blur of arms and legs.

Here a gasp, there a gasp, everywhere . . . Hairpins flew from Miss Thorn's mousy head as she pounded away at her bopped-up version of "Old MacDonald."

"Time, ladies!" Bunty's cry rang out as if this were closing time at her Aunt Et's pub, The Pig & Whistle.

The piano music sputtered away to nothing.

All of me had come to a stop except my heart, which went right on hopping and bopping. Eyes on our leader, the Fully Female ladies stood around like a bunch of ice lollies.

Above us, Bunty paced on her platform. Shoulders back, tummy in, she trailed that mike lead as if she were the Honourable Mrs. Snodgrass walking Peaches the pooch in Hyde Park.

"Bloomin' hell, class, am I ever proud of you! When I was a kid growing up with the toughs and scruffs, all I ever wanted was to go on the stage; and so I did for a while, but I swear this stage right here is the best ever. Up here, I feel like a missionary of sorts. I *know* I can help you change your lives— if I don't trip over this friggin' mike wire or drop my 'aitches' and trip over them. Cripes! What a time to remember my Aunt

Et's warning the day I married Lionel Wiseman: 'Hellocution lessons in't the same as Heducation, so don't you go sticking your nose too 'igh and getting it pecked off by a dicky bird, Bunty, me girl.' "

Laughter.

Scattered murmurs of "Isn't she wonderful!"

A roomful of rapt faces. Talk about idolatry! Anyone would think our leader was a church statue that had suddenly come to life and begun pelting us with rose petals.

I liked Bunty, but let's not go over the top. Miss Thorn twitching on her piano seat was the only one who appeared to share some of my discomfort. A clunk, as she stuck her elbow on the piano, quickly converted into a ten-second medley. I was wondering what the Reverend Mrs. Eudora Spike, would make of all this, when someone whispered, "Shush." Let no one breathe too loud!

"Fellow Females!" Her blonde curls burnished with sunlight, Bunty cupped the mike in her manicured hands as if it were a rose. "Your lives can change forever when you accept the fact that your place is in your husband's arms. Don't get me wrong. This doesn't mean you have to give up being you. Have I given my hair back to its natural colour? Never. But I have given my heart and mind over to my wonderful husband Lionel Wiseman, who has made me everything I am today."

Miss Thorn's hands plonked down on the piano keys, sending a shower of squawking birds—I mean, musical notes—up in the air. Would the woman last the session without being sacked for the second time in two days?

"Most dreadfully sorry!" All atwitter, Miss T rescued her

spectacles from sliding off her nose and sat hunched over the instrument as if expecting to be bombarded with soggy tomatoes from an outraged audience.

"You're doing a lovely job, Gladys," Bunty reassured her. "I'm so glad Lionel suggested you as a change from records. Ladies, how about a nice hand for Miss Thorn?"

Dutiful clapping.

"That's the ticket!" Bunty beamed her twenty-four-carat smile. "Time for Retro-Relaxation, Fellow Females. Everyone please fetch your mats, then lie down and make yourselves comfy."

Embarrassed to the gills, I was about to inch up my hand and confess I didn't have a mat, when the rest of the class came scurrying back into place, leaving one red rubber oblong lolling against the wall. Stepping over the bodies now lining the floor, I introduced myself to the mat and surveyed the room. Not too promising. Rather like searching for available grave space in an overcrowded cemetery. But just when I was ready to take my mat and go home, a pair of eyes looked up at me from the floor, and a voice I recognized as belonging to Mrs. Thirsty—headmistress of the village school—said, "Here, next to me, Mrs. Haskell."

"Thanks. It'll be like parking a lorry in a space reserved for a bubble car, but I think I can manage."

"Hold on a moment and I'll move over." Another voice that sounded familiar, and I found myself looking down into the face of Jackie Diamond, wife of Norman the Doorman. And this was *her* first day too! Amazing how much better I felt knowing I wasn't the only new girl.

"Everyone comfy?" Bunty asked as I flopped down. "Good!

Now I want you all to close your eyes and imagine that you and your sweetie pie are alone in a secret place. A place known only to the two of you . . ."

I lay on my red rubber mat. The sound of her voice washed over me and sunlight crept across my closed lids. The sound of rhythmic breathing became a summer breeze and suddenly Ben was there with me. We were in a rowboat, gliding down a golden river. I was wearing a white eyelet dress and a big shady hat. His profile was dusted with harlequin shadow. Above us the sky had that lovely shimmer you see only near water, and on the banks weeping willows grew, leaning far out to trail their tresses on that gleaming surface of beveled bronze.

My love's shirt rippled in the warm breeze while his muscular arms rhythmically pulled at the oars . . . *clip clop, clip clop* . . . Dreamily, I began to recite from *The Forsaken Merman*. "Now the wild white horses play/Champ and chaff and toss in the spray . . ." Whoa, there! Ugghh! A clip of smelly river water clopped me in the face.

"Sorry, Ellie! The oar got away from me."

"Never mind, Ben, dear," said I, folding my sun-dappled arms. "Romance is wasted on we old fogies."

"I'm not sure I agree, old bean."

"Really? You could have fooled me, Mr. Hearthside Guild Program Chairman. Leafing through Mr. Fisher's coffin catalogue, I got the distinct impression I was being hustled through life so as not to keep the hearse waiting."

"Ellie, we had this same conversation last night."

"And it bears repeating. I had hoped to enjoy a few good years with my children before the lid falls."

Resting on his oars, Ben squinted the sun out of his eyes.

"My dear, we are no longer free agents. Our role as parents demands we protect our offspring from all unpleasant inevitabilities such as our mutual demise." Sensing I was about to open my mouth, he held up an oar. "I'm an old-fashioned chap, Ellie. I don't subscribe to the Die Now, Pay Later viewpoint. The day my parents got married they started putting a couple of shillings a week by for . . . their last outing. And I intend to do as well by Abbey and Tam."

"Very well! But can't we at least wait for a good sale?" My sigh was swept up into the breezes gusting merrily overhead. Suddenly the boat was being spun around in a whirlpool of light and shadow. Faster, faster until Ben's eyes crossed and the boat rolled over, coming down on me with all the weight of a coffin lid so that there was only blackness . . .

"WAKEY, WAKEY!" A disembodied hand was shaking my shoulder and I sat up on my red rubber mat to find a Fellow Female in a zebra-striped leotard kneeling over me. "You were out for the count, ducky."

"Thanks for bringing me back." Still groggy, I stumbled to my feet and joined the tail-end of the class in exiting the room. As I passed Miss Thorn at the piano, she gave me a coy little wave. At the door, Bunty latched on to my arm.

"Ellie, I'm tickled pink you joined."

"Me too."

"And we will do dinner sometime." Her blonde curls shone and a smile danced over her pert features. "Promises, promises! I've been saying the same thing to Li for a month, but you know how it is." Obviously she was kidding. As the founder of Fully Female, the woman who had made husbands Big Business, she had to be kidding, didn't she?

"Never enough time," I quipped back. "In fact I made up a little poem about it."

"Recite!" Bunty seemed oblivious to the fact that we were blocking the doorway.

"Well, if you insist!" Flexing my lips, I began:

"I met myself the other day

As I was going the other way

Not much time to stop and chat,

Was I really getting fat?

We parted on a promise to get together

Some time next year in the never never."

Why do I set myself up for embarrassment? Bunty stood rooted to the parquet, a smile glued to her face, while I wished the river had swallowed me up. Silence stretched into eternity, giving me a pretty good idea what hell would be like . . .

Suddenly out of nowhere, meaning behind me, a gasp was heard, followed by the exclamation, "If that isn't too beautiful for words!"

Came the pitter-patter of Lycra feet and there, standing bang in front of me, was the effervescent Mrs. Bludgett. "I knew it, I knew you were a gentle spirit when we met at the vicarage last night." She held up a hand to stay the rest of the Fully Female crowd who were trying to squeeze past us into the hall. "Everyone stop, you positively have to hear Mrs. Haskell's rhyme. It's so brilliant, I have goose bumps. Just writing a letter about does me in!" Fortunately, while she enthused, the other ladies escaped and I made it out into the hall without doing an encore.

"See you upstairs at Marriage Makeover," chanted Bunty as I wended my way to the changing room with my new admirer in tow.

"Isn't this fun?" Mrs. Bludgett was all ebullience. Her bobbed hair bounced. She had springs in her feet. "Do you know I couldn't believe my ears when Jock came home and told me you had him up to fix the washing machine. 'The Mrs. Haskell of Merlin's Court?' I kept saying it over and over until he thought he'd have to give me a sedative. I felt so awful for calling him off the job that we never did get around to making love. We both just lay on the bed, staring at the ceiling, whispering your name."

"How kind." I pushed open the changing room door to a rush of memories from my school days at St. Roberta's. The smell of old lockers and tired linoleum.

"And then to see you at the vicarage last night. I can't find the words. It was so incredible. I kept wanting to rush over and hand you a coaster. Anything! Just so I could tell people I had spoken to the fairy tale lady of Merlin's Court! But first you were talking to the vicar and then to Mrs. Melrose and then came the program . . ."

At that point Mrs. Bludgett disappeared, sucked up into the crush of women in varying stages of undress like fluff into a Hoover, but seconds later she reappeared, still talking.

"There you are. I was in such a panic! She'll think me so rude, I thought. That lovely woman will never speak to me again! And on this day of all days I don't believe I could bear it. Not after the shock of walking into that room and seeing *her* perched at the piano."

Somehow I managed to squish my face through a gap in the throng. "Gladys Thorn?"

"Jock was carrying on with her a few months back." Mrs. Bludgett was wriggling out of her leotard, her boobs bouncing a mile a minute. "And I'm ashamed to say I came entirely unglued. Instead of focusing on the positive, I phoned her up, yelled all sorts of threats . . ."

"I'm sorry, but I don't get the positive."

"When you think about it, what higher compliment can one woman pay another than to try and steal her husband? That's why I had trouble facing her just now—I felt so small."

"I see."

Untrue. I couldn't see anything. All that was left of Mrs. Bludgett was a nose. Voices floated over the tops of heads, but just as you can't see the woods for the trees, you couldn't see the women for the crowd.

"Marjorie, lend me your comb."

"Someone button me up the back."

"Damn! Where did I put my bra?"

My back was to the wall; I struggled to keep afloat but found myself going under. My dream came back to me, the one about the horror of being buried alive. Panting, I applied traction with my hands, but it was no good. *Plonk.* I thumped down onto a ledge—a bench, I suppose. Cheers! My nose was above sea level. I could breathe. All I had to do was sit quietly and pray I wouldn't have to inspect a row of bare behinds while the lady jocks pulled on their tights.

Heaven be praised! Between one breath and another, the changing room was emptied of all but echoes and Moll Bludgett, who stood sizing herself up in the wall mirror.

"Guess I won't feel right until I face Gladys Thorn and apologize for the awful things I said." Bouncing over to me, the plumber's wife grabbed my hands and clasped them between her own. "Thank you, thank you, Ellie, for being here for me when I needed a friend. You're the *best,* you know that?"

"Well . . ."

"Yes, you are!" Her boisterous laughter evaporated; her face became deadly serious. "Now say it after me: I, Ellie Haskell, am the best . . . the very best."

Hot with embarrassment, my eyes locked to hers, I recited the fatuous nonsense.

"Remember that, Ellie! You are a lovely woman and don't let anyone tell you different."

I mumbled a thank you to the floor.

"Make friends with life!" She waved bye-bye from the doorway and was gone. Thank God! The woman was a vampire. Her energy had drained away every drop of life from me. I hardly had the strength to remove my leotard. As for returning it to the lost-and-found box . . . My knees began to shake, but I couldn't blame Moll Bludgett for that. I felt like a grave robber, one of those black-hearted villains who creep into the crypt at dead of night and steal the rings off the fingers of corpses. The label on the leotard indicated it belonged to the late Mrs. Huffnagle. That fearsome female of the Roman nose and ski-slope chin. That matriarch of Chitterton Fells society. A woman who might be alive today if she hadn't joined Fully Female in hopes of making her sex life sizzle. Poor lass, she had sizzled all right when her electrical appliance fell in the bath.

Dwelling upon this terrible accident got me back into my clothes and out of the changing room. Should I even bother going to Marriage Makeover? By now I must be a good five minutes behind everyone else, which in itself wasn't a bad thing. Having the place to myself meant I could retrieve Mrs. Malloy's gun from the grotto under the stairs. With the *splish splash* of the waterfall sounding in my ears, I knelt down and dipped a hand into the terra-cotta urn. Nothing. Not so much as a pebble. The gun was gone, along with the apron in which it had been wrapped.

I was in the process of getting to my feet, not sure whether I should be terribly worried or not, when I heard footsteps on the stairs. I looked up to see Mrs. Pickle leaning over the banisters.

"Good morning." I straightened up.

As was her way, she took her time answering. Slow as treacle she glided a duster along the rail. "Lost something, have you, Mrs. Haskell?"

Now I was the one who couldn't get the words out.

"Was it"—she drew the words out—". . . a gun?"

"Yes."

"Wrapped in an apron?"

"Yes!" By now I was ready to scream.

"Oh, that!" Her bread-and-butter face was expressionless. We might have been talking about a dropped earring. "I spotted it when I was dusting that there pot this morning and gave it to Mr. Wiseman as he was leaving for work." Another long pause as Mrs. Pickle moved her dusting arm in reverse. "Hope I haven't caused no trouble."

"Oh, no!" Doubtless Mrs. Malloy would be thrilled to know her gun was now in the hands of Chitterton Fells's most prominent solicitor. But in the meantime I had to assuage Mrs. Pickle's curiosity. "Naturally you are dying to know why I put the gun in the pot . . ."

"No."

"But surely . . ."

"Your business is your business." She continued to deal out

the words with agonizing slowness. "I'm glad to have a job. When I rung up Mrs. Wiseman last night to tell her I couldn't afford to come to class no more because of being sacked by the new vicar, she said she'd take me on here."

"I'm so glad." As much to my surprise as hers, I climbed the spiral stairs and gave Mrs. Pickle a hug. My reward was the opening of the flood gates. Words poured from the lady's lips as if she had that instant been released from a vow of silence.

"Vicar said she didn't need me because her husband just loved to do housework. Can you believe that?"

"Well . . ."

"I'd say love came into it, but not for scrubbing floors and the like, Mrs. Haskell. Yesterday, I heard Mr. Spike having a go-round with Gladys Thorn and it was plenty clear to me there was something between them. What's more, he *knew* I heard. You should have seen the flash in his eyes. Talk about if looks could kill! And what do you know? A couple of hours later me and that trollop, Miss Thorn—we both get our walking papers."

Exhausted by this spate of words, Mrs. Pickle fell silent, the duster dangling limp in her hands.

"I suspect you're right," was all I could say.

"And I know you should be at Marriage Makeover." She spoke, if possible, even more slowly. Stepping around me, she plodded down the stairs to stand in the pool of light from the skylight above us both. "Mrs. Haskell"—Mrs. Pickle folded her duster and laid it over the banister rail—"I want to tell you why Reverend Foxworth asked to be relieved of his duties at St. Anselm's. It was all on account of you."

"Me?"

"Bless his shiny white collar, he fell in love with you the day you came to Merlin's Court."

"No!"

"He said to me, 'Mrs. Pickle, I can't go on like this, one eye on my sermon, one on her. I'm going to speak to the Bishop and beg him to send me away, anywhere, so long as I can be free from the torment of her face.' "

"Believe me, I had no idea." Standing on that staircase, I was in no-man's-land. There was no upstairs or downstairs, there was only the realization that kind, sensitive, handsome Rowland Foxworth had cherished for me a Grand Passion.

"Was a time when I hated you, Mrs. Haskell, but I come to see you never meant to hurt him. Life can't be a Fantasy Special Edition Romance for everyone. Take me for an instance. I've been in love with your gardener, Jonas Phipps, since time began."

I left her dusting the banister in slow motion, and wended my way up that spiral staircase. Never in my life had I felt more Fully Female than at that moment. I knew myself to be the object of Rowland's Unrequited Regard. I never gave another thought to Mrs. Malloy's gun. What hit me like a bullet between the eyes when I reached the top stair was the memory of the vicar's surprised expression on meeting me last night. Now I understood she had been anticipating someone much different—a real femme fatale.

MARRIAGE Makeover was taking place in the dining room, which like every apartment in this Hollywood-style house redefined geometric space. Early Druid, Ben would have called it. I followed the sound of voices and entered with the whimsical feeling that I was taking an elongated peep at the room and its occupants through a keyhole. Bunty was seated at the far end of the mile-long table. Ranged down both sides, at strategic intervals, their chins down to their waists, sat a dozen or so members of Fully Female.

I was tiptoeing toward a vacant chair when our leader held up a hand. A hush fell like a blanket over a birdcage.

"Fellow Females, say hello to Ellie Haskell."

"Hello, Ellie!" The voices charged at me as I dropped quivering onto my seat. Everywhere I looked were smiles. I was beset by smiles.

Bunty's smile was as shiny bright as her blonde curls. "No need to break out in a cold sweat, love! All we do here is talk."

My worst fears realised. They would hold me prisoner until I had spilled every last bean concerning my intimate life . . . or present lack thereof. Bunty went on talking in a rush of words that went spinning around my head. My eyes darted here, there, and everywhere, searching for a break in the cover, and finally spied the familiar face of Jacqueline Diamond, wife of my favourite TV celeb, Norman the Doorman. How magnanimous! The great lady was removing her dark glasses to take a better look at me.

My mistake. She was pushing back her chair and rising to her feet. Finally, Bunty's spiel caught up with me in a sort of instant replay. Jacqueline, being one of the new members present, was to get the ball rolling by revealing what had brought her to Fully Female.

She seemed such an urbane woman with her sweep of ash-blonde hair, Lauren Bacall eyes, and twenty-two-inch waist, shown off to perfection by her rhinestone cowboy outfit. It seemed all wrong that she should bare her soul to a bunch of yokels such as us. Across the vast table Mrs. Wardle, the librarian, sat bolt forward as if someone had grabbed the strap of her forty-four triple D, ready to catapult her across the room. Two seats down from her sat Mrs. Thirsty, the headmistress of the village school, click-clicking away with her steel knitting pins like a bloody revolutionary waiting for the guillotine to come slicing down. Not on my neck, by heck! But of course I was deluding myself. As soon as Jacqueline Diamond was through doing a mental striptease, it would be my turn. Desperate for some sort of emotional support, I searched that sea of faces for someone I could even loosely regard as a friend. But Moll Bludgett hadn't made it up here after her talk with Miss Thorn, and Edna Pickle would still be dusting.

Jacqueline Diamond stood behind her chair, gleaming red nails gripping the knobs. "First up, ladies, let me say I'm a perfectionist." Her sleepy eyes roved the table. "My motto has always been, If you can't do it right, kiddo, don't do it at all: which is why Normie and I have never had too much sex."

Bunty got the applause going. "Everyone, give Jacqueline a big hand for honesty!"

I slid lower in my chair.

"Normie jokes that I'm the sort of person who sprays air freshener outdoors. That's the way I am. Everything has to be just so, especially when we . . . have a party, as we call it. I want fresh flowers and dripless candles, the works. Normie's different, he . . ."

"Yes?" The word buzzed like a bee around the table.

"Normie . . ." The red nails picked at the chair knob. "He used to toss his shoes in the air and say, 'How about it, old chum?' But since he got the role of Norman the Doorman . . ."

"Yes?" This time the word was a roar.

"Now he's the one with the headache. He's so into that bloody part, he never takes off his cape. He refuses to have sex with me because he thinks thousands of kiddies would be shocked out of their socks if they suspected their hero was up to tricks when he should be out leaping over rooftops in a single bound in pursuit of the evil Toy Snatcher."

Looking spent, Jaqueline resumed her chair.

"Young woman," Headmistress Thirsty said as she laid down her knitting pins, "you need to be doing your homework."

"But your problem is not insurmountable," warbled Mrs. Wardle.

"Any suggestions from the floor?" Bunty asked.

To my horror, a treacherous right hand inched upward. Mine. Immediately, the eyes of all present zoomed my way. Stumbling to my feet, I bleated out an apology for my forwardness . . . my very existence.

"And you are . . . ?" inquired the librarian.

"Ellie Haskell."

"Our other new member," supplied Bunty.

"It just sort of occurred to me that if Mrs. Diamond were to enact a fantasy in which she was the dolly in need of rescue, Mr. Diamond might feel comfortable in resuming the husbandly role."

The air quickened with the sharp intake of breath. Was I destined to be banished on the spot? Alas, not so. The room was suddenly asqueal with congratulations on my brilliant contribution. What Mrs. Diamond thought was lost in the crush of excitement. Several women left their seats to rush over and hug me.

"Mrs. Haskell, welcome to our little group!"

"You're going to be such an asset!"

"A breath of fresh air!"

"Such insight!"

When the hubbub ebbed a little, Bunty called the meeting back to order. "New members, each week all Fully Female candidates are required to do a homework assignment. Jacqueline, you might like to consider Ellie's suggestion as a possibility. Which brings us to the moment when our second new person will tell us what brought her to Fully Female."

Sunlight came slicing down on the table in the shape of a golden guillotine, but enveloped in the mantle of friendship, I stood undaunted, ready to meet my fate. To be truthful, my only regret as my Fellow Females settled back into their chairs was that my saga would sound tame after Jacqueline's.

Perhaps if I doctored it up by stating my Christian name in its entirety. . . . "I'm Giselle Haskell and I reside at Merlin's Court, Chitterton Fells, with my husband Bentley, our twins Abbey and Tam, and our gifted cat Tobias. These last few months I have been unhappy with my performance as a wife . . . as a human being. I am failing everyone—even my plants . . ."

The going was easier than I thought, but at the crucial moment, when I was all braced to confess that I was not as highly motivated sexually as one might wish, I was jarred out of myself by the distant pealing of a bell.

"Bloomin' heck!" Bunty was on her feet and heading out of the room. "That must be the new vicar. She rang up this morning and insisted on coming round to bestow her blessing on the Fully Female program." Still talking, Bunty vanished. She returned seconds later, followed by a black-garbed figure in lace mitts and a flower-seller's hat.

My emotions were in a turmoil. I resented being stopped midstream, and I was embarrassed at having the Reverend Mrs. Eudora Spike catch me in a place like this. I was beyond thought when I looked into her face and found myself bathed in the sunshine of that smile. Sinking down onto my chair, I clasped my hands in prayer.

"Blessings, dear ladies." Her features shadowed by the hat brim, the vicar swept to the far end of the mile-long table and inducted herself into Bunty's seat. The buzz of voices subsided as the black lace mittens were raised. "My friends"—she paused to allow our hearts to become one—"let us reach out our hands in the circle of friendship and let the love flow."

Love be damned! I ground my teeth in helpless recognition. The "vicar" was none other than my traitorous kinsman!

"And now"—Cousin Freddy piously bent his black hat—"let us talk of multiple orgasms."

Chapter Six

Isn't life wonderful? Horror may fade into memory but there is always some new, exciting torment waiting to take its place. On the morning following my Marriage Makeover session, Mrs. Malloy telephoned to lay down the law.

"Mrs. H, I trust you have your homework assignment prepared?"

"What?" Instantly I was back in the Upper Fourth at St. Roberta's frantically trying to write an essay on the Hundred Years' War during algebra class, all the while knowing that the heavy hand of Miss Clopper would soon descend on my shoulder. "What homework assignment?" I implored.

Mrs. Malloy's heavy breathing turned the receiver into a blow dryer. I had to hold down my hair. "Fantasy night at the old homestead, Mrs. H!"

"That's right!" I slumped down on a chair, mounded with the babies' outdoor togs. "We're to put on a real seduction production—turn the bedroom into an Arabian Nights' tent, spread satin sheets on the bed and dance the Rumba of the Seven Veils . . ."

"You can't have that one," Mrs. Malloy interrupted.

"What one?"

"The Salome schmozzle."

"But . . ."

"I've already taken me net curtains down, so there's no point in blubbering, Mrs. H, you'll just have to come up with your own fantasy."

"What I was about to say," I fumed into the phone, "is that I can't possibly arrange a tryst with Ben for this evening. I have a million things to do. I have to take the babies in for their checkups; I have to write to my in-laws and Dorcas and Jonas; I have Mr. Bludgett coming this afternoon to repair the washing machine; I have to weed the rockery—"

"You're breaking me heart!" I suspected Mrs. Malloy of sarcasm, but she went on with a break in her voice. "I thought we was in this together. You was the one who suggested Fully Female in the bloody first place, when I'd far rather have put an end to me misery—a gentle squeeze of the trigger and peace, perfect peace."

"Enough!" I cried, as memory of the misplaced gun rose up to haunt me. Getting it back from Lionel Wiseman must be added to my Do list, but first things first, the mollification of

Mrs. Malloy. "Truly," I assured her, "I am committed to Fully Female, but do I have to do my homework *tonight*?"

"Our reports have to be in tomorrow."

Impossible to tell her that much of what was said at Marriage Makeover had gone in one ear and out the other after the vicar had put in her . . . *his* appearance. By going to the afternoon session, Mrs. Malloy had missed Cousin Freddy, the wolf in clerical clothing.

"You there, Mrs. H?"

Rising from my chair like a phoenix from the ashes, I promised to do my part for the honour and glory of Fully Female.

"I can't wait to see my Walter in the rude." On which grizzly note Mrs. Malloy hung up, leaving me wracked with despair.

Was there no escape, no loophole in the fabric of my existence? Was I destined to cheapen a love which in its glorious heyday had rivaled that of some of the great duos of all time . . . Paris and Helen . . . Tony and Cleo . . . Charlie and Di? Thus might I have stood all morning, waxing morose in the hall at Merlin's Court, but a reprieve came in the form of an imperious summons from the nursery.

"Coming, my darlings!"

What angels! They partook of breakfast with an enthusiasm to gladden a mother's heart and accompanied me on the drive to Dr. Melrose's office without protest.

The one whose smile occasionally dimmed was mine. After managing a nip-and-tuck parking job in a space clearly reserved for a skateboard, I got through the business of unloading with only the loss of a scarf, which got sucked away by a passing lorry. Next came the trauma of shouldering my way through the double glass doors while gripping the babies' pushchair with one hand and dropping the nappy bag with the other. Waiting for the lift in the brown linoleum lobby, I thought jeeringly of those tough-guy triathletes, the ones who aren't satisfied with making it a one-sport event. Oh, no! They have to cycle up the slopes of Kilimanjaro, parachute onto their dogsleds, and canoe down subterranean rivers with stalactites dropping like spears out of the bat-infested darkness. What these gluttons for punishment need is a day in the life of a mother on the go.

When the lift grudgingly cranked open its doors, I got myself and the pushchair aboard with my usual spry grace, but somehow the nappy bag didn't quite make it. The metal jaws snapped shut, leaving two inches of strap attached to my arm. Why me, Lord? Machinery hates me. Vacuum cleaners, hair dryers, coffee pots, my washing machine . . . they all spend their tinny little lives plotting ways to bring me down. Fortunately, the lift was out of condition. Before it could wheeze upward, I managed to press the Open button with my nose and rescue the nappy bag.

"Mummy saves the day," I boasted, feeling rather like Norman the Doorman, who was performing as we entered Dr. Melrose's waiting room, for the television set had been tuned to my darlings' favourite program. Scooting over to the woman at the desk—a woman who looked as though she had been born for the sole purpose of shouting "Next!"—I gave the twins' names and surveyed the area with its rubber plants and magazine-littered table. Business was certainly brisk this morning. Faces, faces everywhere and not an empty chair. The words jingled inside my head to the music coming from the telly. I was wheeling the Porta-Pram into a corner when a wheezing old gentleman with a tobacco-stained moustache offered me his seat.

I smiled. "That's awfully nice, but really, I'm glad to stand."

He groped a hand toward the pram. "Got your hands full there, Mother!"

Pink with pride, I drew back the covers to let him take a peek at Abbey and Tam sleeping like angels, their sweet little hands clutching the satin ribbon of the blanket, their mouths working as if they were blowing bubbles in dreamland.

A rosy-cheeked woman to my left leaned forward for a look. "Aren't they lovely?"

"Thank you."

"Are they twins?"

Amazing how often this question was asked, but I never found it irritating. One baby is a miracle; two at once is so mind-boggling that people tend to blither. I was recounting the babies' life histories, starting with my heroic labour, when one of the doors off the waiting room opened and Miss Thorn emerged. A black hat was clamped on her head and her coat skimmed the floor in the manner of a downtrodden governess. A squeal from Abbey caused her to look across the room directly at me.

Lifting a hand in salute, I felt my smile congeal. For Miss T looked right through me—actually cut me dead before gliding from the room. Silly of me to feel quite so spooked, even though I told myself her spectacles probably needed cleaning.

"Next!" boomed the keeper of the desk, and away bustled the rosy-cheeked woman.

"Now you sit down," she told me, with a bye-bye wave at the twins. Glad to do as bid, I went to sit in her seat and found she'd left a paperback novel lying there. From the bodice-buster cover it didn't look like something I could read to the twins, so I laid it down on the pram cover and settled down to watch Norman the Doorman. Noble and solitary, he stood in the doorway of Tinseltown Toys, his black cloak swirling about him.

"My word," he said, cupping a hand over his mask, "do my peepers deceive me, or do I see lots of my little friends coming to help in a very important rescue? Yes! Here come Billy and Josie—hope your broken arm is better, Josie—and a big hello to Edward, Nancy, Patrick, Julie, Lisa, and all my special friends. Now"—Norman lifted his cloak as if to draw the children under its shelter—"I really do need the help of everyone. Once upon a time, not very long ago or far away, a nice lady named Mrs. Brown decided to make a special treat for her little boy's birthday. The little boy's name was Barry and Mother made him a red jelly rabbit with licorice whiskers. When teatime came and Mother reached out her big spoon, a voice as sweet as red jelly said, 'Please don't eat me. I am a magic rabbit. All I ask is to be able to live happily ever after in your refrigerator.' Barry's daddy wasn't too pleased at first. 'What? Give up a whole shelf to a plate of plop! Am I supposed to turn my bottles of fizzy pop out on the street?' But at last Daddy stopped huffing and puffing and the Jelly Rabbit became one of the family, until last night when he was kidnapped from the refrigerator by the evil Mr. Melt, and if we don't get to Jelly Rabbit in time, he will be fruit juice—"

"No!" The word whipped around the room, and I came out of my glassy-eyed stare to discover I was not the only one in the waiting room on the edge of my seat. The wheezy old gentleman next to me had almost chewed off his moustache.

I nonchalantly informed him that I was personally acquainted with the star of Tinseltown Toys.

"You know *Norman*?" The old gent almost wheezed his last.

"In a manner of speaking." Rocking the pram with one hand, I smoothed back my hair with the other. "I know his wife."

"What's she like?"

"Friendly, nice . . ."

"And you think that one day she'll get you together with the old man?"

"I hadn't thought . . ." My eyes returned to the television where Norman was propping a ladder up against the moon. Magical, harmless make-believe. Fantasies. Suddenly, on the outskirts of my mind, I heard Mrs. Malloy's voice informing me that tonight was the night for my homework assignment. And I felt a stirring of girlish, *childlike* anticipation. I wasn't embarking on a lifetime of slime, I was rescuing my marriage from the evil clutches of neglect. As if fate so decreed, Norman the Doorman was replaced by an advert for cat food, and my eyes fell on the pram cover, where lay the paperback book *Voyage to Valhalla*. My hands reached out and the book fell open to page 31 as if waiting for me.

The great god Thor, who once drank from the ocean and made the tide, now drew back the clouds with one sweep of his wrathful hands. You could have heard a pin drop upon the field of battle. Cringing mercenaries fell to their knees, their eyes fixed upon a grassy knoll, where stood the warrior princess, Marvel.

Her fiery hair burned like the sun's fierce rays. Her amethyst eyes rivalled the jewels pillaged from her father's castle. The hem of her kirtle was stiff with blood and her creamy shoulders ached from wielding the sword which at daybreak she had removed from the hand of her dying henchman, Bod the Unmerciful. Dry-eyed, Marvel had sworn to hunt down his murderer, that vilest of all Saxons—Baron Derick of Dryadsville. Safe in Thor's protection—one hand trailing the sword, the other pressed to a waist no bigger than a laurel wreath—she paced the knoll all bright with buttercups.

Across the weir, eyes steely as his shield, Derick stood in the shadow of his men and thought her fairer than any flower. By Wodin! Before the moon set over this accursed vale he would make the warrior princess his own. His chiselled lips curved into a boyish smile, which as quickly froze hard as ice. Herold of Leeth was creeping up the far side of the knoll. The scurvy knave was within a hand's breadth of crushing that lovely neck in his yeoman's hands. But suddenly, with the delicacy, the elegance that was hers by right of royal blood, Princess Marvel whirled about and with a flash of silver sword put a period to Herold's existence. In the golden hush of that April afternoon, the lifeless head went somersaulting down the knoll—eyes bulging, lips mouthing Gadzooks! until with a final bounce it came to rest at Derick's feet.

Kneeling, he doffed his helmet and raised his eyes to the lady of the hour. "Ye gods, you've come a long way, baby . . ."

I was laying *Voyage to Valhalla* down on the pram cover when a twentieth-century war cry sounded.

"Next!"

Abbey and Tam bopped up and—yes! Three cheers! We were the chosen ones! Under the envious gaze of the rabble, who looked as though they had been there since the dawn of penicillin, I pushed the pram into the hallowed presence of Dr. Melrose.

My goodness! The good physician was slumped in his chair, eyes closed, leading me to assume he was dead (anything else being completely unprofessional), but suddenly he sat up, scaring me spitless.

"Mrs. Haskell, isn't it?" This from the man who had been my M.D. since my arrival at Merlin's Court. The doctor was a large man, both tall and bulky. He usually wore tweeds which heightened his resemblance to a bear, but today he seemed to have shrunk. His face had caved in and his eyes possessed a glassy look that brought forcibly to mind the severed head bouncing like a football down the knoll.

"Yes, 'tis I," responded *moi,* with all the perkiness that was mine by right of good old peasant stock. "Time for the babies' checkups." The need to remind him why we were here was overwhelming. Still seated, Doc Melrose watched me lift Abbey from the pram as if he had no idea what—let alone who—she was.

"I haven't been sleeping well." His hands were trembling. Unnerving because they were of a particularly hairy sort.

"Oh, dear!" I sat across from him with both babies in my lap. "Lots of middle-of-the-night stuff, I suppose." I meant emergency bunions, that sort of thing; but his response almost resulted in Tam's falling over the precipice of my right thigh.

"Yes!" The doctor squeezed the neck of his stethoscope as if trying to choke himself. "Morning, noon, and middle-of-the-night stuff. Flo hasn't been herself since she joined that Fully Female organization. You haven't joined, have you?"

"Heaven forbid!" I said, flustered.

"For your sake and your husband's, I pray you never do."
His bloodshot eyes darted to the door. "You didn't spot my
wife out there in the waiting room?"

"No."

"She could have been disguised." He was now tying the
stethoscope into knots. Worse, his face was getting tied up in
knots. "Flo likes to stage these little surprises. I have no idea
when she will fling open that door and bare her teeth . . . the
lot . . . at me. The woman has turned into a vampire. She's
insatiable. Last night when I got home . . . before I could take
off my hat, she had flung me across the dining room table.
We were to have played bridge."

"Mrs. Melrose cancelled?"

"No. And thank God the doorbell rang in the nick of time.
I'm too old for this, Mrs. Haskell. I'm looking forward to
retirement and the two of us sitting in the garden, wearing
straw hats and holding hands."

"She does like to sketch." I offered what encouragement I
could while snuggling Abbey and Tam closer. Poor darlings,
they were both rubbing their noses, a sure sign they were
pooped.

"Sketch!" Flinging down his stethoscope, Dr. Melrose
ground his teeth. "Do you know what subjects now obsess
her artist's brain?"

"Uhmmmm . . ." Full well I remembered Flo telling me at
the Hearthside Guild meeting that she was into painting nude
dudes. She had even suggested that Ben would make a lovely
subject. But for all I knew she had told Doc that she was into
still life, which could have passed as a varnished version of
the truth if she instructed her subjects not to move, not even
to scratch their goose bumps.

"Mrs. Haskell, Flo is into Male Anatomy."

"Really!"

"Localized areas of the Male Anatomy."

It took a moment for the penny to drop, whereupon I was truly shocked. Perhaps I have an impure mind. But to my peasant way of thinking, there is a big difference between an artist who paints only hands and those who focus on what books such as *Voyage to Valhalla* address with euphemisms. The Princess Marvel might feast her eyes on Lord Derick's manhood to her little Nordic heart's delight, but Flo Melrose was not getting her paintbrush within an inch of my Ben's—

"And I'm not the only one to be driven crazy!" Dr. Melrose was on his feet and bumbling around a tray of instruments. "Do you seriously believe that Huffnagle woman's death was an accident? Mark my words, her husband couldn't go one more round and ended the high jinks by tossing that electrical appliance into her bath."

"Murder?" I gasped.

"A mere figure of speech." Dr. Melrose pursed his lips and waved a hairy hand. "And difficult to prove, lucky devil."

"Well, as Reverend Foxworth always said, and I am sure the new incumbent would echo, let Heaven be the judge." I popped the babies in the Porta-Pram and began edging towards the door.

"Not so fast!" He held up a syringe, whose wicked point glinted in the sun streaming through the prison-sized window. "This is no fun for Mummy, but Alice and Tom must have their jabs."

Appallingly rude of me, I know, but I wasn't about to let that sleep-deprived man come at my babies with, for all I knew, the wrong serum. Shouldering the door open, I fled through the waiting room and was in the car with my angels safely installed in the backseat before drawing one full breath.

Driving up Cliff Road at a maternally responsible rate of speed, I wondered anew if I had done something awfully silly in joining Fully Female, even assuming Dr. Melrose had lost his professional perspective regarding the Huffnagles. What Ben would say if—*when*—he found out was the big question. The male ego is unfathomable. He might be delighted at my investing time and energy in preserving our marriage or he might think the whole thing an insult to his manhood—in the broadest sense of the word.

I was on that stretch of road where the iron fence of the churchyard breasts the hill when I saw a man emerge from the archway of yews. Unfortunately, he didn't see me and ploughed across the road a hair's breadth from the nose of the car. If not for my ladylike speed, he would either have ended up on the bonnet or gone whopping over the cliff edge into the waiting jaws of the hungry sea, whose belly-rumbles came up to us loud and clear.

The wind ruffled Mr. Gladstone Spike's scanty hair while the rest of him seemed quite undisturbed as he peered into the car window.

"Mrs. Haskell, a pleasure to run into you." His gentle smile informed me no pun was intended. The man had no idea that St. Peter had been standing at the Pearly Gates shouting, "Next!"

"I'm on my way home from taking Abbey and Tam to the doctor."

"Ah, lovely!" he said.

I asked after his wife and suddenly it wasn't only his hair that was ruffled. His eyes took on the glazed look which I would forever after associate with this morning. "Eudora is well, I thank you. Busy, as one would expect."

"The parish is fortunate to have her." My voice was now on automatic. The twins were growing restless. Without turning round I knew that Abbey had Tam by the nose and that any minute a roar would go up equal to anything Cape Canaveral could offer.

"Eudora is a splendid woman." From the sound of him, Mr. Spike might have been breaking the news that she had an allergy to incense which might force her into early retirement. "A saint. I have never stopped counting my blessings that she married me." He stepped back from the car and stood stoop-shouldered, a wintry figure even on this April day, staring straight ahead, as if somewhere on the blue horizon lay the answer to a question of deadly importance.

"Most kind of your husband, Mrs. Haskell, to send over the box of ginger biscuits. My wife will send a note, I know, but do thank him on behalf of both of us."

"I will." Revving up the motor, I explained I was in a rush to get home for the babies' lunch, and he lifted a hand in what appeared to be both farewell and blessing. As I drove away, he stood framed in my rearview mirror. I had assumed that he was out for a midday stroll, but something about the turn of his head, the alertness of his shoulders, made me wonder if he might be waiting for someone.

Some days are full of surprises. I entered Merlin's Court by the garden door with the babies loaded in my arms to find a man in my kitchen.

"Mr. Bludgett," I said, addressing the little man with the Charlie Chaplin moustache, "how did you get in?"

He stopped doing whatever he was doing to the washing

machine and looked at me with his good eye. The one under the puckered lid was doing its own thing.

"Sorry to give you a scare, Missus." He looked as though he would have liked nothing better, but as I am sure the Reverend Spike would adjure, Thou shalt not judge by appearances. "When I got no answer to me hollering, Missus, I tried the door and found it was open. Figured you wanted the washing machine fixed before it was any older, so Bob's your uncle."

"I'm pleased to see you."

"Here, let me take one of the little buggers." Suiting words to action, Mr. Bludgett scooped Tam out of my arms.

"Thanks." I was unbuttoning Abbey's coat. "And please don't mind us. We'll try not to get in the way while you work."

"Don't you worry." Mr. Bludgett might have been looking hopefully at the kettle, or he might not. Either way I didn't have time to make him a cuppa until I'd changed the babies and got them fed.

"If you'd like to make yourself at home," I began, heading toward the hall door with a baby tucked under each arm.

He read my mind like a shot. "No trouble, Missus. I'll brew up."

"The tea's in the copper caddy."

"Say no more. My Moll says I'm like a bloodhound around the kitchen. She can't never hide anything from me. Last week she baked a cake—not for our anniversary or nothing special. It was a thank you cake . . . for the night before. She's a great one, my Moll, for those little extras what make a man feel cherished. Anyway, to make a short story long, she hid it in the top cupboard above the cooker, but I nosed m'way to it.

How we did laugh, the two of us, when Moll caught me holding the tin. 'Someone needs a spanking!' she said."

Oh, my goodness! Now we were getting into the kinky stuff. Hot with embarrassment, I mumbled, "There should be some Dundee cake in the Houses of Parliament tin," and hurried from the room.

After changing the babies, I raked a comb through my hair and sized myself up in the nursery mirror. By no stretch of the imagination was this the face to launch a thousand ships. Not even a few rowboats. Bother. But no time to wallow. One must not forget that time was on the march. If I was not to make Public Enemy Number One of Mrs. Malloy, I must make ready for Fantasy Night with my number one husband. Should I follow the example of Moll Bludgett and bake Ben a cake? That would be like taking coals to Newcastle. Anything I could bake, Ben could bake better, but surely food eaten with the soul comes satisfaction guaranteed. The babies in the twin pack, my eyes on the ticking grandfather clock, I hurried back across the hall to the kitchen. There I found Mr. Bludgett with a cup of tea in his hands and a rubber pipe roped around one shoulder. Was he anticipating a flood?

Abbey and Tam made clear that they were expecting luncheon, spit spot. Doing kitchen drill with a man underfoot has never been a favourite form of recreation for me. Blundering over hoses and navigating the narrow canal between washing machine and kitchen table, I got the babies resettled in the playpen, all the while trying to read the Fully Female manual one-handed. Understand, a Fully Female member must read her manual as faithfully as a Roman Catholic priest reads his office. I wasn't looking for recipes, but at the end of Chapter

Three I came upon a Fully Female Fondue that sounded just the ticket.

RECIPE

MARINADE: Fill a bath with warm water gently seasoned with Fully Female Fantasy and soak for one half hour, turning when needed to avoid pressure points. Remove from liquid, pat dry, and oil lightly with Fully Female Herbal Balm.

DRESSING: We suggest Ranch—a lively blend of cowboy boots and a cute little holster, no additions or substitutions. Or you may choose French—very basic, and certain to appeal to the most finicky husband. Wear your favourite negligee, weave a satin ribbon through your hair and slip your tootsies into your slinkiest mules.

GARNISH: Spray your lovely self and your love nest with Fully Female's *Parfum de Passion* and, if desired, dust your shoulders with powdered sugar.

SERVING SUGGESTION: Set your table with your finest linen, china, and cutlery. Arrange fresh flowers artfully . . .

As recipes go, this one was certainly gripping, but I was beginning to wonder if we would ever reach the climax, the part where we artfully arranged dinner on a serving platter. Ah, now we came to it—Bird of Paradise Fondue, which from the look of it was really an erotic way of saying Fried Chicken. The only culinary challenge I foresaw would be locating the fondue pot. At one time we had owned two, but Ben, being the purist he is, had given away the electric one. I did ask myself whether it was consistent with responsible parenting to deep fry, but . . . oh, what the hell! Do people who make a cult of abstinence really live longer? Or does boredom make it *seem* longer?

Dip chicken portions in batter seasoned with Healthy Harvest
Herbs and cook in hot oil until a succulent, sexy doneness.
Serve with a tasty side dish and veggies from your friendly
frozen foods section. By taking these shortcuts, dear Fellow
Female, we ensure you are not overdone when your love-dove
walks in the door. We want him to find you gently simmering.
Let him bring you to a rolling boil when the fondue candle
begins to dim . . .

"Mrs. Haskell?" Mr. Bludgett brought me back to earth
with a thud. Dropping the manual, I turned to find him with
the coil of rubber rope poised in his hands and, for a sickening
second, thought he was going to lasso me. Ridiculous. He
wanted to talk washing machine, but somehow I could not
separate the reality from Bludgett the Burglar, Menace to
Society.

"Yes?" I kept one eye on the twins who were gripping the
sides of the tumbrel—I mean, the playpen—their periwinkle
eyes unblinking.

"I think I've found the problem, Missus."

"Really?"

"And there's two ways you can go." Mr. Bludgett patted
the washing machine lid, a gesture so poignant he did not
need to spell out his meaning. We could choose to keep old
Nellie alive by artificial means, hooked up to life-support
hoses. Or we could let her go with dignity to the great
scrapyard in the sky. If making a unilateral decision, I would
have opted to boot the old girl out the back door. But Ben
has this obsession with keeping mechanical objects going long
after their day. Take his car, for instance. He plans for it to
outlive him and has made provisions in his will for its ongoing
care.

"Mr. Bludgett," I said, "my husband is devoted to this washing machine. Is there any way to save it?"

To my amazement, Mr. B's moustache quivered and he gripped the rubber hose with unsteady hands. They were not as hairy as Dr. Melrose's bear paws, but I realized two strong men in one day were reduced to trembling in my presence. What was this town coming to?

"Mrs. Haskell, no need to tell me you went and joined Fully Female; I can see it in your eyes, hear it in your voice when you talk about the mister. My Moll's the same. What a woman! Every day's a honeymoon. She'd give me her first waking breath and her last. Only one thing spoils our happiness . . ."

"Oh, dear!"

"I get to thinking about . . ." Mr. Bludgett was twisting the rubber hose as if trying to throttle it. "Thinking how I went and had . . . immoral doings with . . . that woman." No need to identify the scarlet woman. The name Miss Gladys Thorn was etched in the air like a cartoon caption. I didn't know what to say. The old saw, It takes two to tango, sprang to mind, but moralizing takes time and we still hadn't made a decision about Nellie and . . . oh, knickers! Someone was at the garden door.

Rap-tap-tap.

A silly, coy knocking. Fury bubbled into my throat as I peered through the pebbled glass panel and espied the tall narrow figure. Cousin Freddy! How dare he show his face here after his hideous charade at Fully Female! Impersonating a woman of the cloth! It might work as a music hall skit, but I was not amused. Yanking open the door, I hurled my voice in his face.

"Set one foot inside my house, you festering wart, and I kill you."

The person at the door was Miss Thorn.

Before I could find my voice, which had gone into hiding, she was backing down the steps, stumbling over her feet as well as her words.

"So sorry, Mrs. Haskell!" Her mushroom eyes burned into my soul. "I was in this neck of the woods and thought I would return your sweet husband's handkerchief." A flutter of white flag before she clamped it to her lips and fled down the driveway, a gaunt black figure pursued by the hounds of hell. I felt dreadful. I thought about racing after her to the bus stop and laying my apologies at her feet. The spirit was willing but the flesh, alas, was hopelessly out of condition. I took the coward's way out and closed the garden door.

Mr. Bludgett looked as though he would have liked to pin a medal on my chest. "You're a Fully Female woman all right, fighting for your man like that."

"The washing machine," I said sternly.

Mr. Bludgett prowled around Nellie the way a dog prowls its basket before settling down, then he beckoned me closer. Watched by my children, I edged forward. He took time out to scratch his moustache, heightening the suspense, then thumped a fist against Nellie's side as if knocking on wood. "Try that, Missus, and see how you go on."

"What? Give her a thump every time she stops?"

"You got it."

I felt curiously let down, as I suppose one might after picking a coffin ensemble from Mr. Fisher, only to pass the medical with flying colours. While Mr. Bludgett repositioned Nellie in her cubbyhole, I scurried around the kitchen trying to find my *Chocoholic Cookery Book,* the one with the foolproof recipe for devil's food cake.

Not on any of the shelves. Papers went flying as I ransacked the drawers without success. As frustration reached its zenith, I remembered Dorcas had made a cake for my birthday using that same book. Probably it was still in her room.

From the look of him Mr. Bludgett would be a while finishing up and Abbey and Tam were contentedly conversing in goo-goo talk, so it seemed quite safe to slip upstairs for a few moments. But is life ever to be trusted? Those few moments turned into a good ten minutes. Looking through Dorcas's room without invading her privacy was a tricky business. I wasted precious time staring at drawers I couldn't bring myself to open. And all the while I knew that cookery book was there; I could feel its presence; I became obsessed by the need to find it. There is something horribly menacing about lost objects. I always picture them tucked away in their hiding places laughing at me. Typical of the games such objects play!

I had finally given up and was on my way out the door when I saw the *Chocoholic Cookery Book* lying in full view on the lower shelf of Dorcas's bedside table. Grabbing it up, I was suddenly very much aware of being gone longer than planned from the kitchen. Racing downstairs, I prepared my apologies to Mr. Bludgett. The kitchen door went crashing inward with more force than intended and I found the room empty. No Mr. Bludgett. No Abbey and Tam.

THAT wicked man! Why, oh why had I not trusted my first instincts regarding him? He was worse than a burglar! He was a *kidnapper*! He had taken my babies! Without knowing how

I got there, I found myself outside in the courtyard. The soft April afternoon had turned grey. Trees rustled against a sky as ashen as my face. The stable door batted open, and dead leaves, blown from the compost heap, whirled in front of me. Sunshine is no talisman against evil, but somehow the dying of the day made everything more hopeless. When next I got my bearings, I was in the stable. O wild and foolish hope! How could they be here when Mr. Bludgett's van was gone? I didn't deserve to have children. Any mother worth a pinch of sense would have telephoned the police at once. Charging back indoors, I experienced another shock wave as unreality came crashing in.

Freddy was camped out at the kitchen table, a slab of cake in one hand, the Fully Female manual in the other. Staggering toward him, I cried, "Thank God you are here!"

"What'sthat?" he asked through a mouthful of cake.

"The twins have been kidnapped!"

"Have you lost your mind?" Freddy cocked his legs on the table, crossed them at the ankle, and lolled back in his chair.

"I'm telling you, Mr. Bludgett the plumber—"

"Funny-looking chap? Gammy eye?"

"Yes!" My voice hit the ceiling.

Freddy swallowed his last fistful of cake and laid the manual flat on his chest. "He was getting ready to leave when I walked in and I told him to cut loose. Silly sod, he stuck his ugly mug over the playpen to say bye-bye to the kiddies and had them bawling their eyes out. Soon as he was gone, I got them sorted out and down for their naps. Say, why are you looking at me like that, cousin?"

"You idiot!" I screamed, but whether I meant him or me I had no idea. Slamming the garden door I returned to stand, arms folded, looking down at him. Oh, the temptation to grab up a pair of scissors and snip off his ponytail . . . in lieu of something better!

"Sorry if I gave you a fright," he said. He looked genuinely remorseful. " 'Struth, Ellie, I'm one of those hapless individuals who can't do right for doing wrong. And the really pathetic part is that I just wanted to get back in your good graces after yesterday."

Blast him. He could play my heart strings like a harp, and the infuriating, frustrating part was that he *had* meant well. While I was racing around outside like a madwoman, he was probably changing nappies. But I wasn't to be cheated of my wrath.

"I suppose you also meant well yesterday when you did your ghastly impersonation of Reverend Spike—a woman whose name you are not fit to utter, let alone usurp."

"I know it was naughty." Freddy removed his feet from the table—scared, I suppose, that I might tip over his chair.

"Stupid is the word." I was beginning to feel better. "I don't know how you thought you could get away with it. Any one of the women at Marriage Makeover might have met the real vicar. What if Mrs. Pickle had opened the door to you? What if Moll Bludgett hadn't missed the session because she was talking to Miss Thorn? If Moll had been there, you couldn't have fooled her."

"I admit it was risky." Freddy tossed the Fully Female manual from hand to hand. "But at least I knew I could count on you, dear Ellie, not to spill the beans. Must uphold the family honour, what!"

I removed the manual from his clutches. "My concern was

for Ben and the restaurant. Your little masquerade could be very bad for business."

"Ellie, I didn't think." His eyes were brimming with contrition. And, bother it, my heart began to soften.

"Actors aren't like ordinary people, Ellie," he continued. "At times I'm a soul in torment, a madman pursuing his craft in a world where rejection is the name of the game. My part in *Norsemen of the Gods* isn't enough to satisfy my thespian desires and—"

"Don't push it, Freddy," I said.

Smirking, he stood up and plopped an arm around my shoulders. "You're a good egg, Ellie. I'll remember you and Ben when my name is up in lights." A pause. "I don't suppose you have time to hear my lines for *Norsemen*?"

"Freddy," I said, casting a wild glance at the clock, "I'm up to my eyebrows—"

"Enough said," he soothed. "I came by because I remembered I left my horns here."

"Did you?" I averted my eyes from the shelf above the window. "Well, I wonder where they can be?" Before I was reduced to deceiving a deceiver, the garden door banged open and there stood Mrs. Malloy. She was a sight to behold in giant pink rollers and no eyebrows.

"Ever so sorry to barge in, Mrs. H!" Swirling her stole over her left shoulder, she paraded forward as if walking the ramp to the royal yacht.

"Come to borrow a cup of sugar, have you, love?" Freddy bared his teeth in a smile.

He was close. Mrs. M had decided a half hour earlier that the successful seduction of Mr. Walter Fisher hinged on her wearing the purple caftan hanging at the back of my wardrobe. A flashy piece of apparel, dear to my heart because I had worn it the evening I first met Bentley T. Haskell.

"How about the Aladdin slippers?" I asked. "No extra charge."

"Well, just to please you, Mrs. H, and while I'm here, I'll take a packet of Healthy Harvest Herbs. I started to make dinner and got in such a shake when I couldn't remember where I'd put the bloody stuff. No need to write you an IOU, I hope. Anything I borrow, I return. Reliable Roxie, that's me!" Mrs. Malloy surveyed my kitchen. "I don't see your Fully Female Formula, Mrs. H, and out of sight means out of mind." Her mouth was piously pursed. "I'd never remember to take mine regular if I didn't keep it handy at all times."

"Thanks for the tip," I said. What an afternoon! I hadn't drunk my Formula, I hadn't made my cake, and I was never going to get my homework done.

"SPEAK to me of love, dear heart . . ."

The witching hour was at hand. Moonlight silvered the windows. The walls of the matrimonial chamber were blushed with the rosy glow of candles flickering on the mantelpiece. And Tobias had been ousted from the scene after an aborted chicken heist. Garbed in a gauzy green negligee edged with seafoam lace, I paced the stretch of Persian carpet at the foot of the four-poster bed, reciting the lines with which I would captivate my husband anew. "Come to me, my chickadee, and let me soothe your weary brow with kisses moist and sweet."

Fortune for once had smiled upon me, rather than baring her fangs. Abbey and Tam had gone to bed like angels. On looking in on them a few moments earlier, I had found them snuggled in their cots blowing tiny, imaginary bubbles. Funny, that's how I pictured my love for them—shining, hand-held rainbows, filled with a joy that was lighter than air. Mr. Bludgett wasn't the bogeyman. My darlings were safe. They had always been safe. Stroking their downy hair, the colour of candlelight, I had tiptoed from the nursery.

The other vital plus was that Ben had telephoned at a little after six to tell me he was expecting a large party of diners late in the evening and not to expect him home before midnight. Suddenly I was wallowing in spare time. I baked my chocolate cake and it emerged from the oven puffed up with importance. So far so good, but the recipe stated it should now sink down with a steamy little sigh into a sort of hot fudge mousse. Ah, perfecto! Time for the black currant sauce. The remaining culinary preparations were kiddy simple. I rinsed spinach leaves for a salad and made up a bottle of Healthy Harvest Herb Dressing according to the recipe on the back of the reseal packet. I defrosted my chicken parts and left them to marinate in honey and lime juice while I marinated in the bath, reading Chapter Four of the Fully Female Manual.

Husbands want to be wooed, but being stubborn little boys at heart, they don't always know what they want. It is your job—your *privilege*—to lead your darling gently by the hand down Lover's Lane. Be prepared for a little resistance at first. He may think he wants to watch the late night news, he may tell you he is too tired for sex, he may do everything possible to sabotage your attempts at seduction because he's scared. Remember, he's about to embark on an affair with a woman he has just met. The new you. Believe me, he'll probably feel guilty! For your "first time" the bedroom is probably the most nonthreatening environment in which to guide him to that ultimate baring of body and mind in which the soul takes wing, secure in the knowledge that the Fully Female woman would burn at the stake sooner than reveal this side of the grave, what was done—or said—in private and passion. Save your night under the stars for next time. Have dinner in the boudoir, but no TV trays on the knees, please! Cover a *table à deux* with your finest lace cloth and make sure your silver and crystal are as sparkling as your eyes as you wait for the man of your dreams to open that door to find you with arms outstretched.

As the clock struck midnight, I heard Ben's footsteps on the stairs. My mouth went dry. What a time to get cold feet! I couldn't look at the table with the bright yellow fondue pot, the glass salad bowl and earthenware dishes. What was I doing, flaunting my chocolate cake at a man who but a few years ago had been a total stranger? I had never felt so cheap in my life! But as his footsteps came e'er closer, I thought: Knickers! If I've gone this far, I intend to get an A!

On with the Viking horns.

Ben stood in the doorway, staring at me as if he had never seen me before in his life. My cheeks flamed while the rest of me turned into a slab of ice. Say something, I prayed, as he sat down on the bed, his mouth—those lips which I was supposed to rain with kisses—set in a hard, straight line.

"By Jupiter, Ellie, sometimes I think I should have become a monk."

"I . . ."

"That way I wouldn't have to deal with members of the general public who consider themselves gourmands. Would you believe some insufferable sod summoned me from the kitchen this evening to inform me that his prime rib tasted like it was still alive? He wanted it rare, not raw. You would have been proud of me, Ellie. I kept a grip on my temper—and my smile. I brought him the piece of leather he demanded and listened patiently to his suggestions on how the mustard glaze on the brussels sprouts could be improved."

"My brave darling!"

Surely now he would notice . . .

"Hell, tomorrow's another day." He was dragging off his shoes. "Let's get to bed."

"Ben . . ." I went to him in a swirl of green gauze. "Open your eyes, my love. Look around, look at me!"

"What is it, dear?"

"I prepared a special evening for us." The sweep of my wide sleeve indicated the table for two, the candles on the mantel, his black silk dressing gown draped invitingly over the back of the fireside chair.

Wearily, my better half laid his head against me as I stood over him. "That's nice, Ellie, but can't we have it for breakfast? I really am whopped."

The urge came upon me to sit down beside him and cradle him in my arms the way I would have Abbey or Tam, but there was a homework grade at stake here. I couldn't risk an F. Mrs. Malloy would never let me hear the end of it, and I had to think of Bunty. She would think I didn't take Fully Female seriously.

My assignment fell back on the bed, eyes closed, nostrils working like a pair of bellows. Any second now, I would be listening to a stertorous symphony in A minor. Time to take a leaf out of *Voyage to Valhalla*. Surely Princess Marvel would not have stood here dangling her arms and watching her spinach salad wilt? Nay! She who lopped off the heads of her enemies with a flick of the wrist would have seized the mo-ment—seized the man. Reaching down, I took hold of Ben's ears and lifted his head off the pillow.

"Wakey, wakey!"

"What's that?" His eyes cracked open.

"I can't let you sleep."

"Ellie, please!" He moved to roll over, but sat up instead, rubbing his eyes. "I had this nightmare. You were wearing a pair of horns, getting ready to torture me. Good heavens! You *are* wearing horns."

Straightening my headgear to a more becoming angle, I said defensively, "The object of this evening's exercise was to intro-duce a little lighthearted fantasy into our relationship. I was all set to wine you and dine you as a prelude—"

The lift of a dark, inquiring eyebrow. "Is this about sex?"

"In a manner of speaking."

"For God's sake, why didn't you say so!" Talk about fling-ing caution and clothes to the four winds! Ben was off the bed, his shirt unbuttoned, before I could light the fondue can-dle. Five minutes later he returned from a sortie to the bath-room, resplendent in black silk and aromatic with Mr. Right aftershave. I should have been flushed with triumph, but as we took our seats at the linen-covered table, I felt curiously deflated. The man had no eyes for my chocolate cake or the marinated chicken; he sat with hands on his lap, like a good child waiting to be dismissed from table so he could run off and play.

"I hope you don't find me too easy." His demure smile did not match the roguery in his brilliant blue-green eyes.

"Heaven forbid." I went to lengthen the fondue flame and to my horror saw the lace edging on my draped sleeve catch fire. No doubt Princess Marvel would have relished the moment. Her warrior nostrils would have quivered with ecstasy as she inhaled the life-threatening smog. Her mischievous laughter would have quickened the flame. But Ellie Haskell was not ready for the voyage to Valhalla. My mind became one big scream, but I couldn't open my mouth to squeak Help! let alone sing "You Light Up My Life." In hideous slow motion I saw Ben drag his eyes away from my cleavage and lunge across the table to extinguish the blaze with his hands.

All over; both the danger and my precious dinner, which now lay in a mucky, oily ruin on the floor. The good news was that neither Ben nor I had sustained damage. The width of my sleeve had saved my wrist and Ben assured me his hands were not scorched. Perhaps it was the same as with those people who walk on live coals—the absence of fear provides some mystical shield. Even so, I removed my horns and offered to minister first aid to my hero.

"My hands are fine, Ellie." Stepping over the debris, he gathered me into his arms. "You scared me to death."

"I'll fetch the burn cream—"

"No need." He traced the line of my jaw and fingered his way down my throat to part my negligee.

"I do think I should rub some ointment on your hands."

"Sweetheart, there are other parts of my anatomy in more need of attention." His breath was a tropical breeze, gusting its way down my cleavage and, to be perfectly frank, I must say I was no longer thinking in terms of getting an A. What *did* bother me a smidgeon was leaving our dinner on the floor, like the aftermath of some medieval banquet, but Ben—usually such a fussbudget—seemed unconcerned.

"Later." He walked me to the bed.

"Hold on a minute." Breaking free, I hurried to the bath-room and, opening up the medicine cupboard, removed a large pink bottle from the arsenal on the glass shelf. I returned to find Ben lying facedown on the bed. "Ready or not, here I come!" Seated beside him, I drew the black silk of his dressing gown down over his shoulders, shook a dollop of cherry-pink gook onto my hand, rubbed my palms together and began the massage. The scent of an orchard in flower filled the room. Slowly, rhythmically I worked my way down his back.

"Do I get to turn over now?"

" 'Patience is a virtue,' " I quoted, " 'possess it if you can. Found seldom in a woman and never in a man.' "

"Ellie."

"Oh, all right." I watched him flip over on his back and then his smile faded to a look of blank horror. "What's wrong?" I cried.

"I feel so tacky!"

"Darling!" I gurgled a laugh. "We're married!"

"I'm stuck to the sheet!" He tried to sit up but it was as though he were held down by rubber suction cups. "What the hell have you done to me? What *is* that stuff?" He sounded every bit as outraged as Hercules must have been after don-ning the lion skin smeared with lethal gook.

"It's body lotion." Picking up the pink bottle, I began read-ing from the label. " 'A pleasing blend of nature's finest wild cherry blossom and rose hip syrup for your . . .' "

"Continue."

"Well . . . it does say here 'for your bath,' but I'm sure it's really an all-purpose—"

"Bubble bath!" He shot up with a ripping sound, which

could have been the sheet or the skin being torn from his protesting body. "For crying out loud, Ellie! How could you make such a stupid mistake? Couldn't you have looked?"

"Before I leaped all over you? Is that what you mean?" Yanking my negligee out from under his elbow with another ferocious rip, I got up, screwed the lid back on as tight as it would go, and banged the bottle down on the dressing table. "Next you will be accusing me of forcing my unwanted attentions on you."

"My dear, I don't deserve this!"

"If you had an ounce of humour!"

"Thank God I don't, or I'd have died laughing at those damn silly horns." Wrapping his dressing gown around his manhood, towel-fashion, Ben stomped out of bed. "Look, sweetheart, I'm sorry, but this has been a long day."

"And you're the only one who works?" Chasing after him out the door and into the bathroom, I snarled, "For *you* I disrupted my busy schedule, for *you* I bathed and primped!"

"Thanks for making it sound such a bloody chore!" Turning on the shower, he vanished into a cloud of steam which swiftly turned to cherry-pink foam. I was heading into the hall when his voice drew me back. "Ellie?"

An apology so soon? Wonders would never cease. I turned. "Yes?"

"I forgot to ask if you heard from the vicar. I sent round a box of—"

"Ginger biscuits." I didn't get to explain that I had attained this information from Mr. Spike after nearly running him down this morning.

"Not just any ginger biscuits," came the disembodied voice. "They were anatomically correct gingerbread men."

"You didn't!"

"To the pure all things are pure. And we can assume Reverend Spike and her spouse have the most pristine of minds."

Fury choked me. I knew why he had done this! Vanity of vanities, thy name is man. On hearing the vicar boast of her husband's culinary prowess and the accompanying blue ribbons, Ben had seen in Mr. Spike a rival to be bested before he gained ascendancy in the kitchens of Chitterton Fells. But at what cost?

The spectre of excommunication loomed large, especially if Freddy's escapade leaked out. For the first time it occurred to me that the reason Miss Thorn had looked right through me in Doctor Melrose's office that morning might be because she had spotted my dear cousin dressed up as the vicar and suspected me of being in collusion with him. Perhaps she had used the excuse of returning Ben's hanky to come round this afternoon and have it out with me. Whatever her feelings for the new vicar, Miss Thorn might well have been outraged on Bunty's behalf.

In the last couple of days my life had turned into a quagmire. For that I could not entirely blame Fully Female. But it did occur to me as I stood in my Turkish bathroom that there were dangers inherent in becoming the Woman He Always Wanted. Already we had Mrs. Huffnagle accidentally or otherwise frizzled by an electrical appliance. This evening I had almost gone up in flames and—

The ringing of the telephone brought me out of my reverie. I hastened to pick up the extension on the landing before the babies woke up. All prepared for a wrong number, I was shocked when a feverish voice blasted: "Ellie Haskell?"

"Yes—"

"You must come *at once.*"

"Who is this?"

"Jacqueline Diamond. Please! Don't ask any questions. Just get here. Twenty-one Rosewood Terrace. Hurry! And whatever you do—don't bring anyone with you!"

The desperate urgency of the plea numbed my brain. If I ran to tell Ben I was leaving, he would ask all sorts of questions which I couldn't answer. He would insist on going with me, despite instructions to the contrary, which would mean getting the twins up and taking them down to Freddy at the cottage. By the time I had worked out this scenario and voted it impossible, I was in the estate car and backing out of the stable in a roar of exhaust. The gravel driveway vanished under my wheels and I was out on Cliff Road, racing through the night on my way to an unknown house at the request of Mrs. Norman the Doorman. That I was on the verge of meeting my children's idol never crossed my mind. Nor did I fret that my green negligee was unsuitable attire for so momentous an event. Neither curiosity nor apprehension wracked my soul. The desperate urgency of Jacqueline's plea had driven all caution from my soul. I have no sense of direction, but I drove to Rosewood Terrace as if I had a map etched in my brain. If memory served me correctly, Miss Thorn lived on this street. A year or so ago she had invited me over for tea, and we had talked about twins. Prophetic . . . and quite irrelevant at this moment.

Number Twenty-one was a detached Tudor-style dwelling set back from the road in a garden dense with fir trees. Having parked at the curb, I hurried up the narrow path, my bare feet impervious to the chill of concrete, but the rest of me aware of a prickly sensation that was only partially due to those pine trees brushing up against me with their needles. A strip of light showed from an upstairs room but otherwise the place was uncompromisingly dark. The covered porch might have been welcoming in daylight, but the damp had brought out the smell of cats who had left their calling cards. By feel and error I found the doorbell and heard its peal invade the dim interior. No scurry of answering footsteps, but I thought I heard a distant voice call, "Ellie?"

Feeling came back as I stubbed my toe on a rock by the door. The dam was broken. Terror poured over me like sweat. Something was seriously amiss within these walls. Bending down, I picked up the rock with the intention of smashing one of the glass panels, but fortune was with me. I didn't have to resort to breaking and entering. A stray streak of moonlight pointed out the key which had been hidden under the rock. I slipped it into the lock and with a mixture of relief and dread stepped into the unlit hall.

"Jacqueline?"

"Up here!"

My hand found a light switch and I mounted the stairs as fast as I could—given the fact that I was weighted down by legs borrowed from a convict in irons.

"I'm in here."

What a coward! I longed to turn and flee from whatever torment of the soul lay behind the door now staring me in the face, but I grasped the crystal knob and walked into a room dominated by an iron bedstead. On it lay Mrs. Jacqueline Diamond, bound hand and foot—*gasp!*—and naked as the day she was born, save for a pair of cowboy boots and a leather holster.

Speechless, I looked at the telephone half on and half off the bedside table, the receiver dangling by its cord. Moving towards her—wishing I had a scarf, a handkerchief, anything to cover her embarrassment—I almost pitched over the caped figure sprawled on the floor.

Chapter Seven

I would kill for a cigarette ..." Jacqueline rammed her knuckles against her mouth.

Poor dear, I am sure she wanted to bite off her tongue, for we hadn't needed a medical dictionary to clue us in that Norman was dead. She had staggered frantically to her husband's side the moment I had undone her constraints. When I knelt beside her to drape a blanket around her nakedness, she was trying to find a pulse, but her hand trembled so violently she couldn't hold it down. Norman's face was as kind in eternal repose as it had been when talking to children on television. His fixed stare looked upon a distant place where he saw them still . . . young Marcie and Andrea, Philip and John. Surely wherever he had gone there would be a position available for a man who made little ones smile.

"He has climbed the ladder to the moon," I said.

His wife, now his widow, sat huddled on the bed, her ash-blonde hair dragging on her shoulders, her mascara smeared, her cowboy boots protruding below the hem of the blanket. A fat lot of use I was, standing shivering in my stupid negligee. I knew I should right the telephone and call a doctor or the police, but it seemed inhuman not to first fetch her a glass of brandy or a hot drink.

"Third drawer, dressing table." Her raspy voice jolted me into action. I assumed she wanted me to fetch her something to wear, but she had belatedly remembered a hidden cache of cigarettes.

"Thanks." Taking the packet I handed her, she tapped out a king-size filter tip and asked for the lighter on the black oak tallboy. "Want one?"

"No thanks." In all honesty, I—who had never stuck a ciga-rette between my lips, unless you count those kiddy candy ones with the sugary pink tips—would have given my left lung for a puff. Anything to block out the realization that death is always waiting in the wings, a black-cloaked figure . . . like the one sprawled at our feet.

"Norman was always after me to quit smoking. He didn't like me swearing either. But what the hell, doesn't count now, does it?" She screwed up her Lauren Bacall eyes against the smoke rising in a small cloud and looked at the phone. "It took me forever to work my hand loose, and almost as long to reach the operator with the butt of the receiver." Another puff of smoke. "You must be wondering why you're the one I phoned."

"I do see it had to be someone in Fully Female."

"You bet." Her cigarette voice held a wheeze of humour. "And who was it, Ellie Haskell, who suggested at Marriage Makeover that I liven up my marriage by playing the part of a poor little dolly in need of rescue by Norman the Doorman?"

Gripping the iron bedpost, I hung on for dear life.

"Wipe that look off your face; I'm not blaming you." She ground out the cigarette in a crystal dish and immediately lit up again. "All I meant was yours was the name which leaped to mind. What scared the piss out of me was thinking you might have an unlisted number. Luckily the operator didn't even ask me to spell the name." Jacqueline hoisted the blanket up over her shoulders. "Want to know how it happened?"

"Should we take the time?" My mind was backing away like mad from invading the final moments of Norman the Doorman. What had happened in this room to bring about this tragedy should remain sealed within the heart of his spouse, at least until the police and the medical examiner dragged the story out of her. "Don't you think I should telephone . . . ?"

"Not yet." Jacqueline was on her third cigarette. "Telling you will get things straight in my head. I took the idea of dressing up in the boots and holster from the Fully Female manual."

"The Ranch Dressing," I interpolated, "to accompany the Bird of Paradise Fondue."

"Norman doesn't . . . didn't care for chicken. What shocked me was that he went for my fantasy fling-ding in a big way. Not so much as a peep out of him about what his kiddy audience would think if they knew he was up to high jinks. Normie was always at his happiest in the Land of Let's Pretend. The moment he tied me to the bed, I became Babbsie Bang-Bang, kidnapped from her plastic ranch house by the terrible Toy Snatcher. Before I could grow one goose bump, Normie had donned his mask and cape and was scaling the armoire ... with a leg up from a chair ..."

"But didn't you tell me the other day that Norman was afraid of heights?"

"So he was." She looked away from me.

Removing Jacqueline's cigarette before it dropped two inches of ash on the floor, I ground it out on the bedpost and waited for her to continue. Out of the corner of my eye I saw Norman's hand, fingers spread wide as if making one last desperate clutch at life. Awful as it was to be discussing the man while he lay not a yard away, it was worse to think that Jacqueline's voice fell on dead ears.

"Normie was crouched on top of the armoire, caped arms spread, ready to leap onto the bed and rescue me when I aimed the water pistol I had cupped in my hand. You know how it was on the show—Norman the Doorman could only be destroyed by soap or water—and I thought it would be cute to add an element of surprise."

"'But surely Babbsie Bang-Bang wouldn't hurt Norman?" My interruption was a wild pitch to ward off the inevitable.

A smoky laugh. "I'd been brainwashed by the Toy Snatcher. When Norman leaped, I fired. He was bloody surprised all right. The old dear missed the bed ... end of show." The harshness of her voice didn't fool me. The woman was ... had to be ... choking on misery and remorse. I could see the blue plastic gun peeking out from under the bedside table.

"I killed him."

"No." Sitting down on the bed, I put my arm around her. "Jacqueline, you mustn't do this to yourself. It was an accident."

"Think the cops'll see it that way?"

"You'll explain—"

"Before or after you tell how you found me strapped to the bed naked as a jaybird? And what do you think this will do to Normie's Tinseltown image?"

The word tarnished sprang to mind.

NIGHT gathered up its black cape with a swirl of purple lining and stole across the housetops as if aware that dawn was hard on its heels, a ray gun in its hot little hand. Driving through streets more tortuous than my thoughts, I reflected wryly that a few days ago I had worried about lying about my weight on a yogurt survey. Was it possible my conscience was too finely tuned? Was I engaging in hyperbole when sensing the hand of the law ready to descend on my shoulder, the way Miss Clopper's had in algebra class?

"Ellie Haskell, neé Simons, it is alleged that with duplicity aforethought, you did conspire with one Jacqueline Diamond to conceal facts pertinent to the death of her spouse, the beloved television personality Norman the Doorman."

"Your Lordship!"

"Be brief, Mrs. Haskell."

"Learned Counsel is attempting to mislead the jury with conclusions which, while in the main true, do not reflect the motives of myself or the grieving widow. Yes, I left the premises before the police or a medical examiner arrived at the scene because I wanted to help spare Jacqueline Diamond em-

barrassment. What was the harm in her giving an abbreviated version of the facts—that her husband fell and hit his head while practicing one of his stunts? It's not as though there's any question of foul play."

"That depends on your idea of play, Mrs. Haskell. I suggest, ladies and gentlemen of the jury, that on the night in question, Mr. Diamond was not practicing Boy Scout knots. It is my contention that Mrs. Diamond enticed her husband—a man of guileless naivete—into engaging with her in a game of bondage which I submit ended in his untimely death. Your Lordship, I offer into evidence Exhibit Forty-three, the Fully Female manual."

"No *need*, my wife has one."

"I do not question Your Lordship's impartiality—"

"Pray proceed, Mr. Rimple."

"Ladies and gentlemen of the jury, I sorrowfully suggest that Mr. Diamond rebuffed his wife's animal advances—culled from this paean to erotica—and thus doing, so outraged her that she provoked the fall that killed him."

"Objection! Your Lordship, Learned Counsel is accusing my Fellow Female of murder!"

"Mrs. Haskell, I will hold you in contempt."

"I don't care. I refuse to sit still in the dock for this nonsense. Mrs. Diamond loved her husband."

"Hearsay!"

"Are you suggesting, Mr. Rimple, that she tied herself to the bed after giving her husband a fatal shove?"

"Mrs. Haskell, all things are possible in love and law."

EMERGING from my courtroom nightmare, I discovered that I had been driving on mental cruise control. I began praying for guidance, not out of my moral dilemma, but out of the one-way street, down which I was driving the wrong way, intent on going goodness knows where.

When at last I parked under the archway at Merlin's Court and switched off the ignition, it dawned on me that Ben might reasonably expect some semirational explanation of my exploits following my precipitous flight from home. A friend needed me, I would say. Whereupon he would naturally inquire the name of said friend. Harmless, husbandly chit-chat with potentially awkward repercussions. Tomorrow, when Norman's demise was plastered on the front page of *The Daily Chronicle*, it would be difficult to convince Ben that Jacqueline and I had spent the midnight hours exchanging cross-stitch patterns. He would press me for all sorts of tiresome details which would infringe on my loyalty to a woman I barely knew. I would threaten to leave him if he didn't shut up. He would say, Suit yourself, but you get the cat, I get the kids . . . and I would be tempted to take a flying leap off an armoire.

Stepping from the car, I stood in the courtyard beneath a gauzy grey sky, drained by night of its colour as was my face by the sound of footsteps. Ben emerged through the portcullis to stand like Heathcliff, his shirt ruffling in the wind and his eyes blazing black in a face parched as death. Thank God, my name wasn't Catherine. Ellie is no name for a doomed heroine, and as such, I had never feared to hear it hurled against the twilight sky.

"Ellie!" The wind echoed the mournful sound.

"Yes, dear?" I moved toward him, wishing I were a ghost who would evaporate at his touch. But there was no escape, he reached out his arms and crushed me to his manly chest. He bent his dark head, blocking out the moon—or it could have been the sun coming up; at such moments one loses track of time and place. His mouth seized possession of mine in a kiss of such searing passion that it sucked the soul right out of my body. I would like to say that I fell in love with my husband all over again at that moment, but the shameful truth is that I did not use the moment to step outside myself and analyze my emotions. I did not look into my husband's eyes and think, Damn, you're a good provider, and I adore the way you handle our tax returns. I wanted us to take possession of each other out there in the courtyard; I wanted to be his lover, not his wife . . .

Ben wrenched his lips away from mine, but held on to me with his eyes. "Thank God, you came back to me, my love. I thought I would go mad, pacing the house, knowing I had driven you away by my stupid insensitivity. I was planning on putting an advert in *The Daily Chronicle* this morning: 'Ellie, please come home. Things will be different. Please contact and say all is forgiven.' "

My breathing slowed. I was remembering my anguish upon finding the twins gone from their playpen.

"Ben, aren't you angry that I walked out?"

"Sweetheart, the thought of you driving around in circles for hours . . ." He had that part right at least. "I was filled with such shame!"

That made two of us.

He touched my face with fingers more gentle than the breeze that ruffled my green lace negligee. "I kept thinking I didn't have one portrait-sized photo of you with the twins."

"Ben . . ." I couldn't go on. There was so much to lose by telling him the truth.

He drew my hands to him, and through the fabric of his

shirt I could feel his warmth and the pounding of his heart when he said, "Never in my life have I felt such dread."

"Don't think about it," I said hastily.

"How can I not? The thought of having to ask my mother to come down and take over was so demoralizing. Not that there's any doubt she would have done a superb job."

"Sublime!"

"But, Ellie, I wanted my children's mother, not *my* mother."

Laying my head against his shoulder, I asked him how he could seriously have believed that I would stay away forever. Abandon him, abandon my children, just because things had become a little sticky for a while?

"At such times, Ellie, one doesn't think rationally. I've forgotten how to be alone."

The wind chose that moment to step between us like a third presence. Too many powerful emotions too late at night turned the world topsy-turvy. Or that's what I thought had happened until it occurred to me that Ben had swept me up in his arms with my gauzes trailing and, like Heathcliff with his benighted Cathy, was striding across the courtyard into the house through the garden door, which he had left open and now kicked shut behind us, and up the stairs to our bedroom, where the pheasants on the wallpaper awaited us in a flutter of excitement.

I can't say I experienced any qualms upon returning to the scene of my fantasy fiasco. But when Ben settled me upon the bed in a swirl of skirts that would have done justice to a fabric softener advert, I did look with some aversion toward the fireplace area. No need for fear and trembling! Some genie had been at work here. The intimate table for two had been denuded of its oil-soaked cloth and returned to its everyday state. A collage of books and candlesticks was now arranged on its mahogany surface. The ruined rug, the fondue pot, and all other vestiges of our aborted midnight feast had been scraped from the landscape as if they never were.

Joining me on the bed, Ben enveloped me with his arms and spoke into my hair. "We were ready for a new hearth rug."

"Oh, yes! I hated that little family heirloom."

His laughter vibrated down my spine, and if the tingling wasn't one of exquisite passion for my dark and stormy knight, it didn't matter. At that point I was ready to trade up to friendship, with its lifetime guarantee. Shifting around to face him, I cupped his face in my hands.

"Thank you."

"For what?"

"For cleaning up and . . ."

"Yes?"

"For being imperfect."

His blue-green eyes were flecked with the gold of tomorrow's sunlight, and I wanted him to hold me so tight that neither death nor thoughts of six A.M. feedings could part us.

"What's that?" He lifted his head.

"Sounds like Abbey."

"And there goes Tam."

"Perhaps if we lie here and don't breathe . . ." But even as I spoke, I was on my feet, already mentally back in uniform.

"Ellie, you're not leaving this room." He took hold of my arms and walked me backwards to the bed. "I'll see to the twins while you get some shut-eye."

"But you have to go to work in a few hours."

"So do you."

I wove my fingers through his rumpled black hair and whispered, "Why don't we both go? We could make a date of it."

He didn't answer. Instead, he removed my chenille dressing gown from the hook behind the wardrobe door and wrapped it around my shoulders as if it were a sable stole and we were Lord and Lady Fitzuppity stepping out for a night on the town.

LUCKY me, I am blessed with one of those constitutions that bounces back from lack of sleep with no ill effects—other than feeling as though I've just donated eight pints of blood and every drop that is left has migrated to my eyeballs. When Ben left for the restaurant at the inhuman hour of ten A.M. the next morning, I presented as sweet a picture of domesticity as you could imagine. There I sat at the kitchen table demurely sipping coffee while my offspring, identically attired in peppermint green, gurgled and gooed in the playpen. Ah, but what falsehood lurks in the heart of woman! As soon as the garden door closed behind Ben signalling the all-clear, I grabbed up the newspaper and rifled frantically through the pages, desperately searching for a late-breaking bulletin on the late great Norman the Doorman. Not a word.

The death-of-the-week honours went to the recently departed Mrs. Huffnagle. Her husband, a distinguished gentleman of the old school wearing an ascot and a lugubrious expression, was pictured under the caption *Grieving widower learns faulty electrical outlet a factor in bathroom death of spouse.* Did I need this callous reminder that joining Fully Female could prove a fatal mistake?

The last of my energy drained away and I slumped forward,

rocking my coffee cup in its saucer, and was out like a light for all of thirty seconds. Grimace! Something was calling me back to life—an insistent knocking that brought me snarling to my feet.

"Coming!"

Under the watchful eyes of my daughter, who was gnawing on her rattle in a most unladylike way, I staggered to the garden door and opened up.

"What is this, the Royal Mint?" Mrs. Malloy stood on the doorstep, supply bag looped over her arm and the spotted veiling of her hat drawn down over her eyebrows.

Immediately on the defensive, I stammered that the door wasn't locked, only stuck. Before she could open her mouth, my brain had thumped out the anticipated response in a series of jolts that threatened to cave in the sides of my head. But to my perplexity, Mrs. Malloy never said a word about not doing windows or hinges. Her introductory crack seemed to have left her spent. She entered the kitchen as if borne upon a current of air, her four-inch heels seeming to skim the quarry tile. Belatedly, I realized she looked as though she'd had even less sleep than I. Her eyes stared out of a face as white as the roots of her hair into a vast nothingness. They reminded me uneasily of Norman the Doorman's last night.

She paused in the middle of the room, staring down at the red-gold heads in the playpen. "They new?"

"What?"

"The kiddies."

"No, I've had them for some time." Shock turns me giddy. "I got them at a two-for-the-price-of-one sale."

"That's right. I remember now." Mrs. Malloy deposited herself, supply bag and all, in the rocking chair beside the fireplace and began pumping her foot as if working a treadle sewing machine, back and forth, back and forth. I would have gone mad if I hadn't been so desperately afraid she had already crossed the invisible line. Could she have fallen off the bus and suffered a concussion? Should I phone Dr. Melrose or, light dawned, was her state of mind a repercussion of her romantic tryst with Walter Fisher? Had he performed some kind of experimental taxidermy on her? Or were we dealing with a standard case of post-orgasmic trance?

"Tell me," I asked with a brave smile, "how was your evening?"

"None of your bloody business, Mrs. H," she answered in a monotone.

"Sorry." Properly put in my place, I attempted to hide my discomfiture by plopping the kettle down on the cooker and hunting about for the copper caddy. Sure enough, it was where it always was—next to the teapot, right under my nose.

From behind me came a raucous sob and, scattering teabags, I hastened back to the rocking chair to find Mrs. M with her face buried in a black-edged hanky. A gift no doubt from her beloved. And suddenly it occurred to me that what I had read in her face might not have been ecstasy revisited, but the blank look of despair. All too possibly her homework assignment had been the same dismal failure as mine and Jacqueline Diamond's.

"Roxie, dear!" I stayed the arm of the chair to fend off a wave of motion sickness. "So what if your romantic rendez-vous didn't measure up to your hopes and dreams!"

"How's that?" She lowered the hanky a notch to reveal eyes that looked as though they had spent twelve rounds in the ring, but there was a note in her voice that suggested she might be returning to her old fighting form. "I trust you're not suggesting, Mrs. H, that I failed to give satisfaction."

"Heaven forbid!"

"Mr. Fisher was *transported.*"

"Lovely!" I said, sounding like the vicar's husband. Mercifully, my blushes were forestalled by the shrill summons of the kettle. Like a hurky-jerky damsel in a Charlie Chaplin film, I scurried to and fro, steaming up the kitchen as I brewed up, fetching the mugs because I didn't want the hassle of saucers. Ooops! Forgot the sugar.

"There!" I held out Mrs. Malloy's tea.

"What are we doing, sending up smoke signals?" her voice came from far off, causing me to fear I was losing her again, but she spread her hanky on her lap in lieu of a serviette and took the mug. "Walter told me he'd never had it so good. He held me in his arms after he had his way with me for the fifth or sixth time and told me things I can never breathe to a living soul. The floodgates were opened you see and . . . he . . . The man wept, Mrs. H."

Gracious! Now I did feel like a failure. In all the time Ben and I had been together I had never once made him cry for joy during moments of intimacy. Perhaps the occasional sniffle when my perfume didn't agree with him, but that hardly counted. Noticing Tam sleepily rubbing his nose, I plucked him from the playpen and cradled his silken head against my shoulder. All the perfumes, all the creams, and we grown-ups still never smell this good. Eyes on Abbey, who at any moment might demand her turn with Mummy, I asked Mrs. Malloy about Mr. Fisher's wife.

"What about the woman?" Jealousy is a powerful force. The rocking chair almost did a backwards somersault. Tea slopped all over the hanky. "She's been out of the picture for donkeys' years."

"So you told me." I shifted Tam in my arms. "But are they divorced? Is he free to marry again?" Already I could see the announcement of nuptials in *The Daily Chronicle. Mrs. Roxie Malloy wed Mr. Walter Fisher, Chitterton Fells's foremost undertaker, in a simple ceremony at the Chapel of Rest last Tuesday. The bride wore a shroud of white silk with a demi-train and carried a wreath of white roses.*

"Walter didn't promise marriage."

Ah! Herein lay the rub.

The rocking chair started up again. "You don't get it, do you, Mrs. H? I tell you, after last night it don't require a piece of paper to make me Walter's till death do us part." Her voice broke.

"You know what they say," I interrupted. " 'Love is a good servant but a poor master.' "

Mrs. Malloy ignored me. "No need to brand his name on my behind. I knew when my eyes opened this morning and met his across the pillow that I'm his till the end, bound by invisible chains, never to be a free woman so long as we both shall live."

This peppering of the conversation with references to the mortal state didn't alarm me. I assumed that after a night in Mr. Fisher's company, one might begin to think in terms of the Big Sleep. But at the same time, I wished she wouldn't talk that way. It fleshed out the horror of seeing Norman the Doorman dead on the floor.

Watching Mrs. Malloy plod over to the table and begin unloading the supply bag, I felt the full weight of Tam in my arms. Since he and Abbey were born, I had chafed at times against the loss of freedom. I had wondered if I'd ever belong to myself again. But surely lovers weren't as high maintenance as children, although I would concede they were more work than husbands. Inviting a man into your bed is quite different from yawning a "Ready to turn in, old dear?" before toddling around to your own side with a cup of cocoa. In a liaison there are expectations to be met and amenities to be observed. Fresh sheets at the drop of his drawers. Your mother's photo turned to the wall in case her scowl puts him off his stroke . . .

"Time for a drink," said Mrs. M, causing me to curse Mr. Walter Fisher for driving her back to the bottle. But I misjudged the matter—if not the man. She lifted her container of Fully Female Formula from the supply bag and helped herself to one, no, two glasses, and held them under the tap. "You'll join me, won't you, Mrs. H? I haven't heard—and I'm not asking—what you got up to last night. But we both have to keep up our strength. Bottoms up!" In the context of Fully Female, this toast struck me as decidedly risqué, but no time to gape. Mrs. Malloy drained her glass, set it down, and removed Tam from my arms. "There! You sit down and enjoy yours."

"I really can't."

She clearly took this to mean that I didn't wish to horn in on her meager supply. Quickly, she set me straight. "What's a tablespoon of Formula between friends? You can stand the next round. By the by, Mrs. H, what with one thing and the next, I forgot to bring back your Healthy Harvest Herbs and the purple gown."

"Don't worry."

"How the bloody hell can I help it? I can see from your face you're upset."

"It's . . . the Formula," I said through contorted lips. The liquid mush was the vilest stuff imaginable. It looked as though sawdust were the main ingredient and it tasted like glue. I was sure I would never get my tongue unstuck. Unbeknown to Mrs. M, this was the first time I had taken more than a couple of sips before chucking the stuff down the sink. "Perhaps I shouldn't indulge this early in the day."

"Finish it up." Depositing Tam back in the playpen, she stood over me—right down to the last gulp. The beauty spot above her upper lip twitched as she stretched a damson smile. "That's the girl, Mrs. H. Now you can be off to your Fully Female meeting with a clear conscience."

If she only knew what secrets lurked in the heart of her employer.

THERE was no possibility of my making the morning session, and I strongly urged that Mrs. Malloy be the one to attend the afternoon one. But there was no budging her. She returned to her trance state when she picked up her feather duster.

"I was tickling Walter's fancy with this when . . ."

Happily, I was spared the gory details. She exited the kitchen through the already open door, but if it had been closed, I swear she would have walked right through it. Here was a woman elevated above the normal impediments of daily living, as once was Norman the Doorman. When the hall was clear, I went to the telephone and got Jacqueline Diamond's number from the operator.

"Want me to ring through for you, love?"

"Please."

Brrrrrppp . . . Brrrrrppp . . .

At the fourth ring I hung up. To have held on longer would

have seemed as vulgarly persistent as pounding on the front door of the house in Rosewood Terrace. Either the widow was incommunicado . . . or was she visiting Mr. Walter Fisher's place of business? Was he even now showing her the ultimate in relaxing pleasure—Eternal Rest's Chaise Lounge, with the Regency Ribbon lining and scrollwork sides?

Don't worry about the lack of notice, Mrs. Diamond. These spur-of-the-moment deaths are our bread and butter. We'll get your husband fitted out. We are talking made to measure, I assume. We wouldn't want a gentleman of your husband's fame going down in an off-the-rack jobbie, would we?

Disconsolate, I proceeded about my business, feeding the twins, getting them down for their naps, and putting an experimental load in the washing machine. I was in no mood to go down to Fully Female. That is, I wasn't until Freddy walked in through the garden door, tracking in dirt and a glimpse of the outside world.

"Peace offering, cos!" He held out a scraggly bunch of flowers. "I stole these especially for you from the vicarage garden."

"You really shouldn't have . . ."

"For you, nothing is too much trouble." A grin broke through the facial stubble, and he flourished a bow in which his ponytail brushed the floor.

"I meant, O Great Impostor," I said, bunging the purloined posy into a jug, "you shouldn't have set foot within a yard of the vicarage."

"You're right." Freddy strolled over to the table and helped himself to the cheese and tomato sandwich that was to have been my lunch. "Could have been very embarrassing if I'd been spotted lurking outside the French windows. The vicar—

well, I assume it was she, but to be on the safe side, I'll call her Madam X . . ." Freddy paused for dramatic effect and to take a huge bite of sandwich.

Damn the wretch for driving me to vulgar curiosity. "You were saying?"

"Madam was at prayer."

"Freddy!" There are some places I will not stick my nose lest it be smote from my face and cast into the outer darkness, never to be found again.

"She was petitioning forgiveness for the sin of jealousy, which had caused her to act unjustly to a fellow voyager through this vale of tears."

I silenced him by pitching a tea towel in his face. But of course the damage was done. I was unable to put this piece of gossip from me before my mind began toying with it, the way Tobias was pussyfooting at a grey felt mouse over in the alcove by the garden door. Was the Reverend Eudora Spike suffering pangs of remorse concerning Miss Gladys Thorn, whom she had sacked from the position of church organist—not because of any lack at the keyboard, but because Gladys might be singing "Abide With Me" to Mr. Spike.

Freddy tossed the towel back to me. I wadded it up into a ball and began buffing the surface of the counter between the cooker and the sink. Somewhere in the house Mrs. Malloy was singing "John Brown's Body," and the mouldering melody settled like a greasy film on the kettle, the copper bowls, the tea caddy, and the chairs. As for the hanging plants in the greenhouse window, they seemed to wither on the stem as if waiting for the inevitable root rot to set in.

"Who's the merry warbler?" Freddy bit into the apple that was to have been my dessert.

"Mrs. Malloy."

"Does she charge extra for these little ditties?"

"She's in love."

"And who's the lucky chap?"

"None of your business." As soon as the words were out, I regretted snapping at him of whom I was about to beg a favour. I suppose the idea had been at the back of my mind since he set foot in the kitchen, but it had taken old John Brown to make crystal clear that I had to go down to Fully Female and turn in my resignation. "Freddy"—I folded the tea towel over the rail of the cooker—"if I promise to listen to your lines for *Norsemen of the Gods* when I get back, will you stay and mind the twins for an hour or so? Mrs. Malloy is busy and, as you can hear, not really with it."

"My dear Ellie"—Freddy's face lurched into a porcupine grin—"groveling doth become you as the stars the night."

"Is that a yea or a nay?"

"What do you think, cousin?" To my surprise, he came around the playpen and gave me a hug. "Toddle along, old girl, and leave all in my capable hands."

ALL the way into town I practiced my farewell speech to Fully Female. *You're going to hate me, Bunty, but what with the babies and the house, to say nothing of the garden now that Jonas isn't here to help out, I really don't feel I can make the commitment to Fully Female that both you and I would wish. My marriage will undoubtedly be the loser, but at this point I feel I have to settle for getting my bed made every day rather than getting Ben into it every half hour.*

I had my lines down pat by the time I parked the car on the circular drive. But when I was walking around the fountain toward the Hollywood mansion shaded by trees, my mind derailed. All I could come up with was the truth: that I wanted to get out of Fully Female because I was beginning to think of love as a dangerous and possibly deadly pastime.

My feet slowed as I neared the half-moon terrazzo steps, and my heart throbbed with sympathy for all those people who, not having any major problems, have to make do with little ones. With my usual sterling cowardice I began hoping that Bunty would be unable to see me, either because she was at Marriage Makeover or engaged in interviewing Fully Female candidates. Alas, this was not my lucky day. The door opened as I reached the top step and Bunty herself stood on the threshold, looking as fetching as ever in a sleek outfit that resembled a body stocking for fit and exactly matched her champagne curls.

"Ellie! I saw you from the front window."

"Bunty!" Scraping up a smile, I blurted out the first words that came into my head. "Where are the peacocks?" Talk about drivel! If the birds weren't flaunting their fans and doing the royal strut at the front of the house, they would be on the back lawn . . .

Bunty's blue eyes filled with tears that spilled onto her luxuriant black lashes. Drawing me into the house, she closed the door before breaking the news.

"The peacocks have been kidnapped."

"No!"

"That's what I said when I went out this morning to find them buggering gone and a note tacked to the front door. You know what it contained?"

"A demand for ransom?"

"Bloomin' heck! Nothing so civilized. It was a recipe for

Bird of Paradise Fondue, the one from the Fully Female manual. What does that tell you, Ellie?"

"We're not dealing with a vegetarian?"

Taking my elbow, she propelled me through the spacious hall to the white-on-white living room with its skylights and Egyptian pyramid tables and the orchestra pit occupied by the grand piano. "Know what I think, Ellie? There's someone out there who's jealous as cats of the success of Fully Female and is out to sabotage the operation."

"You don't think you might . . ." My voice faltered.

"Go on, spit it out."

Fixing my eyes on the wall hanging with its nouveau Bronze Age design, I made the heinous suggestion. "Might it be possible that you're dealing with a dissatisfied client or the spouse thereof?"

The tear-darkened lashes gave her the ingenuous look of the twins. "Ellie, you're kidding, right? Sure I've had a couple of setbacks lately. First Mrs. Huffnagle kicked the bucket and now Mrs. Diamond is having to resign." A pause. "But I don't suppose you know about that."

I made the sort of helpless response you make to the dentist when he has you in the chair with your mouth full of instruments.

"Horrible shame. Mr. Diamond fell last night while practicing for one of his TV stunts in the bedroom . . . and snuffed it. A real blow"—Bunty seemed impervious to the pun—"but not in any way connected with Fully Female." The very strength of her denial made me wonder if she suspected that Norman's death was linked to Jacqueline's homework assignment.

"What a tragedy!" I managed to say. "Poor Mrs. Diamond. She has been questioned by the police, hasn't she?"

"Yes, but she said they were real loves." Bunty was standing on a llama rug, her coral nails plucking at the gold chain around her neck. "Flippin' heck, into every commercial venture a little rain must fall, and no one can call me insensitive. I cancelled this afternoon's program after talking to Jacqueline. Sorry you fell through the cracks, Ellie. You see why I keep grumbling about the office help. What do you think? Should I take Li's advice and give Miss Thorn a try? She wasn't bad the other day on the piano, and it would be handy having someone who could do both—play accompaniment for Retro-Relaxation and handle the office. If only she didn't look like something Rover dragged in from the graveyard!"

I didn't answer because I was trying to pluck up the courage to tell Bunty to cross another name off her client list. But the moment was lost. Footsteps sounded in the hall and suddenly— talk of the devil . . . and make that plural—we were looking at the handsome silver-haired Lionel Wiseman and Miss Thorn, who looked gawkier and more myopic than ever in the presence of such urbanity.

"Li, Sugar! Home so early?" Bunty gave him a perky smile, but I suspected she wasn't entirely pleased to be caught on the hop by her husband.

"Afraid so, sweetie!" Mr. W was unbuttoning his cashmere coat with his usual savoir faire, while Miss Thorn stood panting down on him from her superior height, her spectacles fogged and her raincoat misbuttoned.

"If this is not a convenient time . . ." She was tieing her hands into knots and trembling all the way down to her sensible shoes. "Perhaps if I come back another time, when Mrs. Wiseman isn't entertaining dear Mrs. Haskell—"

"Oh, I'm just leaving." I sent an ottoman skidding across the floor in my eagerness to be gone.

"Please"—Lionel Wiseman looked at me, while placing a hand on Miss Thorn's arm—"both of you stay. We'll all have a drink . . . and talk things through."

"Just as I suspected," Bunty stage-whispered in my ear, as the other two retreated into the hall with their coats. "Li is about to twist my bra strap. And what the bloomin' heck, Miss Thorn can have the job. A woman with my looks and charm," she continued with a puckish grin, "can afford to be kind. Yes, I suppose I should be cross with Li, but he's such a sweet old chauvinist, always looking out for his Bunty baby."

"But there's no need for me to stay—"

"That's where you're wrong, Ellie. I could tell Li wanted you here so it wouldn't look like two against one, and if you bugger off, we'll spend forty-five minutes talking about Miss Thorn's collection of telephone directories before getting down to pounds, shillings and pence."

"Thank you, I will take a glass of sherry." My non sequitur alerted Fully Female's fearless leader to the return of her husband and the job applicant. While he was busy with the decanters, we ladies seated ourselves—Bunty and I in the oyster-colored leather chairs, while Miss Thorn helped herself to the sofa. In anyone else this presumption might have been deemed bad form, but as always, she was so much atwitter it was hard not to smile . . . until I remembered slamming the garden door in her face yesterday afternoon when she came aknocking and I thought she was Freddy.

Amazingly, her mushroom eyes—when they strayed my way—harboured no hostility. It was as though the incident had never existed outside my imagination. Such magnanimity was both heart-warming and scary. But this was no time for psychoanalysis. Someone had to get the conversational ball rolling before our smiles set permanently.

"How are you, Miss Thorn?"

"Tremulous." She ducked her mousy head.

"I'd never have guessed." Bunty sucked in her smile. "You look cool as a cucumber in that sweetly pretty frock."

"Thank you." Miss Thorn drew the skirt of the hideous garment way down over her knees and raised her spectacles to Lionel Wiseman, who was heading toward us with the drink tray. "Nothing for me, my dear Mr. Wiseman. As you know, hard liquor does not agree with me. I have very sensitive insides."

"You suffer from indigestion?" Bunty asked.

"No, irregularity."

"Ah!" My exclamation went whispering to the lofty ceiling to vapourise on one of the skylights. I accepted a glass of sherry from Lionel and watched him hand one of the same to his wife before depositing the tray on a glass table and joining Miss Thorn on the sofa. As a married woman, I had no business noticing such things but he was one of the handsomest men I'd ever seen on the screen or off. Well into his fifties, he was still getting better. Those heavy dark brows, offset by that wonderful silver hair, promised passion as well as power. Blotting my drooling lips with a cocktail napkin, I waited for someone to say something.

"So!" Bunty, cute as a kitten, raised her glass. "I say the occasion calls for a toast!"

Lionel leaned forward, his handsome hands pressed to his

handsome knees. "My sweet, I never expected you to be so readily amenable, so accommodating. Gladys and I were braced for all kinds of fuss."

"Indeed, yes." Miss Thorn's flush clashed with her sallow complexion. "I have been so frightened and, of course, tension is the very worst thing for my . . . condition."

"Why, you silly goose," said Bunty. "As a Fully Female woman, my husband's wishes are my command."

"So kind! But as I said to Lionel, having waited this long to bestow my hand on the man of my dreams, I wanted everything to be perfect and I stoically refused to become officially engaged until I had your blessing, dear Mrs. Wiseman. Isn't that so, my Lionel, my treasure?"

"It is indeed, my rose without a thorn!"

Chapter Eight

Bunty dropped her sherry glass and I went into shock, whereupon Lionel Wiseman raised Miss Thorn's hand and pressed it to his comely lips. There they sat on the nubby white sofa with its oversized throw pillows, the man-about-town and the mature woman—lost in each other eyes. A moment of hearts and flowers to be savoured and reverently stowed in the Precious Memories Album of their lives.

The discarded wife gripped the sides of her chair and stood up. Her beautiful face was stiff with strong emotion. Suddenly, she threw back her blonde head and pealed out a laugh.

"This is a joke! A belated April Fools joke, isn't it? Li,

darling, you almost had me fooled, and I really would be very cross with you and Miss Thorn if I weren't even crosser with myself for being such a gullible nitwit. Ellie!" Bunty rounded on me as if I were a bodyguard who had failed her in a dark alley. "Stop looking like someone just ran over your grandmother! I tell you they're *kidding*."

"No, my sweet." Lionel's sorrowful eyes spoke more eloquently than his deep-timbered voice. "Your pain is mine, dear one, but these last six weeks, when you have thought me working late at the office, I have been with Gladys, engaging in the affair of a lifetime. Ours is a passion so explosive that I finally understand the principle of fusion."

"Oh, my God!" Bunty's face twisted in anguish. "To think I was so proud of you, carrying that organ donor card around in your wallet!"

Mr. Wiseman's broad shoulders sagged. He murmured, "We never meant to hurt Bunty, did we, beloved?"

Miss Thorn gathered up his hand and pressed it to her nonexistent bosom. "Never!"

This was worse than awful. I had never felt more horribly in the way. It was like opening a door into what you thought was the hospital gift shop and finding yourself in the chaos of a surgical procedure—blood spurting, guts flying, and a senior doctor jumping rope with a large intestine. *Please . . . get me out of here!*

"So," Bunty snarled, "Li wasn't a big enough boy to face me on his own!"

"We thought it best"—Miss Thorn gave one of the titters that were so much part of her charm—"that the three of us talk matters over with the hope that when the dust settles, we can all be the best of friends. I've always been a slave to convention and I said to Lionel . . ."—she paused to kiss his well-manicured hand in a slow voyage from fingertips to wrist— ". . I said I couldn't agree to a formal engagement until you, dear Mrs. Wiseman, agreed to sever the tie that binds."

"Are we talking divorce?" Bunty screeched.

"I've seen a sweetly pretty ring." A dreamy Miss Thorn stretched out her hand, the better to picture the betrothal gem perched on her knobby finger. "A half hoop of diamonds in a Victorian setting with a ruby—"

"To match your eyes?" Bunty lost all restraint. She lunged toward the dovesome twosome and let rip a scream that threatened to bring the skylights crashing down on our heads. "I'll kill you! I'll kill you both!"

Thank heaven for the twins! Toting them around must have increased my upper body strength. For I was somehow able to restrain her from diving across the coffee table and shredding the two of them with her pearly-white teeth.

While I held Bunty at bay, Mr. Wiseman and Miss Thorn exchanged concerned glances. "My dove, you see I was right to be deathly worried," he said.

"Hush, dear heart! Why don't I play one of my tinkles on the piano?" Eyes closed, mousy head thrown back, the lady braced herself for the agony of placing a distance of some fifteen feet between herself and her True Love. Taking the long way round the room in order to avoid coming within fighting distance of the current Mrs. Wiseman, Miss T descended into the orchestra pit, seated herself on the piano stool, arranged her skirts over her knobby knees, flexed her fingers, cracked her knuckles, and began to play a movement so lachrymose, I could have sworn the piano wept.

Miss Thorn raised her spectacles to Bunty's foaming face. "Ah sweet music, your charms do soothe the savage beast."

"*Breast,* my dove," corrected Lionel, his face as tender as that of a father listening to a child mispronounce its first words. "Music hath charms to soothe the savage breast."

"Oh, you couldn't expect Gladys to get that one right!" Bunty twisted free of my grasp. "You're the expert of course, Li darling, but I'd say all your lady love can boast in the way of breasts is a couple of mosquito bites."

"How dare you!" Mr. Wiseman rose up from the sofa. "How dare you impugn the physique of the woman I love!"

Miss Thorn uttered a mousey squeal.

Somewhere in that *House Beautiful* room a clock pinged the half hour, but I mistook the sound for a boxing ring bell, signalling another round about to begin. And, my goodness, with the opponents both up and prancing on their toes they could be letting fly for hours. I wasn't unsympathetic. My heart ached for Bunty, but I did have a life of my own outside these walls. My babies needed me. To say nothing of Freddy, who in return for favours rendered expected me to listen to his lines for that silly play.

But I was the one destined to take part in a two-bit melodrama. Gasp! On this very stage the silver-haired, silver-tongued male lead was pulling a gun from the inside pocket of his suit jacket and aiming it at the the ex–chorus-girl wife and ... there not being a sneeze of space between them ... her dim-witted companion.

Miss Thorn came to an echoing halt on the piano.

"Bunty," I cajoled, my eyes on the gun in Lionel's hand, "promise him a divorce."

"Never," shrilled the blonde numbskull. "I swear I'll see him and his fleshpot dead first!"

"Exactly as I thought." Lionel Wiseman was staring at the weapon, distaste pinching his nostrils, and with the breath lodged in my throat, I waited for him to explain how he knew of no recourse but to do for Bunty before she did for him. I was shaking so badly that I had trouble following what he was saying. "When Mrs. Pickle gave me this gun the other day, after finding it hidden in an apron in the terra-cotta urn by the waterfall, I tried to tell myself you were worried about burglars, but as I sat in my office, sipping cafe au lait and smoking a Brazilian cigar, I became increasingly convinced, Bunty, that you were aware of my liaison with Gladys and bent upon revenge."

"Mr. Wiseman, you couldn't be more wrong!" My voice raced along to get in ahead of him before he could stop—or shoot—me. "I'm the one who left that gun in the urn!"

"You?" A weary smile creased his handsome features. "Dear lady, your loyalty does you credit, while insulting my intelligence."

"But truly—"

"Shut up, Ellie!" Bunty pounced forward and, to a shudder of piano chords, whipped the snub-nosed gun away from her husband. "So, buster"—she chucked him under the chin with the butt before dancing backwards to rejoin me—"what took you so long? Why the bloomin' heck didn't you spill the beans about the gun when you first got your pudgy paws on it?"

In response to the gun swivelling in her direction, Miss Thorn was edging across the room to her loved one's side, hands raised above her head. "Lionel deemed it proper not to raise a rumpus until I had accepted his proposal of marriage."

"How friggin' decent!" Bunty spat out the words. "Never sink the old boat until you have launched the new!"

"One has one's standards," said Lionel.

"Until this very afternoon"—Miss Thorn had reached the sanctuary of his embrace—"I was teetering on the brink of declining the honour of becoming the second Mrs. Wiseman."

"The third, you clot!" Savagely, Bunty closed in on the pair of them. "At least I had the decency to wait until the first Mrs. Wiseman had been put out to pasture. Mark my words, you scraggy-necked bitch, you'll get what's coming to you, and it won't be any diamond ring with a bloody great ruby." A chill smile spread over her face, turning colder yet as she pried them apart with the gun and prodded them toward the hall. "Now get out, the pair of you!"

"You're behaving like a child." Lawyer Lionel managed to retain some dignity, even though he and his amour did resemble a couple of knock-kneed kiddies learning to skate backwards.

"Out, I say, out the pair of you!" Slam went the front door. Bunty returned to the living room, the gun dangling from her hand.

"Here, let me take that." I hurried over to her, but she flagged me away.

"No, Ellie! Give me a moment—I'll pull myself together."

"That's good."

"I can't shoot myself if my hand is shaking, can I?"

"Now stop that!" Without thinking twice, I snatched the revolver away from her. "And don't bother wrestling me for it, because it's not loaded." I devoutly hoped such was the case as I stashed it inside my raincoat pocket, but I didn't have time to worry about blowing off my feet, for Bunty had collapsed on the sofa and was sobbing piteously.

"Can you believe this? Li abandoning me for *that* woman? I adored him, you know that? I thought we had it all. Oh, why didn't I listen to that wise old bird, my Aunt Et? She used to say to me when I was a teenager, 'Bunty me girl, don't you go making my mistake. Don't make sex the be-all and end-all. Don't spend your life worshipping at the shrine of the one-eyed god.' And now look what I've done! Here I am, president of Fully Female, instructing other women on how to hold on to their men—and mine has bunked off with Miss Thorn!"

Unlike me, whose nose takes over my entire face, Bunty cried exquisitely. Tears beaded on her lashes and her cheeks deepened to a damask rose. How in heaven's name could Lionel Wiseman leave her? One could only wonder anew at Miss T's success with the opposite sex and marvel that she had lived thus long without coming a cropper.

"I am so sorry." I sat down next to her latest victim.

"What a laugh! Not satisfied with being a doting dolt myself, I persuaded dozens of other women to turn themselves inside out."

"You meant well."

"What will become of me?"

"You have friends, Bunty."

"I mean, financially. Fully Female is down the tubes. And Li can be generous as Midas or cheap as old Nick, depending on which way the wind blows. He'll blow hundreds of pounds on a tie, but won't throw out a crust of bread. He's always showered me with credit cards but now it wouldn't surprise me if he cut me off without a farthing."

"You'll have to get yourself—"

"A good lawyer?" Tears splashed from her blue eyes, but incredibly, she was laughing too. "You know, Ellie, a cockney brat who grows up dancing for pennies learns a thing or two about survival."

HOME SWEET home. Freddy and Mrs. Malloy had returned to their own hearths. The afternoon had dwindled to dusk and I was feeding the twins late, I am ashamed to say, without putting one hundred percent of myself into the task. Removing Abbey's empty bottle before she swallowed it whole, I rubbed her pink terry-cloth back and deposited her in the bouncer chair.

"That's my good girl!"

"Goo!"

"And now for Mummy's big boy." While Tobias prowled the kitchen sniffing the milky air, I settled with Tam in the rocking chair, tucked a nappy under his chin and whispered, *"Bon appétit!"* Ben, all being well, would not be home until late, which would give me time to accomplish something with the day. Ridiculous this feeling that women have—that they must present the mister with a report card at the end of the day and request that he initial it if satisfied. Behaviorists can say what they like about such things being environmentally based, I know it's a matter of biology. When the caveman came home to find the place still littered with bones from breakfast, he wanted to know why, but don't ask him about the bear he dragged home, whether he trapped it or won it playing pebbleante poker with the chaps.

The rocking was peaceful and Tam was taking his bottle with the methodical zeal that characterized him, but my heart was heavy. I had failed not only myself, but Mrs. Malloy and the rest of womankind in getting involved with Fully Female. A sense of powerlessness and doom settled upon me. Bunty's Aunt Et was right: those who make sex their idol shall pay a horrible price. Look at Mrs. Huffnagle and poor Norman the Doorman. And Mrs. Malloy—turned into a zombie by her Svengali. And now the founder of Fully Female—dumped! They had paid the price, but who was to say when enough pain, enough blood was enough?

"You should be ashamed of your mother," I informed both Tam and Abbey. "What sort of values is she teaching you? And goodness only knows what Daddy will say if—when—he finds out about Fully Female."

"Oooh!" Abbey pressed a hand to her rosebud mouth.

"Exactly." Holding Tam against my shoulder, I massaged his blue terry back, while giving my impersonation of Daddy on the warpath. " 'By Jupiter, Ellie, what am I to you? An object, a toy to be manipulated and mauled for your pleasure, picked up and discarded at will? I don't think I have ever felt so cheap, so utterly used!' "

As soon as I had my wee precious ones tucked into their cots and prayers said, I returned to the kitchen and ransacked the cabinet drawers for the Fully Female manual. Damn, Freddy must have had his disgusting paws on it. Ah, here it was under the toaster.

Hands trembling, I fully intended to tear it into shreds and burn the thing, if it would burn—somewhere I had read that tomes of witchcraft were flame-resistant, and these pages certainly had a mind of their own. The manual flipped open to Chapter Five.

Confess, Fellow Females, how many of you have been making do with love in the dark? What a thrill, huh? Every so often, just when you least expect it, this faceless nighttime creature gropes its way out of the swamp to feast upon your unseen flesh . . .

"Ughhhh!" I was poised, ready to drop the book, when a knock sounded at the garden door. Unable to move, I squeaked, "Come in!" And lo and behold, the Reverend Eudora Spike entered my bawdy house. "What a lovely surprise!"

Every hair, along with her decisive smile, in place, the new vicar stood holding a covered casserole dish in her kid-gloved hands. "Excuse my not phoning first, but . . ."

"You're so right." I blushed. "The best part of having neighbours is never knowing when they will pop in."

"I hope I'm not interrupting your dinner hour."

"Heavens, no! Ben works evenings and I was just indulging in a little inspirational reading." Idiot! She would ask the name of the book.

"How nice."

"Do let me take . . ."—I could hardly ask for the casserole without sounding grabby—". . . your coat."

"Thank you, but I won't stay more than a moment."

"Oh, but surely a cup of tea?" Dropping the Fully Female manual behind the toaster, I breathed more easily, but the same couldn't be said of Eudora; she appeared as stilted as our conversation.

"Well, if you insist, Ellie. And I do hope"—she held out the casserole—"that you don't distrust, as our youngsters say, geeks bearing gifts."

"What an idea! But I should be bringing *you* a house-warming gift."

She returned my smile. "Please accept this as a heart-warming gift. The pleasure being all mine. Your husband was so kind as to send over those delicious biscuits, I will be sending him a note. I should have done so before, but things have been . . . rather at sixes and sevens."

My eyes fell. I was picturing the anatomically correct gingerbread men.

"This afternoon Gladstone poached this salmon and, inevitably, five minutes before tea he received a phone call from . . . someone and had to leave unexpectedly, so I thought I would bring it over in hopes that you might enjoy it—if not tonight, perhaps tomorrow."

"How kind." There was something decidedly fishy about all this. Why couldn't she have saved the salmon until she and Gladstone, reunited, could partake of its coral-colored flesh? Mercy me, I was beginning to think like the Fully Female manual. And, if my eyes did not deceive me, Eudora was glancing over toward the toaster.

"How do you like the parish?" I bunged the casserole in the fridge, knocking over a jar of mayonnaise in the process.

"Very well, thank you." Mrs. Spike peeled off her gloves and unbuttoned her coat. "My, but Chitterton Fells seems a busy place. If the women aren't working outside the home, they are off at this health place . . . Fully something."

"Ah, yes," I said, sidling toward her. "The name does ring a bell. Fully Female . . . I think that's it."

"You don't belong yourself?"

"Eudora, as you can imagine"—I was doing the cat's cradle with my hands—"I am run off my feet with my four-month-old twins, and my cat Tobias is not adjusting well to being displaced." Said feline, hearing his name taken in vain, mewed loudly and swiped a pile of nappies off the work surface.

"And we mustn't forget your young and, unless appearances are deceiving, virile spouse." The vicar folded her regulation navy blue coat over a chair and smoothed her helmet of hair. "I remember how extra demanding Gladstone was of my time following the birth of our daughter Brigitta. In other words, Ellie, I would have thought you a prime candidate for this Fully Female organization." Her protuberant hazel eyes bored holes into my soul. Oh, dear God, I thought. The salmon is a sham. She knows about Freddy's masquerade, and she is here because she thinks I put him up to it.

"All right." I flopped down in the chair across from her and braced my elbows on the table. "I confess! I *am* a card-carrying member of Fully Female, but I had no hand whatsoever in my cousin's impudent charade and though I understand *fully*—hateful word—why you may well want to see the twit brought before the tribunals of Rome, or rather Canterbury, I do beg you to remember Freddy is an impressionable thirty-year-old who does have his good points. He is fond of children, kind to animals, and does not eat red meat to excess."

Alas, the vicar looked as immovable as any of the granite monuments in St. Anselm's churchyard. "Ellie, I am sorry to say this . . ."

"Yes?" My knees were doing a drum roll.

"I've no idea what you're talking about."

"You don't?"

"Well, I do grasp that your ne'er-do-well cousin's name is Freddy and that he's been up to some prank, but what that has to do with me I have no idea. You have to understand, Ellie, I am a cleric, not the public executioner."

"Ah!" In a wild impetuosity, born of my prevailing neuroticism, I had thrown a cousin *and* baby-sitter to the wolves. And much as I would have liked to leave the subject where it stood, I couldn't, lest Eudora suspect some criminal activity on Freddy's part the next time the poorbox came up short.

"Won't you take a cup of tea?"

"No, thank you," she said, as she held up a capable hand, "and please don't look so worried."

Did this mean we were still friends? Head bent, I recited the dreadful tale. "It was like this, you see. Freddy got wind of my having joined Fully Female and at once the possibilities for mischief were infinite—given the peculiar way his mind works. He also knew of your arrival on the Chitterton Fells scene and . . ."

"Yes?"

"He appeared at Fully Female headquarters dressed up as you, in a black hat with a veil, and led the Marriage Makeover session in prayer. Oh, Your Reverence"—I lifted my tear-spattered face—"I felt violated for you. He had us all join hands . . ."

"For the Lord's Prayer?"

What a dreamer. "Not on your life. Freddy closed his eyes, swayed in his chair, and urged us to let the love flow. And when we had reached a state of oneness, he told us to open our hearts one to the other by turning to the person on our right and telling her what we most disliked about her. Oh, it was awful! Mrs. Wardle, the librarian, told the girl from The

Bake Shop that she hated her for having hair that bounced.
Mrs. Sturgess told Mrs. Olsen that she was sick to death of
hearing about her multiple orga— . . . you know . . . and Mrs.
Best told Mrs. Rose, who owns the dress boutique on Market
Street, that she should be ashamed of her mirrors and it was
a wonder more women weren't found hanging from garment
hooks in the dressing rooms. The latter I sympathised with.
Mrs. Rose's clothes always suit their hangers far better than
they do me, but I didn't open my mouth to say Boo! let alone
denounce Freddy. He works with my husband Ben at the restaurant, and I was so afraid if those women knew what he
had pulled, they would blackball Abigail's.''

Reverend Spike's hazel eyes prompted me to continue.

"As a mother—no, let's make that a coward—I didn't say
a word to Freddy until I got him alone."

"I see." The vicar stood, but instead of heading for the
garden door, she crossed the room to the Aga cooker and
turned on the kettle. "I see that this calls for a cup of tea."

"You're not furious?"

"No." She reached for the copper caddy and turned to me
with it clenched in those strong hands. "I'm amused and . . .''

"What?"

"Grateful."

"I don't understand."

"I'm glad that you could be real with me."

"But . . .''

"Most people, in their everyday dealings with the clergy, are
not themselves. They see the image, not the person." Reverend
Spike—Eudora—got busy warming the pot.

"I think I know what you mean," I ventured. "When I was
a little girl, I didn't think nuns wore knickers."

"And I didn't think nuns were women."

"You thought they were *men?*"

"I didn't think they were either. I thought they were just . . . nuns." Ellie was returning to the table with a tray, laden with cups and saucers, milk jug, sugar bowl, and teapot. The window above the sink was dark as a blank television screen and Eudora had to shoo Tobias off her chair before sitting down. A cosiness had joined us in the kitchen, as real as a third person, as familiar as a friend. For the first time that day, I felt safe from the encroaching evil of Fully Female.

"Ellie, I had an ulterior motive in coming to see you." Eudora passed me the milk.

"Tell me."

"This isn't easy." She stirred her tea. "But you came clean with me, so I suppose the least I can do is return the favour. I . . ." She added two spoonfuls of sugar. "I want you to tell me if you think I might find the tenets of Fully Female beneficial in . . . restructuring my marriage."

"Oh!"

"This afternoon I drove very slowly down to that place; I was right behind your car all the way. I saw you turn in at the gates and right then and there lost my nerve, or rather came to my senses. I couldn't go before a group of people, some of them my parishioners, and pour out my heart. The counsellor cannot seek counsel. She must have the answers, not be seeking them. But as I drove back home, Ellie, your face was in front of me."

"Really?" I couldn't lift my cup.

"When I met you on Monday, I was frankly surprised. I had expected the woman who had captured Reverend Foxworth's heart to be, not to mince matters, a vamp. But what

I saw was a fresh-faced country girl who seemed my kind of person. Someone who wouldn't always get it right first time and, therefore, might know something about compassion. So, driving back to the vicarage this afternoon, I came up with a compromise. I could not join Fully Female, but I could pick the brains of one of its members and perhaps"—her eyes strayed toward the toaster—"perhaps even borrow the manual."

"No!" I rattled my cup over onto its side so that it lay in a saucer of tea.

Slowly, she got to her feet. "I see."

"No, you don't! Eudora, I am speaking as your friend. Do not dabble in the workings of this heinous organization!"

Even more slowly she resumed her seat. "Why, Ellie! You make it sound like the haunt of the devil."

"That was never the founder's intention. Believe me, Bunty Wiseman is a bit of a flake, but a nice person. Yet somehow her little venture has gone horribly awry. My first tip-off was that Jonas, who does the garden here, ran away from home, terrorized by the advances of Mrs. Pickle. Now two people are dead, a friend of mine is reduced to a lovesick zombie, and Bunty herself, who tried to turn other women into doting dolts, now realizes she has been the biggest doting dolt of all. Her husband Lionel Wiseman has fallen prey to the machinations of . . . well, I don't suppose it can do any harm to name names, seeing the engagement is about to be made official . . ."

"Yes?"

"The lady in question is Miss Gladys Thorn, your former church organist."

"The woman from Gladstone's past!" Eudora gripped the table with such force that the milk jug and sugar bowl jumped up and down on the tray. "This doesn't make sense. I know there is still something between my husband and that woman. He has not been himself since we came upon her in the church. She was at the organ, thumping out some hymn or other, and the moment Gladstone's eyes met hers and she uttered a squeal of joy, I knew my thirty-year marriage had hit a bump in the road. Then, when I was in the study, I heard them out in the hall. There was no doubt she wanted to pick up where they had left off, while he, poor lamb, was resisting with all his might. I *knew* I had to get rid of her, so I sacked them both— Miss Thorn and Mrs. Pickle—so it would look more like a new broom sweeping clean."

"Miss Thorn said you accused her of frequenting the Methodist Church."

"What I said was that someone, Mrs. Melrose, I believe, had mentioned seeing her going into Unity Methodist, and I wondered if she might not be happier serving that congregation."

"And when the deed was done, you felt awful." I righted my cup and poured us both a fresh cup of tea.

"That nice Mrs. Pickle!"

"If it's any consolation, Rowland was dying to sack her, but he—"

"Don't say it! He was too kind." Eudora looked at me with the wounded eyes of an early martyr roasting on a spit on one of St. Anselm's stained-glass windows. "Everything has changed. Last night Gladstone burned the treacle pudding, and breakfast this morning was a disaster. Only one sausage, no bacon, and the merest dab of scrambled egg."

"But surely," I said, indulging in a teaspoon . . . and a half . . . of sugar, something I never do except in times of stress, "surely if Miss Thorn is marrying Lionel Wiseman, your problems are over."

Eudora shook her head. "Ellie! That's a smoke screen, it has to be. I tell you the woman is in love with my husband."

"Possibly, but what you don't understand is . . ."

I was hunting around for a nice way to say what Mrs. Malloy had phrased so pithily—"Gladys Thorn would throw her legs in the air and give the V sign to anything in trousers"—when a knock sounded at the garden door. And who should come gliding in, but Mrs. M herself.

She had my purple caftan strung over one arm, but otherwise she was all in black, from the supply bag in her hand to the turban on her head. Even her damson lipstick had a blackish cast, as if it had grown old and mouldy in her service. Her complexion, robbed of its rouge, was the colour of death, and her eyes still had that faraway haze.

"Good morning, Mrs. H."

With a sideways glance at Eudora I started to stammer that it was six in the evening, but Mrs. Malloy had gone sleepwalking into the pantry, the way a character in a farce will walk into a cupboard thinking it is the exit. Several awkward seconds later, she reappeared and without looking left or right, coasted past Eudora and myself to vanish through the hall door.

"And that"—I smiled gently upon Eudora Spike—"is the work of Fully Female. Are you sure you still want to borrow the manual?"

WHEN BEN, the evening shadow on his chin matching the darkness at the window, came home from a hard day at the restaurant, he found me seated in the drawing room which was beginning to seem more than ever like a museum documenting the lives of an unknown couple living sometime B.C.—Before

Children. These cream silk walls and Queen Anne furnishings had as much to do with my present lifestyle as my Aunt Astrid had to do with modelling naughty undies at lingerie parties.

Loosening his tie, my husband crossed the rose-and-peacock Persian carpet to stand gazing, not at me, but at the portrait above the mantelpiece—Abigail of the auburn hair and periwinkle eyes, the Edwardian mistress of Merlin's Court.

"Sweetheart?"

"Are you talking to me?" I roused myself off the sofa, shook the creases out of my washerwoman skirt, and braced myself for questions regarding my day's productivity.

"Every time I look at this portrait"—his dark head was tilted so that the light from the wall lamps brushed his face like a watercolour paintbrush—"I become consumed with desire."

"For Abigail?"

"No! For a portrait of you with the twins."

"Ben, you know how I hate having my photo taken."

"So you do." A thoughtful gleam darkened his eyes to the peacock blue of the vase on the leaded-glass bookcase.

"I would rather be hanged in the good old-fashioned sense of the word than strung up for posterity on some wall of this house. I hate the thought of a complete stranger gawking up at me somewhere down the years and saying, 'Don't you think she looks like a bulldog?' "

"Ellie!"

"Don't tell me I am depriving Abbey and Tam of the opportunity for immortality and your mother and father of their rights as grandparents, because I have every intention of taking the twins down to Belamo's Studio in the—"

He did not let me finish. His hands found me and in one

swift jerk I was in his arms, his breath warm upon my lips, his voice raspy as the feel of his shadowed face beneath my fingers. "Are you crazy?"

"You don't like Belamo's?"

"I don't give a hang about the place." He held me away from him. "What I care about is having you take a good hard look at yourself."

Uncertain what he was getting at, I escaped into banter. "Sorry, dear! I don't have a hand mirror on me."

"You don't need one." He cupped my chin in his hand and suddenly we were rubbing noses like a couple of passionate Eskimos. "Make my eyes your mirror, sweetheart. Look into them and see yourself as I see you."

"I'd rather not." I managed a laugh.

"Stop that!" He gently shook me until his face blurred. "I won't let you sneer at the woman I love."

"You blind fool!" My smile hovered on the verge of tears. "You're the one who needs to face facts. I'm not the girl you married. I'm a frumpish hausfrau. Oh, let's stop prettying up the truth—I am *fat*."

"No."

"You see what you want to see."

"I see a lovely woman."

"Then you're looking with the heart, not the eyes."

"So," he said, then drew my braid over my shoulder, removed the rubber band, and began undressing my hair with slow, deliberate fingers. "Isn't that how you look at me?"

"Don't be silly." For some unknown reason, I was having trouble breathing. "We are not talking about the same thing at all. You, Bentley T. Haskell, are gorgeous."

"My poor blind fool!" His mouth came down on mine and

I was enclosed in an embrace that sent my senses reeling. Perhaps it was the spicy clean scent of his Mr. Right aftershave that made my head spin. All I knew was that the moment became eternity and nothing existed but his heavy breathing and the pounding of my heart. And no one existed but the two of us, fully clothed but moulded into one being made out of scalding wax.

At last he lifted his head. "Ellie, I have an idea."

"Me, too."

"What I had in mind was a little moonlight adventure."

"Sounds good to me."

"A picnic."

"A *what?*"

Gently he disengaged my arms from around his neck and ignored my lips, aching to be reunited with his. "Sweetheart, remember how in the early days we used to enjoy dining al fresco under the beech tree?"

"Yes," I said, rubbing my arms, already feeling the nipping spring wind, "but in the daytime."

"Ah, my love." He raised my hand an infuriating inch at a time to his lips. "Where's your sense of adventure?"

"Defunct." Impossible to tell him it had died in the service of Fully Female, which reminded me—I hadn't told Ben about Mrs. Malloy. And this wasn't to be my chance. I was being hustled into the hall and told to go and slip into something comfortable, like a coat and a wooly hat, while the master of the manor retreated to the kitchen to rustle up our midnight feast.

"The babies!" I whined.

"Not to worry. I'll give Freddy a ring."

"Really, Ben. We can't keep imposing."

"Nonsense. The old chap dotes on those kiddies, almost as much as he dotes on the opportunity to raid our refrigerator."

"He may be in bed." Obviously I was now reduced to talking nonsense. My cousin boasted that he never slept more than three hours a night, rarely turning in before three or four in the morning.

So Ben went whistling off to the kitchen, and I reluctantly wended my way upstairs, crossing the landing on tiptoe to enter the bedroom. Never had that old four-poster looked more alluring, but I tore my eyes away from it and opened up the wardrobe, bent on hunting out my navy duffle coat with its windproof hood. But the garment staring me in the face was none other than the Purple Peril, the caftan which Mrs. Malloy had borrowed and, bless her heart, returned.

Standing at the wardrobe with my hands full of faux silk and gold braid, memories came flooding back of the night I first met Bentley T. Haskell. There I had been, about to slip into my Aladdin slippers, when he came through the door, his long scarf flapping with every stride, his hair made blacker by the wet night, a glitter to his fine eyes, eyes that boded ill for any woman who would keep him waiting while she made a last-minute hike to the bathroom, closed the door, swooned against it and informed the dazed woman staring at her from the mirror: 'The man's a devil, but God knows I never wanted to be a saint.'

"Ellie!" Back in the present the bedroom door opened and banged shut and I turned to find Ben swooning against it.

"What's wrong?" I tugged so hard on the Purple Peril that the hanger snapped.

"I've just had most damnable shock."

"Tell me!"

"The babies are fine." Ben found the strength to lift his right hand and press it to his brow. "I came upstairs to get the travelling rug from the Blue Room so we wouldn't have to sit on the damp grass and what do you think I found? Ellie, there is a strange woman in that bed snoring her head off."

"Oh, her!"

"What's that supposed to mean?"

"Darling, I'm sorry! I forgot to mention that I suggested that Mrs. Malloy stay the night."

"I didn't recognize her."

"You're just not used to seeing her in curlers and a chin strap. Then, too, she hasn't been herself lately. She turned up late this afternoon and hinted that she was nervous about going back to her house. She's involved with a man—Walter Fisher, your undertaker friend—and I think she's frightened of him."

"That Milquetoast?"

"Ben, she told me he has aroused passions she never knew she had . . . and to be honest, I can remember and empathize. There's nothing to equal the delicious terror of going over the rapids into the whirlpool that first time."

"Is that so?" Ben opened the door and held out his hand.

"Yes, but . . ."

"Sweetheart, I like to think there may be several first times in the lifetime of a love affair."

"You took the words out of my mouth." Tossing aside the hanger, I closed the door on the Purple Peril. "Ben, dear, after the fright you just received, I will understand completely if you wish to cancel the picnic."

"Not a chance."

"I hate men who play hard to get."

"I'm thinking of you!" Taking my arm as if we were strolling down Lovers' Lane, he walked me along to the nursery. "That was a fine salmon I found in the fridge and it deserves the right ambience in which to be fully enjoyed." He opened the door and we crept in to peek at our offspring. Sweet darlings, they were both magically asleep, watched over by Mother Goose, the Calico Cat, and Tommy and Topsy, the twin bears. Silly of me, but I half believed that as soon as we were gone from the room and the door closed, those toys would come alive and whisper the secret words: Norman the Doorman.

Heading downstairs, I said, "About that salmon . . . I didn't cook it. The vicar brought it round; her husband had prepared it for their evening meal, but he was unexpectedly called away and she wanted to be neighbourly."

"Very kind."

"You sound peeved."

"Not a bit of it." Ben snorted a laugh. "I'm delighted to have the chance to sample another of the chap's blue-ribbon recipes."

I had feared this reaction, but I'd had to tell him. I wasn't prepared to live my life skirting the word salmon whenever we were in the company of one or another of the Spikes. My existence was already chock-a-block full of things I hadn't told Ben. And as I stumbled down the last stair, one of them caught up with me.

"Ellie, I found a packet of Healthy Harvest Herbs in the pantry."

"Really?"

"A nice blend."

"You don't say."

His dark, enigmatic glance confirmed my worst fears. He had read the label from front to back and was about to accuse me of being a covert member of Fully Female. Standing as still as the twin suits of armour positioned against the staircase wall, I braced myself for what was to come. "Ellie, I don't quite know how to put this . . ."

"Please, just spit it out."

"Very well, but bear in mind my intent was not malicious. Far be it from me to attack the culinary integrity of Mr. Gladstone Spike."

"What are you talking about?" My heart was lifting even as I sank down on the bottom stair.

"I used the packet of Healthy Harvest Herbs to make a glaze for the salmon which naturally I thought you had prepared." He paused to looked at me suspiciously. "Why are you smiling?"

"I've no idea."

"Ellie, I am not for one moment suggesting Mr. Spike made a bland and boring job of that fish."

"Heaven forbid."

"Within his limitations . . ."

Oh, bother! The rest of Ben's charitable commentary was forestalled by Freddy opening the hall door and carolling, "Mary Poppins reporting for duty. By the by, which one of you bright souls left that salmon alone and unattended on the kitchen table?"

"Don't tell me you helped yourself?" I tried to sound severe.

"Not me, Your Honour, but you might want to have a few words with Tobias Cat. He just skulked out with half a pound of fish on his whiskers."

"I'll kill the varmint!" Ben's shout tore through the rafters.

*   *   *

MOONLIGHT painted pictures on the courtyard worthy of
the niftiest pavement artist. And within moments of exiting the
house I could tell from the quickening of Ben's stride and the
airy way he swung the picnic basket that his spirits had begun
to lift. He had made a half-hearted attempt to persuade me
there was no earthly reason why we should not finish off what
was left of the salmon, but the look in my eye must have
made clear that even for the privilege of sampling the Healthy
Harvest glaze, I would not partake of my cat's leftovers. Halfway down the gravel drive I caught a glimpse of Tobias brows-
ing among the trees. Oh, goody! From the droop of his furry
head I suspected the wretched feline was already ashamed of
himself.

"May you have indigestion," I bellowed through cupped
hands, before hastening to keep pace with Ben. Rather than
returning upstairs to fetch my duffle coat, which I had forgotten when Ben burst into the room and told me about Mrs.
Malloy, I had grabbed an old cardigan coat hanging in the
alcove by the garden door. The wind nipped through it, but it
was a teasing, almost sensuous type of nipping, and suddenly I
couldn't wait to be camped out on the travelling rug, watching
Ben uncork the wine with those elegant, dexterous fingers
while I ached to have him touch me even if only to place a
brandied cherry between my parted lips.

We passed Freddy's cottage and went through the iron
gates, so solidly familiar in daylight, but now with a magical,
fantasy quality about them, as if they, like the shadows in the
courtyard, had been painted by some phantom artist of the
night. Only when we were on Cliff Road, walking in the direc-

tion of St. Anselm's church, did I say, "Ben, I thought we were going to picnic under the beech tree in the garden."

"Changed my mind." He put his arm around me. "Since Jonas hung the rope swing from that old tree, I've thought of it as the twins' special place."

"Even though they're still too little to swing?"

"Ellie, it's out there waiting for them. An integral part of their childhood. You and I must find a new special place. All suggestions are welcome, but I thought of that little knoll next to the churchyard."

"The one with the grotto of silver birch trees that looks as though it is just waiting for a miracle to happen?"

"Right." Ben's smile, captured in the beam of the torch, was golden. Without another word, we followed our lighted arrow up the rocky incline, which in summer would be ablaze with wildflowers. Halfway up I sensed, rather than heard, the pad-pad of paws behind us, but if Tobias were tagging along I chose to ignore him. I had yet to forgive his bad table manners; besides, two's company and any third party, even a cat, would be an intrusion.

"Here we are." Ben set the picnic basket down on a moss-grained rock; the silver birch trees encircled us as his arms closed around me. We might be only a few yards above the road, but we were king and queen of the castle. Ours was a veritable fortress, a place where no evil could touch us, because love was our shield. There! I had finally dared think the word that had been lurking in the shadows of my mind all night. And I was still afraid. The feeling was so fragile, like a ballgown worn and loved, then put away in a dark trunk until one day the lid is lifted, and there it is—more beautiful, more shimmering, more radiant than remembered. But have the moths been at it? Will it crumble to dust when touched?

"Look at the moon," said my love.

"Yes!" I whispered.

Pure as the dreams of childhood, perfect in its symmetry, it appeared to be elevated directly above the church—God's very own Eucharistic wafer. And when my eyes returned to Ben's, I knew with a quiet, luminous certainty that love is more than satin sheets and a pair of Viking horns. It's a gift that is not ours for the grabbing. Try, and it will slip through our fingers like a handful of water.

"Hungry, sweetheart?"

"Passionately." I stepped away from his arms and in a dreamy haze watched him spread the travelling rug on the ground and start unloading the picnic basket. The air smelled of cowslip wine. Just breathing could make me drunk.

"How do Cornish pasties, spinach salad, grapefruit mousse, and a mature Camembert grab you?"

"Delectably." Out the corner of my eyes I noticed one of St. Anselm's stained-glass windows blaze into jewelled light. Emerald, ruby, sapphire. Was the vicar prowling her domain? Or did a ghost walk?

Ben's hand reached up to draw me down onto the blanket, but I resisted. To our right, down on the road, two amber orbs pierced the dusk, a throaty growl tore at the night, and a car came around the curve at what seemed to my pastoral state of mind a fearsome speed. A scurry from the bushes directly below our birch grotto, and I saw the dark shape of an animal glide toward the road. My torch was in my pocket, but a chill crept up my sleeves and clutched its icy fingers about my throat.

"What's wrong, Ellie?" Ben was on his feet.

"Tobias!" I was already stumbling over rocks and honeysuckle briars in a desperate race to scoop up my pet before he was crushed under the wheels of that chariot of death. Too late! I hit the road on my heels in time to see my darling furball lurch, mesmerized, toward that rush of lights. Before I could hurl myself forward, Ben grabbed me from behind and a second—a century—later, there was the hideous squeal of brakes as the car slammed to a standstill.

I saw Tobias lying inches from the front wheels, I saw his tail flicker then lie still. To hope was fairy-tale folly . . . The door opened and out stepped the dark figure of a man wearing a Dick Tracy hat.

"Murderer!" I screamed.

"Ellie, you wait here."

"Please, keep holding me."

The man in the hat was opening up the boot of his car. Was he getting out a spade? No! He . . . oh, my heavens! This was worse than Tobias. Indeed, poor Tobias, R.I.P., faded from memory when I saw Mr. Road Hog lift out a body . . . the body of a human. Then, knees bent, he hoisted its sagging weight over his shoulder.

"By Jupiter!" Ben muttered. "Something fishy going on here."

"You don't say!"

The man was across the road on the brink of our vision, a creature distorted by horror and distance into the Hunchback of Notre Dame. The realization hit me and my spouse simultaneously: we were about to witness the horror of a dead body being hurled over the cliff edge—down, down, to bounce off the jagged teeth of the rocks below into the foaming mouth of the sea.

"Stop!" Ben took leaps that never touched the ground. "In the name of the law! This is a citizen's arrest!"

Only the sea answered, in a surge of crazy, crashing laughter, and then . . . the villain of the hour turned around and even in the partial darkness I recognized his face.

"Oh, no!" I cried. "Not you!"

Chapter Nine

W hy, Dr. Melrose!" My torch picked off his buttons on its way up to a face shadowed by the brim of his hat. "What brings you here?"

A bloodless smile creased his lips, and while the night crouched down like a patient policeman to wait and listen, he shriveled before our eyes until he was no more than an overcoat blowing in the wind. "Why Mrs. Haskell . . . and Mr. Haskell . . . this is a pleasant surprise. I was out for a moonlight drive when I decided to stop and smell the roses . . . I mean, the seaweed," he said with a hollow laugh.

"And who is your charming companion?" Ben placed himself squarely in front of me although I do not think the folly of intercepting a murderer had occurred to either of us. "Could it be your wife Flo?"

The wind pitched a mournful sigh, echoed by our quarry. "Astute of you, sir." The doctor shifted his burden so that the dangling foot whopped him where I hoped it hurt the most. "She suffered an attack of car sickness, to put it in layman's terms, and . . ."

Ducking my head around Ben's, I spoke in tones of dulcet bitterness. "Flo has my sympathy. Travelling in the boot of the car does that to me every time."

"Oh, dear God!" Dr. Melrose stepped backwards and might have ended the discussion there and then by taking a flying leap over the edge of the cliff had Ben not lunged to the rescue.

"Not so fast!" He grabbed the doctor by the scruff of his coat collar. "My wife and I would like to pay our respects to Mrs. Melrose."

All fight, all hope had gone out of the beleaguered man. He laid his burden down on the cold, dark sod and stood, head bowed, while the trees closed in like a troop of professional mourners. Garbed in black, they writhed and moaned and lifted their rended tresses to the unfeeling night.

"They'll bring back hanging just for me."

"I wouldn't count on it," I said nastily, afraid to look, yet irresistibly drawn to Flo's shuttered face. Friar Tuck fringe smooth on her brow, she lay feet together, arms straight at her sides, as if ready to be boxed up by Walter Fisher, Undertaker. And yet I didn't feel that Death was present in person as I had when gazing down at Norman the Doorman. Maybe it was the way the wind pinched her nostrils, but I could have sworn she breathed.

"Believe me, I never meant to kill her, but ever since she joined that crazy organization, Fully Female—"

"That what?" Ben asked.

"A health club," I said, informing his feet.

"Oh, yes, I saw the name on the packet of Healthy Harvest Herbs." The lift of his left eyebrow chilled me to the bone.

"Mrs. Malloy is a member." A lie by omission spoken within the shadow of the church, but one could only pray God had bigger sins on his mind.

Dr. Melrose drew a shuddering breath. "Mrs. Haskell, I told you when you brought little Tabby and Tom in for their checkups that I was being driven to madness by my wife's awakened sexuality. Never a moment's peace. Never knowing when she would pounce upon me next. The other day it was in the men's room. Last evening when I got into my car to drive home, there she was on the backseat, wearing only her safety belt. And then this morning! I was summoned to the morgue to identify a patient, and when I pulled open the drawer, I couldn't believe it—there was Flo twinkling up at me and moving over to make room for two."

"Unnerving." Ben looked at me. Was he calling up the memory of his wife in a pair of Viking horns, bent on seduction?

"You can't know what it was like." Dr. Melrose wrung his hairy hands.

"True enough. My wife and I are too recently married and far too deeply in love to have need of the artificial stimulus provided by this Fully Female place." Ben paused. "I do vaguely remember seeing something about it in *The Daily Chronicle,* but it didn't register because it didn't apply." A half-smile touched his lips like the imprint of a remembered kiss, and I knew with dreadful certainty that my spouse did not suspect my personal involvement with Fully Female. But if he were to find out, would things ever be quite the same between us?

"Are you telling us, Doctor"—Ben spoke with utmost contempt—"that you *killed* your wife because you could not keep up with her sexual demands?"

"Your understanding, please!" Dr. Melrose's eyes were rimmed with woe. "I was desperate to the point of resorting to tactics of intimidation. I even arranged to have a pair of peacocks kidnapped from the Fully Female premises and sent a letter indicating they would end up in the soup if the place didn't close down."

"That wasn't kind," I said.

"Believe me"—the doctor's voice broke—"I have been punished. The chap who did the job demanded extra money for smuggling them into the zoo. But never mind that. Try, if you will, to picture this evening's scene. I arrived home to find Flo absent. I knew a feeling of peace that was indescribable; then came a ring at the door and I opened it to be confronted by a woman in a Halloween mask. Shocked, I asked what I could do for her, and to my horror she cried, 'Trick or Treat,' then flashed open her raincoat. Naked! Completely naked! And something in me snapped. I picked up the doorstop and brought it down on her head. I didn't need to remove the mask to know it was Flo. I would have known that appendix scar anywhere. I didn't have to look at her or touch her to know she was dead." Whether Dr. Melrose was touting his professionalism or talking his way through the pain was not clear. His monotone washed over us the way the dark waves below would have washed over poor

Flo had the grieving widower succeeded in his scheme to rid himself of her body.

"Doctor," I said, my voice as chilly as if I had just emerged from a midnight dip, "heaven forbid that I question your medical judgment, but I think you might be well-advised to get a second opinion."

"What are you saying, Mrs. Haskell?"

"That your wife isn't as dead as you think."

"Ellie!" Gripping my arm, Ben stared down at the body. "By Jupiter, I think you're right!"

"Impossible!" Dr. Melrose appeared to be coming back to life himself. Indeed, I sensed a slight annoyance that his diagnosis had been challenged.

"She moved!" My shout shook the earth and sky. "Look!" Dropping beside Flo, I hardly felt the pain of the pebbles that poked through my slacks to embed themselves in my knees. "She's opening her eyes. Oh, thank God! She's squeezing my hand."

"John . . . ?"

"I'm here, old dear!" Dr. Melrose pressed a fist to his mouth to hold back a sob.

"Where are you?" Flo's fingers broke away from mine to grope the air for a more familiar touch.

Still Dr. Melrose did not move. "I must have been in shock," he kept muttering. I stood and joined Ben in forcing the man down into the penitential position. Finally he snapped back into focus. Removing his hat, he folded it into a makeshift pillow and placed it under his wife's head before unbuttoning his coat to use it as a blanket.

"John . . . ?

"Quiet now, while I examine you." Watching his hands gently probe her head, then work their way down her neck, I wondered if he was resigned to that moment when she would look him in the eye and ask, "Why did you try to kill me?"

"Squeeze my hand with your right one."

"John . . . ?"

"Now the left one."

"Please . . . !" Flo's head thrashed from side to side, but if the poor woman saw Ben and me, she gave no sign. "Why does my head ache? Why am I here, lying by the side of the road at dead of night?"

"I don't expect your forgiveness."

"The last thing I remember is sitting on the sofa; the sitting room window was open and a breeze stirred the net curtains. I was reading the Fully Female manual and came to the chapter on Holiday Treats. My word, Halloween sounded jolly! What a pity it's only April, I thought, and then . . . it hit me."

My eyes met Ben's. So her timing was a little off. Who could expect perfect chronology under the circumstances?

Dr. Melrose buried his head in his hands. "I'm so sorry, old dear."

"It hit me," Flo continued, over and around him, "that pulling my Halloween stunt now would give it extra pizzazz, like Christmas in July. I seem to remember putting the manual down and after that . . . nothing."

Lifting his head, Dr. Melrose pressed praying hands together. "What did you say?"

"Everything is a complete fog."

"Thank God!" The words came out in a roar sufficient to jolt awake an audience sleeping through the opera.

"What?"

"Amnesia," Dr. Melrose hastened to explain to his unsuspecting wife while Ben and I stood rooted to the ground like a couple of trees, "is Mother Nature's way of cushioning a person from the memory of trauma."

"What trauma?" Flo pressed a hand to her presumably throbbing head.

"Lie still, old dear, and I will explain." Dr. Melrose glanced upward at Ben and me. "Do you see Mr. and Mrs. Haskell standing over there?"

"Where?" Flo strained her neck to see, but she still appeared to have trouble bringing us into focus. "Oh, yes, but John, what have they to do with . . . everything?"

"Let me start at the beginning. After you put on your Halloween stunt"—the doctor could not restrain a shudder—"I suggested we continue . . . the foreplay with a drive up Cliff Road. Everything was perfect, from the music on the radio to the love words you were whispering in my ear, when abruptly the idyll was over. We came to the bend in the road just past the church and a cat darted out in front of the car."

"Poor pussy!"

"Your very words at the time, old dear." Dr. Melrose, still on his knees, squirmed. "Seeing you so distressed, I couldn't flatten that animal into a hearth rug, and so I did what no motorist should do, particularly on such a road as this. I swerved, hit the brake . . . and when I lifted my head from the steering wheel, it was to find you thrown from the car, wondering how you came by that lump on the back of your head."

"Wasn't I wearing my seat belt?" Flo was visibly fighting to keep her eyes open.

"You said you found it too constraining."

"What a fool I've been!" She reached up her hand to her husband, but looked at me and Ben. "Was it your cat?"

I nodded, unable to speak, and turned away with Ben at my heels. There had been a macabre blessing to the "death" of Flo Melrose; it had numbed me to the loss of my beloved Tobias. But now feeling was returning with the painful, prickling sensation of pins and needles to a sleeping limb. No more would I watch my furry friend tiptoeing through the summer grass with a lei of butterflies about his neck. The twins would neither babble his name nor stalk his tail. And never again would I sit on winter evenings with my furry heating pad on my lap.

My eulogy was interrupted by Ben, who had reached the car a pace ahead of me. "He's gone."

"Yes," I mumbled, wishing he wouldn't state what we already knew.

"Ellie, have you forgotten I gave up euphemisms after the twins were born? When I say Tobias is gone, I mean he is not where we left him."

"Oh, my heavens!" Dropping on all fours, I stretched prone on the road to peer under the car, and sure enough, I saw not so much as a whisker. "You know what this means?" I started blubbering as Ben helped me to my feet. "Some wild animal has made off with him!"

"Sweetheart"—his voice was a blend of exasperation and tenderness—"this is Chitterton Fells. The hyenas aren't tucking in their napkins for a late-night snack of Tobias. Clearly, his death was of the same temporary variety as that of Flo Melrose."

"He was so still!"

"Agreed. But he afterwards recovered and ... Ellie!" he

shouted, leaping two feet in the air and punching the air with his fist. "I think I see him over by that rock where the grass is moving!" Still shouting, Ben dodged a few yards to our right, was transformed into a dark silhouette, and returned moments later with his arms sprouting fur. "Damn!" Scuffing his shoe. "Poor blighter, he'd been sick and I stepped in it."

"What a night!" I gathered Tobias into my arms, still unable to believe he wasn't a ghost. Certainly he was cold enough to have been haunting this spot for centuries, but that could be alleviated by tucking him inside my cardigan coat so that all that was visible of him was one ear and a dopey-looking eye.

"Ben . . ."

"What?" He was staring across the road, to where Dr. Melrose was still huddled over his wife.

"I've been thinking."

"Same here."

"Well," I said, giving Tobias a hoist, "I've been remembering that old joke about the cat and the salmon. You know the one—a woman prepares a salmon for a dinner party and leaves it on the table while she goes upstairs to dress. When she returns to the kitchen, she discovers her cat has been eating the salmon. Not having anything else to serve, she does a patch job with radishes and chopped egg, and the dinner party proceeds as planned with everyone tucking into the salmon and declaring it fit for a king. When it comes time for dessert, the woman returns to the kitchen and suddenly realizes she hasn't seen the cat for a while. She opens the back door and there he is, stone dead. Convinced the salmon is the culprit, she goes in and confesses the whole story to her guests so everyone troops off to the emergency room to have their stomachs pumped. But later, when the woman returns home, a neighbour walks over and sheepishly confesses that he ran over the cat when backing out of his garage earlier that evening."

"What are you saying, Ellie?"

"Saying is too strong a word. I am wondering, that's all, whether what happened to Tobias could be a reverse of the story. We assumed he was hit by the Melroses' car, but suddenly I am wondering if it was the salmon that almost did him in. I'm not saying it was bad—just too rich for his blood. Ben, I saw him when he stepped into the road, and I swear there was something wrong with him then. He was lurching, and when the car was almost on top of him, he stood there and gawped."

"Probably mesmerized by the lights."

"That's what I thought, but . . ." I gave an uneasy laugh. "Oh, never mind. The late night is probably getting to me. Why don't you get the picnic things together and we'll head home."

Watching Ben race up the slope to the birch grotto, I hugged Tobias closer for his warmth and my own. Talk about someone walking over my grave! Suppressing a shiver, I glanced toward the churchyard and saw what was either a short tree or a tall person standing near the gates. Was Mr. Gladstone Spike taking the night air because he could not sleep, or was I once again letting my imagination run away with me?

"Ellie?"

Unlike Ben and most normal people, I have never been able to leap several feet in the air, even when startled. A sort of bunny hop is the best I can manage. Dr. Melrose was ushering his wife into the passenger seat of the car, and it was she who had called out the greeting.

"So sorry about the cat." She lifted her hand in a wave as

wan as her smile, and before I could reassure her that in the midst of death there is life, her husband had closed the car door and was heading toward me.

"A parting word, if I may?" Removing his hat, he clamped it to his chest and bowed his head. "Mrs. Haskell, I am completely at your mercy and that of your husband. If this evening's events become known, I shall be ruined."

"One would suppose so," I said coldly. "A doctor who cannot tell whether his wife is dead or alive does not exactly inspire confidence."

"I was beside myself."

"Good!"

"Do I have your promise of silence?"

"For a price." Looking him in the eye, I could see all the way inside his head to where the wheels turned.

"Blackmail, Mrs. Haskell?"

"Sticks and stones, Dr. Melrose." Opening up my cardigan coat, I shifted Tobias into his arms, crushing his hat in the process. "As you see, my cat is alive. What I want to know is whether he will stay that way."

"This is your price?"

"Coupled with your promise that you will never lay a hand on your wife again."

"Mrs. Haskell, I've been married to Flo for over thirty years—"

"And that gives you one turn at bat?"

Making no reply, he got down to the business of examining Tobias, raising first one eyelid, then the other before exploring the abdominal area. "Given the circumstances, this may sound fishy"—Dr. Melrose's sheepish expression had given way to one of surprise—"but I'd say this animal has been poisoned."

"Fishy's the word!" My eyes strayed toward the churchyard, but before I could say anything more, Ben emerged from the shadows, complete with picnic basket and travelling rug. Dr. Melrose quickly returned Tobias to me and clapped his hat back on—to look taller, I suppose, as he braced himself to grovel anew.

THE TELEPHONE was ringing somewhere on the outskirts of sleep and I shot up in bed the following morning to find Ben gone and the hands of the clock pointing accusingly to eight o'clock. Hair all over the place like a St. Bernard's, I did not pause to grab my dressing gown before panting out to the landing to pick up the receiver.

"Hello?" I fussed with the collar of my flannel nightdress, hating the thought of anyone hearing me, looking like this.

"Ellie, this is Bunty Wiseman."

"Oh . . . how are you?"

"Heavenly!"

"Really?" Dragging forward a stool, I sat down with a thump.

"What do you expect, a year's mourning?" Bunty's laugh bounced off my eardrum. "Bloomin' heck, love! I've had a whole night to pull myself together. The way I see things, Gladys Thorn gets Li and I get his wardrobe."

Such savoir faire boggled the mind. My eyes turned to the photograph of my mother-in-law Magdalene Haskell and read her mind. Marriages aren't dissolved like flavoured gelatin in hot water; they are torn apart limb from limb like charred flesh at a pig roast.

"If there is anything I can do . . ." My lips paraded out the worn cliche.

"There certainly is," said Bunty blithely. "You can come to the party I am throwing for Li and his luscious fiancée."

"The *what?*" The stool shot out from under me and I ended up on my knees clutching the telephone cord as if it were a lifeline.

"You heard me. I intend to show the world how the Fully Female woman behaves when the impossible happens. Does she crawl into bed and hibernate until the divorce is final? Not on your Nellie! She paints her nails and the town. So, Ellie, can I count on you tonight at seven?"

"Uhhhmmm!" Staggering to my feet, I tried to come up with an excuse to avoid what had to be the antisocial bash of the season.

"It won't be an engagement party without you."

"All right."

"And do bring Ben."

"That I can't do!" The very thought made the banisters fade in and out. "If he doesn't have to be at Abigail's, I would need him to stay with the twins. I can't keep imposing on Freddy; he's far too good-natured. He baby-sat last night, and by the time we got back, it was so late he ended up sleeping here."

"Did he go home yet?"

"I don't know."

"Could you check?"

"Certainly." My curiosity piqued as to what she could want with Freddy, I put the receiver down and headed for the top of the stairs, only to discover my cousin, his hair in a much neater ponytail than mine, bounding toward me three treads at a time.

"Good morrow, cos! Ben sent me to tell you he has the

babies up and fed and breakfast will be ready in twenty minutes."

"Thanks, Hermes," I said. "Bunty Wiseman wishes to speak to you on the phone."

"To *moi?*" Freddy mounted the last stair, and rather than stoop to eavesdropping, I walked—taking teeny little steps—back to my bedroom. Bother! His voice didn't carry and the only thing I heard clearly was the receiver being replaced. Slipping on my dressing gown, I went back out onto the landing and along to the Blue Room. Ben's breakfast alert had made no mention of Mrs. Malloy, so I knocked on the door not knowing what to expect.

"Who the bloody hell's there?"

"Only me!" Thoroughly humbled, I opened the door and approached the Vatican throne . . . I mean, the bed.

"Oh, it's you, Mrs. H!" Mrs. Malloy was propped up against a snowbank of pillows, hands folded over the eiderdown. "For the moment, I thought I was back home and the paper boy had come knocking for his money."

"Did you sleep well?" I could feel myself twitching into a half-curtsey, reminiscent of Miss Thorn.

"Not specially. This wallpaper's enough to give anyone nightmares."

She was right about that. Ben and I had not got around to redecorating the Blue Room, and everywhere you looked there were girls on swings—girls with braided hair and straw hats going up and down, back and forth, until the room itself succumbed to an attack of vertigo. Probably the original idea had been to cheer up the furniture, which seemed to take a baleful pride in being ugly. I could swear the dressing table was looking down its long mirrored nose at Mrs. Malloy. The striped nightdress I had lent her made her look as if she were out on parole, and the absence of makeup heightened the impression of someone who had not seen daylight for a twenty-year stretch. Amazing what eyebrows will do for a woman. But as always, Mrs. Malloy's demeanor was that of someone prepared to meet the Queen on her own terms.

"I hope you're not about to bring me breakfast in bed, Mrs. H. I like my bacon and eggs at the table."

"Ben has everything ready and waiting downstairs."

"Very nice, I'll remember you both in my will. But don't expect me to sit around gossiping all morning with you and Mr. H. I have a lot to do."

"Admirable," I said, and meant every syllable. This was the old Mrs. Malloy before she went to bed with Walter Fisher and took to gliding around like the victim of a vampire's love bite.

She swung a striped leg out of bed. "I intend to seize life by the balls."

"Splendid."

"After I leave here, I'm going to nip down to the vicarage and volunteer my services waxing the altar steps and what-have-you."

"How kind."

"From now on, Mrs. H, I spread sunshine every step of the way. No beggar will go away empty-handed, and all the kiddies will call me Grandma. Every moment will be lived to the fullest. What do you say about them apples?"

What could I say? I could hardly inform her that my heart had plummeted, that I viewed these ramblings as yet another, perhaps more insidious, manifestation of the cursed love sickness.

"Lovely," I said, sounding just like Mr. Gladstone Spike; and suddenly the room was going up and down with the swings.

"A penny for your thoughts, Mrs. H?"

"Oh, they're not worth that much." I grabbed hold of the bedpost. "I was thinking about Tobias, that's all. And reminding myself to watch his diet today. He wasn't very well last night."

WHAT IS your average housewife to do when she is privy to one attempted murder and suspects another? She sinks her teeth into bite-sized problems and gets on with the day. The moment Ben, Freddy, and Mrs. Malloy were out of the house, I piled a load of baby clothes into the washing machine, turned it on, gave it the requisite thump, and got one belch in the face for my efforts. Mr. Bludgett, the plumber, would be hearing from me.

"How about it, my angels?" I lifted Abbey out of her feeder chair and beamed down at Tam. "Shall we all toddle down to the launderette and put money in the machines just like Las Vegas?" Naturally before we could embark on this great adventure, two of us had to take baths in the kitchen sink. Then came the challenge of stuffing stiff legs into floppy leggings before we could head for the car, only to find I had forgotten to check on Tobias one last time and, oh, yes—my handbag was goodness knows where in the house.

An hour later when I pushed the Porta-Pram into the Crystal Palace, it was to find half of Chitterton Fells encamped around six machines, two of which wore cardboard aprons bearing the legend Out of Order. The twins squealed and I was all for heading away from the din of the dryers and the sweaty detergent smell in search of a babbling brook and some nice smooth stones, when who should walk in but Mr. Walter Fisher.

Immediately, people started drinking their coffee faster or poring more intently over their magazines, that is if they weren't so fortunate as to have washing to fold. But they need not have flattered themselves. Walter was feasting his fish eyes on me.

"Good morning, Mrs. Haskell and family," he said as he flapped a fin at the twins. "I saw you come in here and thought I would nip in and have a quick word."

"That was friendly." I lowered my eyes and fussed with the brushed wool pram cover. How could Mrs. Malloy stand this man who looked as though he spent most of his time in an aquarium? From his slicked-back hair to his guppy lips, he was pale and glossy.

"Please don't think I'm rushing you, Mrs. Haskell . . ."

"What?"

A scraping of chairs as my fellow launderers put down their coffee cups and magazines to have a listen.

Mr. Fisher lowered his voice. "On Monday night at the Hearthside Guild, I sensed an interest on your part—and particularly that of your husband—to make your funeral arrangements."

"I really don't think"—I gripped the Porta-Pram handle—"that this is the time or the place . . ."

"Never any time like the present." Mr. Death-Warmed-Up waved a waxen finger. "We none of us know when we will be snuffed out like a candle. And do we want to burden our survivors with all the details necessary for giving us the send-off we deserve?"

"Personally," I said, my insides heaving and foaming like the washing machines until I was certain bubbles would start coming out of my nose and mouth, "I don't give a hoot what happens to me after I am dead. For all I care, my husband can put me on the compost heap."

"You're not serious, Mrs. Haskell!"

"Absolutely."

The pale face winced. "You do at least intend to adhere to the conventions by being cremated."

"I suppose so." Anything to shut him up.

"In that case"—Mr. Fisher did not look quite as crestfallen as I had hoped—"possibly you would be interested in something entirely new at Fisher Funerals. We call it the Show Case—a presentation which features the economy . . ."—he wiped his sullied lips with a black-edged handkerchief—". . . the economy of cremation with the formality and richness of a traditional funeral. We offer a choice of two cabinets—the Royal Mahogany and the Virgin Queen, in which the corpse can repose for viewing prior to and during the memorial service."

"Are we talking Rent-a-Coffin?"

"In a manner of speaking." Mr. Fisher's eyes bulged annoyance. "After the final viewing, the client is removed for cremation and the cabinet is put back into service."

"I'll have to think about it." I smiled at the twins in case they suspected from the tone of my voice that I was cross with them. "Lovely talking to you, Mr. Fisher, but I think I see a vacant washing machine."

"Yes . . . mustn't keep you." Too bad he wasn't as good as his word. As I turned away, he followed, moving past a grey-haired man balancing his coffee cup on his tum and two women stretching out a sheet for folding. "One final word, Mrs. Haskell."

"Yes?" Bundling out clothes from the pram bag.

"Would you mind telling me how you find Mrs. Malloy? I know she works for you, and I wonder if you have noticed anything different about her these last few days?"

"She's . . ." I started to say that Mrs. M was right as rain, but Mr. Fisher's face stopped me. My goodness, the man was all atremble and I was suddenly heartily ashamed of myself. Here was a member of an honourable profession and all I could do was screw up my nose because talk of coffin linings made me uncomfortable. Such prejudice was as shameful as that directed at the overweight. And could the man help it if he wasn't Cary Grant . . . or Ben Haskell? Had there been a hair shirt handy, I would have pulled it over my head.

"You were saying, Mrs. Haskell?"

"Sorry." I stood hugging an armful of clothes. "But I really don't think it's fair for me to discuss Mrs. Malloy with you."

"I see."

"Except to say"—impossible not to toss him a few crumbs of hope—"she's been going around like a woman in a trance."

"Thank you for that piece of information." The expression in Mr. Fisher's eyes as he took his leave was several fathoms deep, and the guppy lips stretched into a smile that promised all sorts of exciting things in store for Mrs. Malloy.

HONESTLY, I haven't a clue where the rest of that day went. It seemed to slip under the doors and through cracks in the windowframes in wisps of misspent time and harried moments, until suddenly there I was at a little after seven in the evening, standing like a potted plant in Bunty Wiseman's early

Egyptian drawing room. Persuading Ben not to accompany me should have earned me the Lifetime Achievement Award for Deception in Marriage. Informing him that I had joined Fully Female almost seemed easier at one point, but somehow I couldn't bring myself to say the words. I knew that he would rather have me bare my bosom in public than strip our intimate relationship naked at Marriage Makeover.

Mrs. Pickle had admitted me to the house, and everywhere I looked were women I recognized from my one attendance at Fully Female. Most of them had a man in tow, all of whom, from the doting looks on their faces, were still under the influence. But oddly enough, I had yet to see hide or hair of our hostess, let alone the guests of honour. The room was so blindingly white that you almost expected masked surgeons to rush in and start sharpening their scalpels. Indeed, there was one medical man present. Standing in the orchestra pit next to the grand piano was Dr. Melrose . . . and spouse. From where I stood it was hard to tell if Flo was in tip-top condition, but she was on her feet, which I suppose was something. My gaze veered away from the Melroses to a mirrored screen angled across a window corner. The screen hadn't been present on my former visits—a parting gift to Bunty from Lionel? Or had she gone on a shopping spree to cheer herself up?

"Champagne, madam?"

"Mrs. Malloy!" I almost jolted the tray out of her hands. "This is a surprise!"

"Nice frock." She looked up and down at my bronze and olive shot silk dress. "Sort of thing you could wear to a funeral and not look too done up."

"Thank you."

"But for pity's sake, Mrs. H, what have you done to your hair? Looks like you combed it with a rake."

Aware that the people to my right were all ears, I lowered my voice. "I was in a hurry—and for your information, Mrs. Malloy, the tousled look is in."

A derisive sniff. "Yes, at Crufts maybe, but not here." She placed a glass in my nerveless hand. "I like to be proud of my ladies and it's not as though I'll always be around to keep an eye on you."

Probably not. Mr. Fisher was no doubt a chauvinist of the old school who would not wish his wife to polish other people's tables when she could be polishing coffins.

"You look very nice," I said. And so she did with her two-tone hair just so, every beauty spot in place, and her cranberry apron adding a splash of colour to her black-beaded frock.

"Well, no rest for the wicked." Mrs. Malloy jostled the glasses around on the tray, took a sip from one—to even it out with the others, I suppose—smacked her butterfly lips in approval of the vintage, and teetered away on her six-inch heels. The next couple she approached was the Bludgetts. I was thinking about wandering over to join them when who should come up to me but the ever elegant and recently widowed Jacqueline Diamond.

"Still no sign of our hostess or the guests of honour." She twirled the long stem of her glass and appraised me with her Lauren Bacall eyes.

"No," I stammered.

"Spooky, don't you think?"

What I thought was spooky was that she—a widow of a

couple of days—should be attending a party . . . especially a party on the premises of Fully Female.

"How are you doing?" I managed.

"Still blessedly numb." She fished into her tapestry evening bag for a packet of cigarettes and, ash-blonde hair trailing on her wrist, tapped out a king-sized filter tip. "Hope you won't clutch your chest and gasp for air if I smoke"—she lit up— "not that I care much if anyone minds. That's one of the nifty things about grief. For your future reference, you don't give a crap about anything, such as what people think about my being here tonight. All I know"—her voice was as smoky as the puffs clouding our space—"is it beats being home alone with only Normie's capes for company."

"Did the police give you a hard time?" I pushed back my hair because it was getting in my eyes and making them tear.

"Soft as butter."

"Do you know when the inquest will be?"

"Nope, but at the moment I am concentrating on the fun stuff, like making final arrangements. Normie was God-fearing but not religiously observant."

"The new vicar of St. Anselm's is very nice," I babbled, and speak of coincidence, who should enter the room at that moment but the Reverend Eudora Spike and her husband.

"Thanks, sweetie." Jacqueline looked around for an ashtray. "But Normie was Jewish."

"Really?" I could feel myself breaking out into a cold sweat that had nothing to do with my faux pas. The Spikes were heading our way. Gladstone looked such a dear, sweet man, with his stooped shoulders and nearsighted eyes, that I felt I should beat my breast and say three mea culpas for suspecting him of trying to murder his wife in order to pick up where he left off years ago with Gladys Thorn, the woman of the hour, who had yet to make her appearance.

Before the Spikes could reach us, they collided with the Bludgetts and were inevitably trapped into conversation with the exuberant Moll.

"Smashing to see you, Reverend."

"Our pleasure." Eudora tucked a hand into the crook of her husband's arm and immediately they were like a cup and saucer, separate but complete.

"Nice party!" Jock Bludgett cleared his throat and elevated it to an upper crust falsetto. "A real classy dame, this Bunty Wiseman. Not too many women'd put their hurt feelings in the old tucker bag and throw a shindig for the tomcatting husband and his bit of fluff."

Any woman less fluffy than Gladys Thorn I could not imagine, but that was neither here nor there. Was Mr. Bludgett remembering how he had done his Moll wrong with this same femme fatale? And were the Spikes wishing themselves anywhere but in this room?

"I was surprised when Mrs. Wiseman rang and invited Gladstone and myself to the party." Eudora accepted a glass of champagne from Mrs. Malloy who was back doing her rounds. "And even more surprised when she explained her reason for the get-together."

"A most Christian endeavour," interpolated her husband.

"Love at its purest." Eudora blinked as if she had something in her eye. From where I stood, her complexion appeared as beige as her silk blouse. My heart went out to her.

"Wonder where Mrs. Wiseman is?" Mr. Bludgett chewed on his moustache.

Moll, all bounce from her head to her toes, lifted her glass.

"Wherever! I say we drink a toast to Bunty Wiseman, the ultimate Fully Female woman!"

"To Bunty!" The unified shout rocked the room, then dropped to a whisper that couldn't peter out fast enough. For standing at the entrance to the room were the lovebirds themselves. Lionel Wiseman was resplendent in a silver-grey suit that complemented his hair, while his dark tie was a perfect match for his black brows. As for his fiancée, what she lacked in beauty she made up for in maidenly modesty.

"Dear, dear friends of Chitterton Fells, this is all too much!" Drawing her black lace shawl about her sallow shoulders, Miss Thorn lowered her head so that the daisies peeked out of her mousy tresses. "My beloved Lionel never expected such a turnout to bless our union." Choked with emotion, Miss T cast herself into Mr. Wiseman's arms and he was holding her thus when a gasp went up from the guests.

Bunty had made her dazzling entrance.

"Hello, boys and girls!" Batting her baby blues, Bunty undulated into the room, blonde head held high, a hand on her scarlet satin hip, her face ablaze with more light than the room. "Hello, Li, darling! And greetings to the woman you love. As guests of honour, if you would like to make yourselves comfortable on the sofa facing the mirrored screen, I am sure everyone else can find a cosy spot so that the entertainment may begin."

"What now?" Jacqueline Diamond tapped out another cigarette.

"Isn't this a gas?" Moll Bludgett moved up close and squeezed my arm. "Aren't you on pins and needles with suspense?"

"Shush," whispered Mrs. Wardle, the librarian.

As instructed, Mr. Wiseman and Miss Thorn sat, champagne glasses in hand, on the white sofa with the huge throw pillows, while Bunty held the floor. Lifting a lily-white hand, she trilled sweetly, "The scrapbooks of all our lives are filled with the memories of cherished events, special to us as individuals, and so, Gladys Thorn, on this auspicious occasion when you announce your engagement to my husband and to the world . . . I bring you a voice from your past because Miss Thorn: This Is Your Life!"

"Oooohhhh!" The gasp rippled round the room, while the lady of moment covered her gaping mouth with a hand on which sparkled the most enormous diamond I had ever seen. The flash made me feel quite giddy, and all at once I was overcome by an overpowering sense of doom. I wanted to shout at Bunty to stop this madness before it was too late. I wanted to dash from that room with all its false brightness and go burrowing home to Ben and the twins. But I couldn't move a muscle, for I was hemmed in by Moll Bludgett, Jacqueline Diamond, the Spikes, and my stupid sense of decorum. Then between one breath and the next it was too late.

A sepulchral voice was emoting from the mirrored screen. "Hugs and kisses, dear Miss Thorn. Remember me, my sugar cube?"

"I don't think I recognize . . ."

"Surely, O sweet delight, you recall how you danced naked in the wooded night, my nymph . . . omaniac." Death-rattle laughter. "Or do I ask too much, considering I am but one of a hundred husbands you have lured into your sticky web, thou Spider Woman."

Not a chair creaked, not an eyelash quivered, until the spell was broken by Lionel Wiseman rising to his feet in a rush that transformed him into an avenger twice his size. Thank God he was going to put a stop to this obscenity. Miss Thorn might not be a lady in the strictest sense of the word, but no one deserved to be subjected to such fiendish cruelty . . . except perhaps the woman who might make off with Bentley T. Haskell.

But before Lionel Wiseman could find his voice, I received the shock of the evening, if not a lifetime. The mirrored screen swayed, then steadied itself. And out stepped my cousin Freddy.

"I'm sorry, Mrs. Wiseman, but I can't go through with this! When you spoke with me this morning on the telephone, I told myself that an actor must take the parts that come his way, but I find I cannot use people's lives as stepping stones on the path to stardom."

"A little late to turn high-minded!" Heading over to him, I would have hurled champagne in his face, but for the fact my glass was empty.

"No talent scouts here, by any chance?" My cousin produced a grin that did nothing to calm me down. The room was in an uproar, or rather Bunty was making enough noise for the whole room. She had gone completely to pieces, pounding her fists against her husband's chest, then clawing them free of his grasp to tear at his hair, while off to their side stood Miss Thorn, her eyes mushrooming behind her spectacles.

"How can you leave me for that knock-kneed trollop?" Bunty screeched. "I tried to be everything you wanted. I blistered my lips reciting *How Now Brown Cow* so I could talk proper. Everywhere I turned, the world was telling me that to be a fulfilled woman I had to be a working woman. You told me, Li, you wanted me to be a contributing member of society, and look where all this got me. I taught other women how to hold on to their husbands, making life tough for the likes of Gladys Thorn." Sobbing, Bunty staggered backwards. "Did I put the wind up you, Gladys, old girl? Did I make you see you might be better off with a husband of your own than continuing to borrow them like books from the library?"

Miss Thorn didn't answer. She just stood there clutching her abdomen, and the next moment the question of response was moot. Bunty whirled about and made a beeline for the hall. Seconds later the front door opened and slammed shut behind her. Talk about ending a party with a bang. With hardly a word being spoken, the women began gathering up their handbags and the men, including Freddy, headed off to collect coats. As for Lionel Wiseman and his fiancée, my last glimpse was them standing by the coffee table lost in each other's arms.

"How are you feeling, my dove?"

"Not too bad." She crushed his hand to her lips. "Of course this sort of upset is disastrous for my digestive system, but the path to true love is paved with milk of magnesia."

"My own brave darling!"

"Tomorrow is another day, and with Bunty gone we can think about redecorating this room." The mushroom eyes strayed around the white-on-white perfection. "What do you think of the boudoir look, lots of black satin and chartreuse lace?"

Terrified that Miss Thorn would catch sight of me and ask me to assist in the renovations, I scuttled out into the hall. There I caught sight of Mrs. Malloy peering around the corner of the kitchen.

"What's all the argy-bargy?" She went back to stirring a glass of what I gathered, from the container standing on the counter, was Fully Female Formula.

"Bunty walked out."

"What? Abandoned ship?" The expression was made for the galley-style kitchen, which like the rest of the house was white as a seaman's uniform. Indeed, it was so compact that when Mrs. Malloy set down her glass and stood with her hands on her hips, her elbows touched the walls on either side.

"She has me worried," I confessed.

"Bloody hell! You think she might do herself in?"

"That or something equally disastrous."

"There's a tide in the life of man"—Mrs. Malloy wiped her hands on her cranberry apron—"that's naught but fuss and foam."

"Probably," I said. "But I think I'll drive around and look for Bunty."

"You do that," she said as she set a couple of wineglasses to bob in the sink, "and after you don't find her, perhaps you would be kind enough to come back and give me a lift home. You know me, Mrs. H, I'm not one to ask for favours, but one of these days you'll treasure our moments together."

Touched to the core, I went to give her a hug, but the moment was not propitious. Mrs. Malloy discovered that her Fully Female Formula had set solid.

"Now look what you've made me do!"

"I'll mix you another."

"Don't put yourself out, Mrs. H." With a long-suffering sigh, she plopped the glass in the sink. "Don't ask me why, but I'm right off the stuff."

*   *   *

MY GOOD intentions met with dismal failure. After driving around in circles for who knows how long, I nipped into the Black Horse and checked out both the saloon and the public bar, but saw no sign of Bunty drowning her sorrows with a lager and lime. Why, oh, why had I even thought about drowning? I could comb miles of beach without finding a pathetic pile of clothes or spying something that might be a buoy—or a body—bobbing upon the horizon. In the end, I drove up Cliff Road to the place where Dr. Melrose had planned to unburden himself of poor Flo. But there was no sign of Bunty's car. Swamped by a feeling of hopelessness, I turned tail lights about and drove back to the Wiseman house. Were its days as the headquarters of Fully Female over?

Walking up the marble steps to the front door, I prayed Bunty was home safe and sound. Before I could ring the bell, Mrs. Malloy, buttoned up in her fur coat, a feather hat perched on her head, opened up for me.

"No luck?" She pulled on her gloves.

I shook my head.

"Well, you did what you could. And just after you left, Mr. Wiseman went out looking for her."

"What about Miss Thorn?"

"Taken over as Lady of the Manor from the looks of things." Mrs. Malloy sniffed. "Went poking into the kitchen and then disappeared down the hall. What do you think, Mrs. H? Should I go up and tell her I'm leaving?"

"Well . . ."

"There is the little matter of payment."

"In that case . . ." I stepped over the threshold and the next thing I knew I was following Mrs. Malloy down the corridor to the master bedroom, where earlier I had left my coat.

"Miss Thorn?" Mrs. Malloy beat a tattoo on the door.

No answer.

"Probably asleep," I offered. I was all for making a quick exit, but my companion had other ideas.

"If it's all the same with you, Mrs. H, I'd like to find her so I can get my money." So saying she opened up the door . . . and promptly fell back into my arms.

Miss Thorn was lying on the bed, wrapped in a transparent plastic wrap toga, with a cherry in her navel. Even more shocking than her night attire was the fact that she wasn't wearing her specs, giving her an obscenely naked, glassy-eyed stare that looked right through me to the doorway . . . of eternity.

Chapter Ten

She's dead!" Choking on tears and eau de toilette, I stumbled away from the bed, with its cupids and tulle canopy.

"And whose bloody fault is that?" Mrs. Malloy flashed back.

"No one's, I hope."

"Let anyone point the finger at me—"

"Oh, for heaven's sake!" I pushed her down onto the bed-side chair and wished I could strap her in the way I did the babies. How could she rant on in this silly way when we had no reason, other than Bunty's threats, to suspect that Miss

Thorn was the victim of foul play? That the deceased had been in fine fettle merely an hour ago meant nothing. Neither was her mode of undress evidence one way or the other. Any of us can have a heart attack any time, especially when we are subjected to the stress of too many men wanting first dibs on our bodies.

"Lord save us, she looks 'orrible!" Mrs. Malloy chomped down on a knuckle.

Uncharitable, but undeniably true. There was a snarl to Miss Thorn's lips and a bulge to her eyes that suggested she had told the Grim Reaper what he could do to himself. To be fair, the bedroom did not set the scene for heavenly harps and celestial voices humming in the background. The white-on-white, stark modernism that pervaded the rest of the house had not set foot in here, probably because Bunty had not permitted an interior designer through the door, choosing instead to model the place on her old chorus girl dressing room. Flounces and fripperies were everywhere. But most horrible of all was the flash of mirrors parading around the walls and across the ceiling, so that everywhere I looked, the deathbed scene was blazed before my eyes like scenes from St. Anselm's stained-glass windows. No wonder Mrs. Malloy was clutching her head and saying she didn't feel well.

"Why don't you go back to the living room and lie down," I suggested.

"What, leave you here on your own, Mrs. H?"

"Oh, go on with you," I said as I herded her out the door. "She won't bite, will she?"

Bravely spoken, but the moment I was alone with Miss Thorn, a chill enveloped my bones like a shroud. Those teeth looked ready to chew off a couple of fingers if I moved a hand in her direction. And the bulging eyes promised another kind of vengeance; they would haunt my dreams for many nights to come.

"Look"—I sidled around the bed on my way to the telephone—"I don't blame you for being thoroughly cheesed off, but please don't look daggers at me."

Amazing how the sound of my voice breathed life not only into the room, but into the body of Miss Thorn. I don't mean she returned from the dead with the aplomb Flo Melrose had shown the previous night. But talking to her dignified her personhood.

"Excuse me." I picked up the phone and dialled Dr. Melrose's number. Force of habit. It never occurred to me to waste time asking the operator for the number of the Cottage Hospital's emergency room.

"Dr. Melrose, this is Ellie Haskell."

"Yes?" I could almost hear the alarm bells going off around his head before he converted them into a hearty laugh. "Flo's fine, as you must have seen yourself this evening at the Wisemans' aborted party."

"Oh, for heaven's sake!" I snapped. "This isn't about blackmail; it's about Miss Gladys Thorn."

"Splendid!"

"She's dead!"

"Super!"

Words failed me. But presumably my shocked breathing brought Dr. Melrose out of his euphoria at realizing that all he was being asked to do was pay a house call. After telling him I was phoning from the Wisemans' home, I hung up and returned to the bedside to keep the late Miss Thorn company.

"The doctor will be here in a few moments," I soothed. Enough said; I could have busied myself praying, but typical of yours truly in times of stress, I went babbling away like a mindless brook. "Miss Thorn, I haven't always harboured the kindest thoughts toward you, not so much because I disapproved of your amorous lifestyle, but because I viewed you as a figure of fun. And a person of my insecurities and physical shortcomings should have known better. Tell me, Miss Thorn"—I smoothed the sheet, well aware those vile cupids were smirking at me from the headboard—"did you decide to revenge yourself upon all womankind by proving that sexiness is more than skin deep?"

Voices out in the hall. A scurry of footsteps. Opening the bedroom door I fully expected to see Dr. Melrose. Instead, I found myself face to face with the missing blonde in red satin. Welcome home madam.

"Ellie!" Bunty's hair stood all on end as if it had been pulled through one of those bleaching caps with the tiny little holes. And her eyes were equally wild. "What's bloomin' going on? Has Mrs. Malloy been at the booze?"

"Not as far as I know."

"Then why's she talking rubbish?"

"Bunty!" I stood blocking the view to the bed, while the pillar of Fully Female sagged against the doorway as if her legs had turned to rubble. Not much doubt as to who had been at the bottle. "I know it's an awful shock, but Gladys Thorn is dead." I put out a hand to touch Bunty, then lowered it. As a child, I had found the pressure of anyone's touch unbearable when I fell down and scraped my knees. And when I was in labour, even the weight of Ben's breath on my face had been too much. Every ounce of energy had to be directed toward the pain.

"I don't believe you!"

Before I could say "Look for yourself," poor Bunty did just that. She staggered and would have collapsed facedown on the corpse if I had not corralled her under the armpits.

"Bloomin' heck, Ellie! They'll say I *murdered* her."

"Nonsense." I bundled her down on the same chair upon which I had positioned Mrs. Malloy earlier. "She died of natural causes."

"Are you a bigger sap than you look, or what?" Her shriek sent me hurtling halfway across the room. "Natural causes are never this convenient. I threatened to kill her and she's dead. Does that sound like a heart attack to you?"

"Life is known for its coincidences," I babbled.

"Oh, talk sense!"

"Bunty, you have to get a hold of yourself. Dr. Melrose is on his way." Tiptoeing up to her, I smoothed down the haywire blonde hair, and after a few moments her breathing evened out.

"Where's Li?" she said meekly.

"Mrs. Malloy said he went looking for you."

"Hell's bells, Ellie!" Tears rained down from the heavenly blue of her eyes. "Li will hate me for this. He'll never believe I didn't murder her. But you believe me . . ." She grabbed hold of my hand, crushing my fingers. "You think me innocent, don't you, sugar?"

"Yes, Bunty." The words were propelled by compassion not conviction, but the moment they were out there in the open I knew I meant them. Murder had been committed, that I didn't doubt, but the culprit wasn't the wronged wife. Bunty was the hands-on type. I could picture her in a white-hot rage pushing Miss Thorn down a flight of stairs or cracking her over the head with a bronze candlestick, but I couldn't imagine her slipping a deadly compound into the woman's champagne glass. And if we were indeed looking for a poisoner—which seemed a possibility considering the absence of a bullet hole in the middle of the deceased's sallow forehead or a dagger protruding from her sunken chest—did I have to look any further than last night? If a human agent were responsible for Tobias's near-death experience, wasn't that person the most likely murderer of Gladys Thorn?

Shivering, Bunty stood up. "By golly, I'm cold, so imagine how she must be feeling!"

We were both staring at the bed when the door opened and in walked Dr. Melrose, little black bag in hand and a furrow to his brow. He waved us out of the way, setting the tone for the brisk examination of the corpse delectable that followed. Not a word was said about her plastic wrap or the cherry in her navel.

Bunty was the one who spouted off on that subject. "Bloomin' cheek really! She stole the idea for that getup from my manual to use on my husband. . . . But what the hell, so long as they were happy in each other's arms, I had no complaints. I'm in the business of spreading love, not hogging it for myself."

Dr. Melrose eyed her with dislike verging on hatred. If he could slip the noose around her neck and yank it tight, I had no doubt he would do so with alacrity. To have the head of Fully Female at his mercy must be sweet revenge indeed for all he had suffered as a result of his wife's passionate quest for sexual awareness.

"Have you phoned the police?"

"Not yet," Bunty and I stammered in unison.

"Then I will do so!" Laying Miss Thorn's hand down on the bedspread, Dr. Melrose stood up. Was he smiling? Or was it the light from the overhead bulb flickering over his face that created the illusion of a puckish lift to the narrow lips? He was heading for the telephone when Bunty dodged around him, picked it up, and held it behind her back.

"Wait!" She stood there like a child at bay, her face framed by tufts of angelic blonde hair. "Why all this fuss about one middle-aged woman who dies in her sleep? Why can't you just write out the death certificate and—"

"Mrs. Wiseman!" Dr. Melrose clicked his black bag shut and came at her, holding out his hand. "Please hand over that phone," he said sternly. "You are obstructing me in the fulfillment of my Hippocratic duty."

"She's upset!" I bleated.

"Understandably so."

"Then you do think—"

"My suspicions, Mrs. Haskell, must await the results of the autopsy." Plain speaking from a plain man. It was unjust of me to think of Dr. Melrose as the enemy. He had always treated me well and was now doing his job as queen and country would have him do it.

"Please . . ." Bunty dropped the phone with a terrifying thud. "Can't we talk about this? Doctor, I didn't kill that gift-wrapped baggage, but if you turn me in, I'm done for! Why look further for the murderer when I'm right there under everyone's nose—with a motive sky-high?"

"A difficult position to be in." Some humanity had edged into Dr. Melrose's rusty voice and Bunty immediately picked up on it. Her voice took on a wheedling tone and I detected a wiggle to her scarlet satin hips as she stepped up to him. "Doctor, dear, haven't you ever found yourself in a situation where the whole world was about to cave in?" she pouted prettily up at him. "But you could be saved if someone would be sweet and kind and keep his . . . or her . . . bloomin' mouth shut."

"Yes." Voice of a robot.

"So couldn't you possibly"—Bunty reached out a hand to smooth down his coat collar—"couldn't you find it in your heart to write out that death certificate, citing, say, a nasty old heart attack for finishing off dear Miss Thorn?"

"If you insist." As slowly and stiffly as the world spinning on its axis, Dr. Melrose turned to look at me, and the contempt I read in his eyes made my knees go wobbly. The man thought I had betrayed him to Bunty. He thought she knew about his attempt to dispose of his wife's body and was now blackmailing him into silence. The enemy here was his guilty conscience because I hadn't said a word to anyone, let alone Bunty, about the Flo fiasco. And Ben, having given his word, would definitely have kept mum. Which only left Flo . . . assuming she had regained her memory of the incident and had felt called upon to report it to Fully Female. So what now? Should I do my civic duty by whispering into the doctor's ear that he had nothing to fear by picking up that telephone? Or should I remember the bond of fellowship between one Fully Female woman and another?

WHEN I went home that night to Merlin's Court, I longed to run straight into Ben's arms. But how could I seek shelter in that sweet haven when I felt like a criminal? Keeping quiet

about my involvement with the death of Norman the Doorman had almost done me in, and my complicity in that regard
was nothing in comparision to the role I had played tonight.
Silence can be unbelievably foul-mouthed. I wouldn't feel halfway right until I had gargled with salt water, but alas, the
path to the bathroom was blocked by my husband standing
guard at the top of the stairs.

"There you are, sweetheart! I was starting to worry about
you." Many a man would have been taken for a ward orderly
in those hospital-green pyjamas, but wouldn't you know Ben
looked as though he had been clipped from a fashion magazine
featuring gentleman's loungewear. Every syllable of his concerned voice was a dagger through my heart. And deeper anguish was to follow when he drew me to him and lifted my
hair out from under the collar of my coat. These last weeks
had been a wasteland parched of passion, and now that love
bloomed anew, I was cut off from it by a barbed-wire fence
built of my own deceit. But did it have to be that way? Could
I go on living in the same house with myself, let alone Ben, if
I didn't tell him I had joined Fully Female and where such
folly had landed me? In a heady rush of relief I opened my
mouth—all set to spill the beans—when an inner voice piped
up: *Great, Ellie! Unburden yourself by burdening him. Put
Ben in an impossible position! Tell him that you stood silently
by while Bunty persuaded Dr. Melrose to falsify the death
certificate. Then leave the decision up to him. What will it be,
Ben dear? Will you tear your heart out and cast it at my feet
before shuffling sorrowfully down to the police station to report the whole sordid mess to a desk sergeant whose wife has
just left him? Or will you bow to my woman's intuition that
Bunty is innocent and concede with a bittersweet smile that*

silence is golden and a murderer on the loose is a small price to pay for her freedom? Oh, my darling . . . gently prying myself loose from his arms . . . No marriage is an island.

"Are you asleep?" Ben's laugh rippled through my hair.

"Almost."

"Must have been some party."

"The worst."

"Poor darling."

"How are the babies?" Head down, I followed him into our bedroom.

"They were a little fretful on and off, but when I checked five minutes ago, they were sound asleep."

"Then I won't go in and risk waking them."

His smile enfolded me. "Do I get a gold star for waiting up for you?"

My throat closed and my eyes stung. How easy it would have been to drop my cares and woes in a pile on the floor along with my coat and let him lead me gently by the hand to the four-poster with the blankets turned down and sheets as smooth and cool as the feel of his skin under my wistful fingers. But it was no good. I would only hate myself in the morning. While I remained a fugitive from the law, Ben and I could not be Man and Wife in the sublime sense of the words, which on a positive note provided a pretty compelling reason for tracking down Miss Thorn's killer on the double.

"What's wrong?"

I put the bed between us. "Ben, I respect you too much to make love to you when I am in mourning."

"What?"

"For Miss Thorn. She died tonight at Bunty's party."

"By Jupiter!" Hand smacking his brow. "When you said

the party wasn't up to snuff, I thought you meant lousy food, which didn't surprise me considering they didn't ask me to cater it." I knew what he was doing, of course. He was talking himself through the shock. "What a rotten business. What was it—a heart attack?"

"That's . . . that's what Dr. Melrose wrote on the death certificate."

"Sweetheart!" Ben reached out for me, then withdrew, recognizing with that exquisite sensitivity of which I was so undeserving that I couldn't bear to be touched. "Did she just keel over in the punch bowl?"

"She was found in the Wisemans' bedroom."

"Who found her?"

"Mrs. Malloy and . . . I."

"Oh, my darling."

"The whole situation is rather a mess." Somehow I managed to lift my head to see my misery mirrored in his eyes. "Lionel Wiseman was leaving Bunty for Miss Thorn."

"You're not serious?"

"Could I make up something like that?"

"The announcement was made, out of the blue, at the party?"

"Bunty knew it was coming."

"Whoa! Given the emotional climate, I'm surprised Miss Thorn was the only one whose heart gave out."

"Ben," I said, sinking down on the bed, "I really am not up to talking about it."

"Sorry!" He stood over me, tenderness flowing from every pore until I was submerged in remorse and self-loathing. "I am an unfeeling brute to press you for details. Bed is the place for you, my love. As soon as I have you snuggled safe and sound under bedclothes, I will go downstairs and fetch you some hot milk. Just what the doctor ordered."

A shudder passed through my body as Dr. Melrose's gaunt image rose up to haunt me. Assuring Ben that I wanted nothing to drink, I went through the motions of getting ready for bed, and five minutes later, he turned off the light.

"Good night, sweetheart." He reached for my hand and I clung to his fingers until I felt him slip away into sleep. Lying on my back, staring into a darkness where the familiar shapes of daylight, the wardrobe and the dressing table, were transformed into hulking monsters from hell, I had never felt more alone. So how about it? Was I going to wallow or was I going to compose a file of suspects? Damn! Put like that, I squared my shoulders and waited for the lineup to parade before the window of my mind.

First comes Miss Thorn herself. *Look me in the eye, madam, and tell me whether you took your own life in a fit of remorse. Did you stick a cherry in your navel and drape yourself in plastic wrap in hopes that your beloved would always remember you as the ultimate dessert?*

Away flits Miss T and in her place stands the ever-handsome Lionel Wiseman. *Did you, sir, have second thoughts about the engagement and decide to take the gentlemanly way out?*

And who comes next but Mr. and Mrs. Jock Bludgett. He licks his moustache and she epitomizes the old saying, Beware the woman with the perpetual smile. *I haven't forgotten that you, J.B., once engaged in an affair with the irresistible Gladys, providing you and your spouse with ample motives for murder. Yours is remorse, and Moll's is good old-fashioned jealousy.*

Away with you both. Make room for the widowed Jacqueline Diamond. *Excuse the question, dear lady, but was your husband's recent demise the embarrassing misadventure you described to me? Or did you punch out his lights in the heat of quarrel, and upon realizing he was dead, stage the Fully Female scenario with you tied naked to the bed and he a crumpled cape upon the floor? Yes, Jacqueline, I know you made much of withholding the lurid details from the police, but was I the ace up your sleeve, to be produced in the event your story did not go over as planned? And what if Miss Thorn proved to be an unexpected fly in the ointment? I know she also resided on Rosewood Terrace. And I remember on the fateful evening noticing a light present in an upstairs room of the house across the road from yours. What if that were Miss Thorn's house and she just happened to be doing some bird-watching from her window at precisely the wrong moment and casually mentioned sometime later that she had seen you bump off Norman?*

Fade out Jaqueline. My goodness, it's Mr. Walter Fisher! *I suppose it is stretching things a bit to suggest that you were having a slow week and decided to drum up some funeral business. What's that you say? I'm the one guilty of stalling for time because I am not ready to face my chief suspect?*

Deep breath. Bring on Mr. Gladstone Spike. *Yes, sir, I know it goes against everything most British to suspect a man who wears grey woolies and bakes the perfect madeira cake of being a cold-blooded killer. But I don't see how I can let you off the hook. Not after the salmon. My contention, sir, is that you first attempted to murder your wife because you wanted to be free to take up where you left off years ago with Miss Thorn. Happily for everyone but Tobias, circumstances neutralized that endeavour, but tonight you succeeded in doing away with the femme fatale. Why the change of victim? Simple. You discovered that Miss Thorn was going to wed Lionel Wiseman. If you couldn't have her, neither would he.*

Getting drowsy. A yawn split my face in two, and for a brief instant I thought Mr. Spike had reached out from behind the doorway of my mind to make sure I never opened my mouth again.

"You're playing a dangerous game, Mrs. Haskell." Gladstone's voice whispered its way down, down, into the very depths of sleep, where Miss Thorn sat on a clay pot by a waterfall, playing "Abide With Me" on the organ, while off to the side, robed in shadow, stood the Reverend Eudora Spike— reading from a black book that was either the Bible or the Fully Female manual. *"The first shall be last, Ellie, and the last first!"* How dear, how professional of her to point out that she should have topped my list of suspects. And how I wished for her—and all my Fellow Females—that love could be one long bubble bath.

MORNING turned up like a bad penny.

"Ellie, tell me I am not abandoning you in your hour of need?" Ben bent over the bed, a quizzical smile on his lips and a glimmer in his eyes that made me think of sunlight taking a peek into a pirate's treasure trove. "I would take the morning off but we are expecting a large luncheon crowd."

"Excuses!" I coiled my arms around his neck and held on to him for as long as I dared. "Off with you. The children and I have a full day planned."

At the doorway he looked back and I knew he wanted to pocket the moment and take it with him. But then he said, "I wonder how Flo Melrose is doing?"

"She was at the party last night," I replied, "and seemed fully back from the dead."

"Good." Pensive look. "See you tonight, sweetheart." The door closed on a final glimpse of his heart-stopping profile, and I climbed out of bed all fired up to catch Miss Thorn's killer, before celibacy did me in.

But half an hour into the routine of getting the twins up and fed, the flame petered out. Spread out in daylight, last night's convictions seemed a sorry lot that didn't amount to a handful of coffee beans. What horrible irony if Miss Thorn had legitimately died of a heart attack and Bunty and I had placed ourselves in the insidious position of hushing up a murder that wasn't. As for that guff about Gladstone Spike, it was surely my imagination that was poisoned, not the fish.

"What do you say?" I appealed to Abbey and Tam who sat in their feeder chairs looking like the offspring of Apollo with their sunbeam hair and sunshine smiles. "Tell me the honest truth, my darlings. Do you think Mummy should phone Bunty Wiseman and try and talk sense into her? We could then go to Dr. Melrose and ask him to tear up the death certificate. With luck no one need ever be the wiser."

Straining at their straps, the twins goo-gooed words of wisdom.

"You think I'm copping out because I don't have a clue how to trap the murderer?"

No response to that one. And dogged by indecision, I plodded through the morning. By noon I was still as much at sixes and sevens as the kitchen, which was once more stacked to the ceiling with washing that wasn't getting done because the washing machine had grown hardened to the thumps and kicks that were supposed to make it go.

"Masochist!" I taunted to no avail, finally throwing up my soapy hands and heading into the hall to telephone Mr. Bludgett.

"Good morning, this is Mrs. Haskell of—"

"Ellie," the voice shrilled in my ear. "What a thrill to hear from you on this glorious April day."

"Excuse me?"

Squeals of laughter. "Now don't go pulling my leg and pretending you don't know who this is. We Fellow Females stick like glue, right?"

"Moll?"

"My Jock's one-and-only." Some of the fizz went out of her voice, but not all of it. "Have you spoken to Bunty?"

"Not this morning."

"Then you don't know it's flags at half-mast?"

"What?" Sometimes I think I have a natural aptitude for playing stupid.

"Gladys Thorn is *dead!*"

"That . . ."—I paused to take a deep breath—"I did know, but I'm afraid I can't talk about it right now. My babies are alone in the playpen, so if you would ask your husband to come back and look at the washing machine . . ."

"Will do!" Not a hint that she felt rebuffed. Could any woman be that unfailingly cheerful and never come apart at the seams or keep from driving other people bonkers? "Just one thing more, Ellie?"

"Yes?"

"Be happy for Gladys. Think about it, what could be lovelier than to die when you're bubbling over with happiness?"

"Moll," I said, struggling to keep all traces of acid out of my voice, "you do deserve a medal for looking on the bright side."

"Thanks!" Her merry laughter drilled a hole in my head. "It doesn't hurt, does it, that the lady was a thorn in my flesh. And I don't suppose Bunty will be putting on black."

"I suppose not."

"She said Lionel was devastated. Spent half the night crying in her arms, which isn't all bad."

"No."

"Oh, one last thing, Ellie! There's a little prayer service scheduled for six tonight at Fisher's Funerals."

"Lovely," I said before I could help myself. It was as though Gladstone Spike were hiding inside my head.

SOMETHING was missing at Merlin's Court and it took me until midafternoon to figure out what. Mrs. Malloy. The twins kept cocking their heads as if listening for her step in the hall. And even Tobias had a droop to his tail that suggested he missed the saucer of milk she would slip down for him when my back was turned. Last night, when I dropped her off at home, she hadn't said anything about coming in today, so to worry about her absence was really quite presumptuous. I could almost hear her voice. "Is this the thanks I get, Mrs. H, for giving you extra of my valuable time? Can't call me bloody soul me own!"

"Quite right, Mrs. Malloy," I said, and kept saying, all the way down the hall to dial her number. But I needn't have worried about getting one of her earfuls. Is there any lonelier sound on earth than the ringing of an unanswered telephone? And is there ever a less welcome sight than someone walking into your house unannounced and uninvited, when your mind is already a cellar peopled with all sorts of bludgeoners and riffraff? Pardon me while I say the F word.

"Freddy!" The receiver leaped from my hand. "You really must pop in and scare the wits out of me more often."

"Save your raptures, cousin! And spare my blushes!" Before I could blanch twice, he dropped down on one knee like some Shakespearean trouper in doublet and hose and smote his breast once, twice, thrice, before tottering toward me at horrible speed, still on his knees, hands outstretched. "Ellie, lend me your ears!"

Ridiculous, but it was the scruffy beard that got to me. "Freddy, what would I do without you? I'll listen to your lines . . . and afterwards, even if it puts me in your debt forever, will you watch the twins for me for a little while?"

MRS. MALLOY didn't answer my knock. The house on Herring Street looked back at me as snooty as you please from its tight-lipped letter box to its wary lace curtain eyes. *Who do you think you are, Mrs. High and Mighty Haskell, to come poking your nose round here?*

"I'm a friend, that's who!" My whisper went spiralling up into the sky like smoke from some of the chimney pots round about. There was no smoke coming from Mrs. Malloy's chimney and suddenly I got the absurd idea that this was because the house had stopped breathing. And what I had taken for awareness of my presence was in fact the fixed stare of rigor mortis. Returning to the car, I realized I had time to kill—lovely expression—before turning up at Fisher Funerals for Miss Thorn's prayer service. And like pulling a rabbit from a hat, I came up with the bright idea of going to visit Flo Melrose. I'm not sure what I hoped to glean from her, but I felt there might possibly be something.

I had been to her house once a couple of years before, for a workshop connected with the St. Anselm's bazaar, and I found my way back to it now with the almost spooky ease I had encountered when driving to Jacqueline Diamond's home on the night of Norman's death. Goodness, was that only a couple of days ago? Traumatic events certainly stretch time out of all proportion. Ah, here was the familiar drive leading to the building that looked more like a school or a fire station than a house. No lace curtains here. No curtains at all from what I could see.

The front garden was a concrete parking lot dotted with fir trees like cones to be maneuvered in a driving test, and I crossed this expanse with quaking footsteps, convinced I would somehow fail to pass muster before reaching the front door. Guilty conscience, Ellie! If Dr. Melrose is struck off for falsification of medical documents you will never forgive yourself. And that's so silly. You're a victim of circumstance. An innocent bystander caught up in events bigger than yourself. A pawn in the cosmic scheme of things.

What a picture! There I stood on the Melroses' doorstep, flushed with an overwhelming sense of unimportance. I didn't so much as lift a finger to ping the doorbell before it was opened by Flo, looking like Friar Tuck in a brown robe, which, from the way it moulded her free-flow form, hid not so much as a hair shirt.

"Ellie Haskell!" Her stare was as blank as the unadorned walls of the hall, even as her outstretched hands, made monstrous by reddish-brown stains, beckoned me over the threshold. "What brings you here?"

"I . . ." I dug my hands in the pocket of my beige linen coat and took them out again. "I . . . was in the neighbourhood and wondered if you might need a ride to Miss Thorn's prayer service."

"That was dear of you." Flo's smile seemed to slide over her shoulder. I realized that even though she was looking directly at me, her attention was fixed somewhere behind her. Fair enough! I had trouble dragging my eyes away from those hands and focusing them on . . . the trail of spatter spots . . . of that same grizzly brown . . . leading from where Flo stood, across the pale green linoleum to one of the rooms off the hall. "Yes, very kind indeed, Ellie, but I am not going to the prayer service."

"Oh!"

"But one of these days"—the Friar Tuck hair bobbed against her cheeks—"you and I must meet for coffee or lunch." No doubt about it, her voice was shooing me out the door, which she had left strategically open. The woman couldn't get rid of me fast enough, which meant she was hiding something. Which meant I had to play dense—a role, Freddy would say, which I perform to perfection.

"What fun!" As punishment, this smile would be stuck on my face for good. "Why don't we strike while the iron is hot? And—" I closed the door with my elbow—"go and take a peek at your calendar."

"This really isn't the best time—"

"No time ever is! That's why it always gets away from us."

"You may be right." With a hunch to her shoulder, which could have been a shrug, Flo glanced toward the stairs, then turned about and glided with a surprising fawnlike grace toward a door on the far left-hand side of the hall. "Time certainly got away from Gladys Thorn. I wonder if she had a premonition that sent her to the church that night?"

"What night?"

"The night before last—when I was in the car accident involving your poor cat. When we were driving back home very slowly down Cliff Road, I saw her standing just inside the churchyard gates with her bicycle propped up against the yews and the moon behind her . . . like a halo. After what I had just been through, it gave me quite a creepy feeling."

"I'm sure." So it hadn't been Gladstone Spike that I had spotted while waiting with Tobias in my arms for Ben to return with the picnic basket! Which meant—I stared uncomfortably at Flo's rear—that Dr. Melrose must be added to my suspect list. Miss Thorn's presence on the scene—her old organ stomping ground—that night meant she might have seen him poised on the cliff edge with his wife's "corpse" slung over his shoulder. And knowing how our Gladys tended to twitter, she might well have gabbed to him about his midnight marauding, perhaps during her engagement party, and thus sealed her fate. Assuming I was correct in my evil suspicions, then what a chuckle for the doctor— listening to Bunty's pleadings that he cite natural causes on the death certificate!

"My calendar should be in here." Flo pushed open a door into a room that reeked of turpentine and oil paints. Unlike the hall walls, these were virtually papered with portraits . . . of nude men.

"Be honest." Flo sidestepped her way between two tables made out of sawhorses and sheets of plywood. "Be brutal if you like. Won't bother me. I thrive on criticism."

"They're wonderful," I gushed. "Such form and definition!

My eyes were riveted to a blond chap who had obviously been a good boy about eating his corn flakes. "Are they . . . anatomically correct? Or, are some . . . drawn larger than life?"

"No. All done to scale."

"My goodness!" Skirting a carousel stacked with paint tins, my foot skidded on a patch of wet floor, and I would have gone crashing down if Flo hadn't grabbed me by the upper arm.

"Sorry." She held up her stained hands. "Had a bit of a spill moments before you came."

"Ah!" Another of life's little mysteries cleared up. The ghastly spatters were paint stains.

"And here's the calendar." It was produced with a flourish that said more clearly than words: *A couple more minutes and I can bustle you out the door, Mrs. Haskell.* Then a look came into her eyes that cried out, *Too late.* Turning to see the door being pushed open from the hall, I braced myself for the entrance of Dr. Melrose . . . and saw instead a far handsomer gentleman, one sporting a maroon dressing gown.

I didn't faint. Fainting is an art which I never mastered, but I prayed for oblivion, as I backed perilously close to the paint pots.

"Hello, Ellie!" Ben said with a smile as crisp as his towel-dried hair. "What brings you here?"

"I . . ." Croaking voice. "I get to ask the questions."

"You know what," Flo said as she glided around us, "I think it might be best if I left the two of you together." The door clicked shut behind her.

"Well, isn't this nice." Arms folded, my errant spouse stood tapping a bare foot on the bare floor.

"How can you stand there . . . ?"

"My dear, I don't know what you are talking about."

"Have you no *shame*?" I was practically jumping up and down with rage.

"Why, sweetheart"—his eyes had a glitter that riveted me in place—"are you in any position to impugn my honour when you have been living a lie for days, if not weeks?"

"*What?*"

"Flo shocked the socks off me"—he looked down at his bare feet—"by mentioning what you have signally failed to mention, Ellie: your membership in Fully Female."

"Why . . ." Guilt fired up my voice. "Why shouldn't I join if I wish."

"Ellie, you didn't exactly take up tennis. This was something that involved the two of us." He cinched the maroon dressing gown more firmly around his Apollo-like waist. "And it so happens that I object to being treated like a trained seal."

"That was never the idea."

"Really? Think back to the night when you wore those damned silly horns. I'd call that a circus act all right."

"You didn't say so at the time!"

"Because I've grown used to craziness from you."

"Thanks a lot."

"You don't get it, do you?" Ben was now looking at me more in sorrow than in anger. "I like expecting the unexpected when it comes to our relationship. What I don't want is to be paragraph one, page ten in a How To sex manual. How would you like it if I came to you complete with instruction booklet: 'Hold right breast firmly . . .' "

"You know what I think?" Sounding like a shrewish fish-wife, I flung out an arm to include the portraits on the wall.

"I think you are trying to turn the tables, Bentley T. Haskell, so I can't say a word about your state of semiundress, the reason for which is appallingly obvious. But if you think I will permit you to flaunt your maleness on these walls, let alone those of Merlin's Court, you have another think coming!"

"Ellie—"

"I refuse to take Abigail's portrait down from above the mantelpiece!"

"Would you stop talking rubbish!" Two strides and he was nose to nose with me. The blaze of his eyes scorched my skin. "I didn't come here today to have my portrait painted. I came to ask Flo to paint one of you with the twins from a snapshot I brought along. We were discussing the project when I clumsily knocked over a tin of paint and got the stuff all over me and the floor. Whereupon I accepted her gracious offer of a shower and . . . here we are."

"Oh!"

"I came down to request some cleaning fluid for my clothes."

"Say no more!" I cried. "You're a saint and I am a total idiot!" Wracked with remorse, I fled the room and made my escape down the hall and through the front door, not really flattering myself that Ben would pursue me outdoors in Dr. Melrose's dressing gown. But he did, whereupon I took off in the getaway car, with the sound of his voice almost drowning out the roar of the engine.

"Ellie!"

So many nuances in a name. Was he calling me back or saying good-bye?

THE FISHER Funeral Chapel was sufficiently well lit that I didn't have to grope my way down the aisle to join the group assembled in the front pews, but no one could have accused the place of any lack of sobriety. The windows were draped with the most mournful of purples and the air was heavy with the scent of gardenias, possibly from a spray can, but let's not be snippy. *Focus on the accoutrements, Ellie! Feast your eyes on the neat little pews and the ceiling painted with the pearly gates. Don't look at the coffin.* But even with my eyes lowered to the mosaic floor I saw it, taking pride of place before the dollhouse altar. The face propped up on the satin pillow could belong to anyone dead or alive. Was she wearing her spectacles? One step in front of the other. And sooner than I would have liked, I was sidling into the pew alongside people I didn't know from Adam, which was better I suppose than being next to Moll Bludgett, who was two rows in front of me with her husband. Who knew, the ever-jolly Moll might send me into nervous peals of laughter, which would never do. I took a brave peek between the heads in front. Yes, Miss Thorn was wearing her specs, which looked a little silly with her eyes closed, but I had to admit, given what Walter Fisher had to work with, she did look positively radiant in her bridal white. She was holding a bunch of white violets, and as someone moved, causing a shift in the way the light hit the coffin, I caught a flash from those clasped hands and saw, straining forward, that she was wearing her diamond engagement ring. How romantic of Lionel Wiseman to wish it buried with her. Out the corner of my eye I saw the fiancé in question, standing in the front pew next to his wife. I hoped that Bunty would look my way so I could get an idea of how she was holding up. But she didn't. My roving eye picked out Gladstone Spike and Dr. Melrose, but no sign of Mrs. Malloy. Silly of me to have counted on her being here . . .

The scent of gardenias was overpowering. Gripping the rail of the pew, I lowered my head for a moment and when I looked up, Walter Fisher had made his appearance along with the Reverend Eudora Spike. Was it the lighting that turned her face to wax? Or was her dark robe responsible by way of contrast? This wasn't the well-corseted woman with the finger-waved hair who had sat in my kitchen drinking tea. She was a being set apart from the laypeople. Stepping down onto the first altar step, she bowed her head and let out a breath that seemed to fill the chapel like the beat of angel wings. Getting herself spiritually primed, I supposed, to address the bereaved. But before she could speak one word of balm, Mr. Fisher stopped fidgeting around the coffin, fluffing up the pillow, prinking at the violets, and came padding down the altar steps to get his spiel in first.

"Mr. Wiseman." Deep bow to the chief mourner. "Ladies and gentlemen, I trust each of you will savour these last moments in the presence of a truly lovely lady. If I say so myself, I think I've done Gladys Thorn proud. Everyone by all means come up after the prayers and bid her a personal farewell. But let's have no kisses on the forehead, we don't want to mess up her hair, do we? And, one final admonition. If you must smoke to steady your nerves, I ask you not to drop ash in the coffin; we wouldn't want to cremate the dear lady here and now."

Was the man trying to be funny? The moment he had bowed himself off-stage—I mean, off the altar—the Reverend Spike called us all to prayer.

"Heavenly Father, we ask your blessing on our departed sister, Gladys Thorn. Grant her your heavenly redemption and look also in mercy on those who mourn her passing. Free those of us who continue on this our earthly journey from the burden of sin, and let us confess our faults one to the other in the certain hope of your bountiful redemption."

She raised her head and looked into the faces of those assembled. Her eyes roved the pews and met mine. They would have passed on, but in that split second I was struck by . . . call it a bolt of heavenly lightning, call it what you will. Without meaning to, without wanting to, I stuck up my hand and cried out in a ringing voice: "Please, Vicar, I have a sin to confess."

All heads turned. All eyes flashed toward me.

"Ellie, dear," Eudora Spike said gently, "I didn't mean now. If you would like to come to me after the service . . ."

"No, I can't hold it in a moment longer. I can no longer keep silent. I haven't felt myself since I realized that a foul murder had been committed."

"*She* should be committed." The words came from somewhere in the crowd, but I didn't search out the speaker; I didn't wait to hear more. Gathering up my handbag, I raced out of that chapel. My goodness, I did seem to be making a habit of this sort of exit. But even when I was in my car and driving up Cliff Road at an unusually reckless speed, I didn't feel I had made good my escape. The scent of gardenias was on my hands as they turned the steering wheel. The sound of that word—murder—still drummed in my ears. But for all the names I called myself, I didn't really regret my mad outburst. By supporting Bunty I had left a killer at large, so whose place was it but mine to reel him . . . or her . . . in. And all this did help take my mind off my problems with my darling husband.

I had every intention of going straight home. But seemingly of its own volition, the car turned in at the gates of St. Anselm's. I knew I had to put my thoughts in order—subconsciously, I suppose—the way a dying person puts his affairs in order. Before I knew it, I was wending my way between the moon-washed tombstones and up the steps to the heavy oak door. I was sure it would be locked—but wrong again, and there went my feet, walking me into the dusky nave. I didn't question that there were lights on. I only wished that there were more of them. There was a ghostliness to the pews and fluted columns as if they were no more of this day and age than those people who had worshipped here hundreds of years ago.

Did I hear footsteps behind me? I told myself not to be silly, but hark—the sound came again and this time I could not convince myself it was only the echo of my own tread. The shadowy distance from where I now stood, with my back to the door, seemed to stretch from yards into miles. No good thinking that I had set myself up for this terror. My eyes dodged this way and that looking for an escape while the footsteps got louder and closer—possibly because I was confusing them with the pounding of my heart. But perhaps I was in luck; to my left I spied the confessional that Reverend Spike had mentioned having installed. Quick as a flash, silent as a shadow, I opened one of the two doors—I had no idea whether it was the priestly or penitential one—and slipped inside, leaving the door ajar so as not to be trapped in the pitch dark. A feathery touch brushed my neck and I almost screamed. Stupid me. It was only my hair. Slowly my breathing steadied and I had just told myself that I had imagined those footsteps . . . when I heard the door on the other side of the confessional creak open and shut.

A muffled voice filled my darkness, and before I could help myself, I had reached out a trembling hand to draw back the wooden slot, exposing a small grille . . . and the face of Gladys Thorn.

Chapter Eleven

P lease don't cry," I begged. Absolutely useless. I might
as well have pleaded with a bat to stop batting its wings.
We sat in the pew immediately outside the confessional, taking great gulps of stale air that tasted as if it had been there
since the eleventh century. High on their pedestals, cloaked
in shadow, the stone saints waited breathlessly for something new in revelations.

"Miss Thorn?"

"Yes?" The soggy handkerchief was lowered an inch and
the mushroom eyes met mine. Flinchingly.

"You're really you?" I couldn't go on. My tongue had turned to dust and ashes.

"Who else?"

"But you're dead!"

"Oh, dearie me, no!" The tittering laugh almost sent me over the edge of the pew. "You must be confusing me with my sister Gladys."

"You mean . . . ?" I had to hold on to my head to keep it from flying off.

"I am Gladiola Thorn."

"Her twin?"

"Actually"—the tip of her red nose twitched with pride—"we are . . . *were* . . . triplets."

"Three of you! All identical?"

"Not exactly. There was Gladys, myself, and our brother Gladstone, with whom I believe you are currently acquainted."

"I—"

She didn't give me room to finish. "Gladys and I . . . if you will pardon my mentioning so delicate a subject . . . we were hatched, so to speak, from the same egg—making us identical twins. But all similarity ended with our looks. In the days of our girlhood I was the wild one, breaking with the C. of E. to join the Methodists."

"I remember Gladys mentioning . . . So it was *you* Mrs. Melrose saw entering Unity Methodist—providing the vicar with an excuse to give your sister the push."

The new Miss Thorn stared through me into the past. "My parents disowned me and I regret to say I quite relished being the black sheep until that distinction was wrenched from me by Gladys taking up a life of . . . slime. One man after another. There was no keeping count—except of the price paid by dear brother Gladstone. His anguish was terrible to behold. He had, at the time Gladys's lifestyle came to light, begun paying his addresses to Eudora. Could there be any doubt that a woman bent on entering the Church would spurn his proposal of marriage if she found out about Gladys? My poor brother! He came knocking on my door one day, and never a word about my harbouring Wesleyan sympathies. He begged for advice and I gave it."

"You told him to change his name to Spike?"

"It was the closest we could come to Thorn. And men are the sentimental sex, so I have been told. I personally know nothing of them—in the biblical sense. Unlike my sister, may her soul . . . not burn in hell . . . I am entitled to be addressed by that noblest of titles: Miss." Noble words that seemed destined to end in a flourish of heavenly music. Which indeed proved the case. From somewhere in the musty swirls high above our heads came the discordant *plonk, plonk* of organ keys.

"Oh, my God!" Miss Gladiola Thorn dropped to her knees, hands clenched in prayer, making it clear that far from blaspheming, she was paying her respectful addresses. I would have liked to have done the same, just on the off chance; but I had this nagging suspicion that we might be contending with God's creation. Not the Almighty Himself—pardon me, Fully Females—Herself.

"Miss Thorn," I said, tugging at her arm, "I think we should get out of here on the double."

"But Mrs.— Oh dear, I never asked your name?"

"Ellie Haskell."

"And you are suggesting?"

"That we have an intruder in the dusk."

"Then I'm doomed!" Miss Thorn's squeal blew her hanky out of her hand. "This can only mean that Gladys's murderer is after me, too!"

"Shush!" I took her hand and we tiptoed into the aisle.

"Do you really think—"

"Without a shadow of doubt."

She stumbled over my feet. "Gladys was healthy as a horse, apart from the occasional"—her voice descended into a whisper—"constipation, which she brought on herself by refusing to take her syrup of figs as a child. I was always the delicate one. Forever at the doctor's. Surely you remember seeing me at Dr. Melrose's office the other day. I noticed you because of the babies."

"So that explains why you passed me without saying hello!" Ridiculous as it sounds, the conversation had become so fascinating that I stopped midaisle, momentarily forgetting that the object of the exercise was to escape the clutches of the Ill Wisher Above. Gladiola rammed me from the rear, booting me into the pew across the way, and I made a grab to save myself, with the result that a stack of hymnals fell to the floor. O Merciful Father, save us! The noise that went shuddering every which way was worse than the walls of Jericho tumbling down. I was having trouble breathing—let alone moving— when a voice boomed out of the twilit upper regions.

"What the bloody hell's going on down there?"

Gladiola Thorn got ready to swoon, but I blocked the path to the floor. Unless my ears deceived me, there was no need for histrionics.

"Come on, out with it! Why all the bloody rambunction?"

"Mrs. Malloy?" By straining my neck and cupping a hand

over my eyes, I was able to make out someone, who could have been my household employee, leaning out from the choir loft.

"Well, who else would it be? I come in here to do me good deed for the day buffing up the place, not asking for pay, just a bit of peace and quiet, and what do I get? All this argy-bargy! It's enough to make me throw in me duster! Really it is!" Whether she suited the action to the words or whether the polishing cloth took a leap of faith, I have no idea. It came fluttering down, causing Gladiola to cower to her knees and hug the edge of the pew.

"Mrs. Malloy, it's me, Ellie Haskell!"

"I know that, Mrs. H." Heavy footsteps. "I may be blind as a bat up here, but I'm not deaf nor ever was."

"So silly of me! I should have guessed someone was working here when I found the church door open and some of the lights on. But never mind the confusion . . ." Stepping around Gladiola, I saw the familiar figure break through the gloom. "I'm just so glad to see you, Mrs. Malloy. After last night with what happened at the Wisemans' party, I've been a little jittery and when I couldn't get in touch with you . . ."

Unlike Mrs. Malloy to let me rattle on this way! Perhaps it was the sanctified atmosphere that kept her mum. But her face spoke volumes. I saw her mouth sag open. I saw her eyebrows vanish into her hair. But it wasn't until she slowly lifted her arm and pointed a shaking finger that I realized she was looking over my shoulder at Gladiola Thorn, who had risen up behind me.

"It's all right," I cried. "It's not what—*who*—you think." But Mrs. M wasn't listening. She plunged forward and would have ended up like her duster, a crumpled heap on the floor, but luckily ... *grunt, grunt* ... I managed to catch hold of her in the nick of time.

"Oh, deary me!" Miss Thorn clutched at my arm, nearly bringing all of us down. "If only she had given me a moment to introduce myself. I could have explained that I only came to these parts to be near my brother in his hour of need. And I would never have darkened the doors of this church had it not seemed the proper place to bid my sinful sister adieu."

"Could we discuss this later?" I gasped. "If you will help me settle Mrs. Malloy in this pew ... That's the ticket. I will fetch some water from the font. Surely there's a dispensation for works of mercy. After we bring her round, perhaps you would help me get her out to my car. Hush there, Mrs. Malloy!" She had opened a terrified eye a crack. "I'm taking you home with me for the night."

THE WINDOWS of Merlin's Court were blurred with morning mist, or maybe they only looked that way because my eyes were blurred with tears. I had been asleep—well, almost— when Ben had arrived home the night before. But now we faced each other across the bedroom and I was saying things I didn't want to say, stiff words poked into awkward sentences that turned him speechless.

"Please!" I cried, when I couldn't stand the silence hanging over my head like a sword any longer. "Don't just stand there! Tell me you understand."

"But I don't!" He paced the hearth rug, head down. "You're asking me to leave ..."

"Not for always!"

"Ellie, this isn't the way to solve a disagreement."

"But this isn't all about Fully Female." I was clinging to the bedpost as if it were the mast of a sinking ship. "It's about my needing a day or two alone. There's never any time just for *me*. Not since the babies came along, and I need time—now, today. I want you to take Abbey and Tam to visit your parents. You know how your mother's been on and on about seeing her grandchildren. Give her this treat. She'll love you for it and so will I."

"There's more to this—"

"You're wrong!" Fingers crossed behind my back.

"It would be difficult for me to leave Abigail's at a moment's notice."

"Where there's a will!"

"I suppose," Ben said as he rubbed his harried brow, "Freddy could squeeze by for a couple of days."

"You're not thinking," I said. "You'll have to take Freddy along. You couldn't possibly drive up to London with the twins without a backup. They're bound to get fussy at times and you might have to stop en route to feed or change them."

"So who runs Abigail's?"

"I'm sure the staff would pull together."

"You make this whole business sound simplicity itself."

Then I was more of an actress than I knew. Mustn't spoil things by letting Ben see the tears in my eyes. Ridding the house of my adored family was a horrible task. But it had to be done. For their sakes. A sense of unreality took over as I went along to the nursery and packed up the babies' supplies while Ben got them dressed and ready to go. Freddy, true to form, put up no resistance to being practically kidnapped. The way he looked at things, Ben would be *his* captive audience for several hours. And I had high hopes that his reading from

Norsemen of the Gods would lull the babies to sleep and keep them that way till journey's end.

At a little before nine o'clock I stood in the courtyard waving the little party bon voyage.

"Ellie . . ." Ben stuck his head out the car window for the third time.

"Go!" I whispered. And because I wanted to make things easier for both of us, I turned and walked toward the house. When I looked back just before going inside, the gravel drive was empty and what I thought was the distant throb of the engine might have been the sea. Heading up the stairs I heard the *plip plop* of raindrops on the windows. But my face was dry. I'd got so chilled out there that maybe I would have to thaw out a bit before I could cry. Besides, there was still one person remaining in this house whose feelings had to be considered: Mrs. Malloy. She had suffered a great shock last night and did not need to be awakened by the face of gloom and doom.

I knocked on her door. "Good morning!"

"Enter!"

Well, that sounded perky enough! I walked in to find her dressed in the black taffeta frock with the jet beading which she had worn last night. Every hair and beauty spot was in place.

"Don't worry, Mrs. H, I wasn't forced to wear my knickers inside out. I found a pair of men's underpants in one of the drawers. Good wool ones, and not a sign of moth."

"Splendid."

"No need to go patting yourself on the back." She bustled over to the bed with a pile of woolies. "I was never more shocked in my life. Haven't you heard of mothballs?"

"Sorry, Mrs. Malloy, I'm forever letting you down."

"Bloody hell!" She dropped the woolies on the bed in a slow-motion bounce that would have done credit to a fabric softener advert. "What's wrong with you, my girl?"

"Well . . ." I sat down on the bed and began pleating my skirt. "I've been feeling a bit hemmed in lately. The upshot being that Ben just left with Freddy and the twins to visit my in-laws for a couple of days and . . ."

Mrs. Malloy lowered her neon lids and smacked her butter-fly lips. "There's more here, ducky, than meets the ear. My guess, Mrs. H, is that you wanted the coast clear because you're cooking up some scheme to catch Miss Thorn's murderer."

Springing up from the bed, I cried, "What choice do I have? It wouldn't be right to leave such a person on the loose. He or she might strike again. In keeping quiet to protect Bunty, I prevented the police from doing their job."

"And you have to bloody do it for them?" To my amazement, Mrs. Malloy looked close to tears.

"I don't see I have a choice."

"Very well, Sherlock," she said resolutely, her shoulders back, her chest out, "just call me Watson."

"Absolutely not."

"Mrs. H, I don't do ceilings, I don't do drains, and I don't walk out on a friend who needs me. Now"—she marched me by the elbow to the bed—"tell me The Plan."

I sighed. But experience had taught me there was no sense in arguing with her. "As simple as ABC, really. Last night at Miss Thorn's prayer service I made a public confession. I said before running out of the chapel that I was guilty of keeping silent about a murder. Of course the villain may not have been present, but Chitterton Fells is such a small place that things get buzzed about in a hurry. And I am counting on the murderer acting quickly to silence me. That's why I had to get Ben and the babies out of the house. I couldn't take risks with their safety, and really, Mrs. Malloy, I would feel lighter of heart with you gone, too."

"Never heard such twaddle! You subdue this murderer?" she said, choking on the words. "All on your lonesome?"

"Certainly!" I sat up taller on the bed. "I have your gun. Lionel Wiseman gave it back to me after I mislaid it at his house and it's . . . let me think . . . still in my raincoat pocket."

"Have to hand it to you, Mrs. H, you're brimming over with competence."

A put-down to be ignored. "My plan is to produce my trusty weapon, hold the Evil One at bay while I telephone the police. By the way, the gun *is* loaded, isn't it?"

"There you have me." Mrs. Malloy looked quite crestfallen, and I hastened to assure her that it didn't matter a whit. I wouldn't be called upon to fire the thing, just brandish it about and look as though I knew one end from t'other.

"That's as may be!" Hands on the black taffeta hips. "But you can't tell me the chances of success aren't a heap better with two of us to one of . . . whoever."

"But it isn't fair to you."

"Yes, it bloody well is."

"Why?"

"Because I say so!" Without deigning to look my way, she stalked to the door, saying she'd go and brew up. Heaven help the murderer who came knocking before Mrs. Malloy had had her cup of tea. To say I wasn't glad to have her would be a lie. Had she still been wandering around in a post-erotic stupor, that would have been a different matter. But who can live on Cloud Nine forever? Her feet certainly seemed back on the ground. I could hear them trundling around the kitchen as I headed downstairs in search of my raincoat. Until I had that gun in my hip pocket I wouldn't know a sane moment. It crossed my mind that I might be readying myself for a confrontation not destined to happen. But deep in my heart I knew the murderer was coming for me. Perhaps he or she was on the way even now. The rain didn't help my nerves. It sounded like a person strumming on the windowpane to relieve tension . . . or deliberately annoy.

My raincoat wasn't in the hall armoire or in the cupboard under the stairs. When I entered the kitchen, I was getting jumpy, and by the time I had searched the jumble of coats on the rack by the garden door, searched them twice, I was borderline frantic.

"Can't find it?" Mrs. Malloy set her cup down with a rattle that started my teeth chattering.

"I haven't been looking very hard." So saying, I dived back into the hall, raced up the stairs, and began flinging open doors, peering behind chests, even crawling under beds. Most places I looked didn't make sense, but I was no longer rational. My raincoat had become the enemy engaging me in a deadly game of hide-and-seek. And time, damn it, got into the game. I looked at the clock at ten o'clock, then again two minutes later to find it was twenty past. Would it have hurt Mrs. Malloy to come up and lend a hand? Coming from the bathroom where I had checked the clothes hamper and the medicine cabinet, I heard a thump . . . then another . . . followed by the sound of a door being closed ever so softly. Heart pounding, I edged across the landing. Nothing now, but the *spitter spatter* of rain on the windows and the creaking of the stairs under my feet. We should have stayed together from first to last. The temptation to call out her name was overwhelming, but without the gun, all I had for an ally was stealth! Oh, come on, Ellie, don't be such a pansy! Pick up that perfectly hideous vase Aunt Astrid gave you for a wedding present and creep down the hall at the ready.

Someone was whistling a tune fraught with spine-chilling merriment while pushing open the kitchen door.

Crash! I smacked that vase down on a flash of forehead and through a shower of shards saw a body go reeling backwards to land with a wallop that shook the house. Behind my closed lids, the list of suspects rose up in grim procession, like the ghosts of a drowning man's past—all the old regulars, with Gladiola Thorn bringing up the rear. But when I forced my eyes open I saw a set of grey overalls spreadeagled on the flagstones, a spanner still clenched in the hand.

"Jock Bludgett!"

The sound of my voice startled me back to life but, luckily, did not do the same for Mr. B, the Bad Guy, for I'd always known in my heart that plumber was a killer. Chances were he could come round at any moment. I should look for something to tie him up with before I went looking for Mrs. Malloy. So I told myself, as I fought down waves of sickness and stared at the study door which was open just an inch. A telltale inch, because surely it had been closed when I went upstairs? Was my sidekick crouched behind that door, afraid to move, afraid to call out because she had no way of knowing whether the intruder had got me, or the other way round?

"Mrs. Malloy!" I found myself standing at that door, my hand on the knob, my voice creeping through the crack into the dusk within. No answer but the rasping breath of the wind and the *drip drop* of the rain. Unable to bear the terror of uncertainty a moment longer, I stumbled into the study to see Mrs. Malloy . . . sacked out on the floor in front of the hospital-green gas fire.

"Oh, my heavens!" I took two steps toward her before hearing an ominously soft sound from behind me. A shadow stepped from the wall.

"Mrs. Haskell?"

"Yes?"

"I think we should have a little chat." The voice closed around my throat, squeezing the breath out of me as effectively as a powerful pair of hands. My chest hurt, but a merciful numbness was spreading through the rest of me as I turned to face . . . Mr. Walter Fisher.

"My thanks." His guppy smile chilled the whole room. "My heartfelt thanks for taking care of the plumber. The plumber could have spoiled everything. But two down, one to go."

"I don't understand," I bleated.

"The female sex is always so impatient."

"What have you done to Mrs. Malloy?"

"I gave her something to make her sleep."

"Oh, dear God! She thought you loved her."

"So I did, for an entire night." His eyes grew filmy with memory. "She cast her Fully Female lure. Her smile beguiled. And those throbbing thighs drove me to a frenzy of desire which could only be satisfied by giving myself totally into her power. And at the moment of epiphany, I told her about Madge."

"Madge?"

"My wife."

"The one who left you one dark night?"

"The one . . ." At last his smile warmed his eyes. "The one I throttled one dark night because I couldn't stand her noisy merriment one hour longer. She was like that dreadful Bludgett woman. Always smiling. Always laughing." A shudder passed through Mr. Fisher's gaunt body. "Fortunately, in my line of work I had no trouble getting rid of the body."

"Don't tell me," I pleaded.

"Cremation isn't for everyone. But I have never denied it has its place."

"Poor Mrs. Malloy!" I meant only that she had been so woefully taken in.

"Now don't worry," Mr. Fisher hastened to reassure me. "In the cold light of day I realized I couldn't let Roxie Malloy live to babble at one of her cosy Marriage Makeover sessions that I had done away with Madge, but don't worry, I have no intention of disposing of Roxie's body the way I did the wife's. Two women disappearing on me is one too many. Yes, indeed, but no need to fuss and fume. In one of her more passionate moments Roxie told me how she intended to take her life here at Merlin's Court, but you talked her out of it. A pity"—he rubbed his nose—"that you won't be available to attest to that at the inquest. But being a Fully Female woman, she will surely have bragged about her suicide attempt at one of the meetings."

"Where," I stammered, "will *I* be?"

"You, Mrs. Haskell, are coming with me after I turn on the gas and position Roxie a little more comfortably."

"No!" With a burst of furious energy, I lashed out with my fists. But if ever there was an exercise in futility, this was it. He reached into his pocket and drew out a gun, whose mean little eye did not waver from my face while Mr. Fisher turned on the spigot. And with that dreadful hiss sounding in our ears, he herded me into the hall. I was duly surprised that he chose to leave the house by way of the kitchen, which meant circumventing the prone figure of Mr. Bludgett, but he explained that his car was parked outside the garden door. For one wild, flickering moment as we trod around Jock's grey overalls, I was convinced that the plumber would come to life and grab hold of Mr. Fisher's legs, bringing him down. But no such luck. And, anyway, Mr. B could hardly be expected to view me in the light of a damsel in distress. He'd turned up here in response to my phone call of yesterday to fix the washing machine and had got bopped on the head for his pains. I could almost hear him saying, "Lady, couldn't you have put your complaint in writing?"

By now, as must be obvious, my thinking was fuzzy in the extreme. When Mr. Fisher halted at the garden door, I watched him help himself to a couple of raincoats from the hook in the alcove and realized with a wry sort of amusement that one of them—the one that had been hanging underneath the other—was the very coat I had been hunting for while he had been making himself at home, doping poor Mrs. Malloy.

"Here, put this on." He handed me the old one belonging to Dorcas, while he slipped on mine, changing gun hands as he went. My heart sank. "Nice to know, isn't it, Mrs. Haskell, that the age of chivalry isn't dead? As for myself, I can't risk a drenching; I suffer with my chest."

I didn't answer. Once outside, the rain brought the stinging relief of acupuncture, deadening the surface of my mind, as well as my skin, still further. I knew I was in his car, and I guessed where he was taking me. But I wasn't afraid. I wasn't anything . . . or anyone. Not Ellie Haskell. Not Ben's wife. Not the twins' mother.

But Walter Fisher was apparently in the mood for a chat. "I didn't expect to find Roxie at your house when I arrived, Mrs. Haskell."

"Well, she was expecting you." Staring at the windscreen, I saw Mrs. M's face in the rivulets of rain, the corners of her mouth dripping downward. Would I ever speak to her again? Would I ever get to tell that I didn't blame her for anything, that I blamed myself for misreading the signals she had been sending me?

Mr. Fisher—nothing would make me call him Walter—rested the gun against the steering wheel as we purred down the drive and out onto Cliff Road. "Roxie's presence was a bonus, although you understand I've been trying to do away with her for several days now. It was only a matter of time before she went to the police. Never trust a woman. Just now, shame on her, she lied to me—said you had left the house with your husband and children. Most annoying of her to complicate matters. Particularly when I thought it would be so easy."

A light went on in a shop window and inside my head. "You put something in her Fully Female Formula?"

"Yew leaves." Another of his pale smiles. "So felicitously available at the vicarage."

"Yes," I said, speaking automatically. "Mrs. Malloy mentioned there was a move afoot to cut down the yew trees because of fears about their toxicity."

"I chopped the leaves up and put some in the jar of Formula. Simplicity itself. I can't think what went wrong. Roxie claimed to be religious about taking the stuff."

"So she was," I said. "But we each had several bottles of Formula. It would have taken her a while to get to the one you'd doctored up. I do remember seeing her opening up a new one the night of the Wisemans' party. She even mixed herself a glass, but it turned to goop before she could drink it. Instead . . ." I stared out the misted window. "Instead Gladys Thorn must have gone into the kitchen. She must have mistaken the Formula for a fibre laxative and . . ."

"Dear me!" Mr. Fisher shook his head. "What a waste!" Whether he meant a waste of good yew leaves or Gladys Thorn I hadn't the foggiest. "Am I to understand," he asked, steering cautiously around a bend in the road, "that when you confessed last night in the Chapel of Rest to being privy to a murder, you were talking about Miss Thorn, not my wife?"

"Certainly."

"That shows you how naive I am." Mr. Fisher tut-tutted. "I truly thought she had expired of natural causes."

"Mrs. Malloy never said a word to me about your wife. And the bitter irony is that if you had left well enough alone I don't think she would have gone to the police. The Fully Female manual instructs that all confidences exchanged during lovemaking be accorded the sacred seal of the confessional, and Roxie wasn't only religious about taking her Formula. She was a dyed-in-the-wool convert, prepared to uphold the code if it killed her." I didn't add he'd had something else working in his favour—namely that his Roxie had truly loved him. Love! A good servant but a poor master. Poor Mrs. M. My throat tightened. May she re . . . live in peace.

Chagrin showed on Mr. Fisher's waxen features. In misjudging the lady he had complicated his life as well as hers and mine. Get him unsettled—that's the ticket, I cheered myself on. He wasn't used to having the bodies he transported talk back to him, so I would keep talking. The topic didn't matter just so long as the lips kept moving.

"The morning after her tryst with you she was in a complete daze, and later turned up at my house out of the blue, but I never suspected she was in fear of her life. Even when she took up good works—helping out at the church—I put it down to the power of love. It never dawned on me she might be preparing to be putting her life in order."

"No need to rub it in, Mrs. Haskell." He pursed his thin lips. "Roxie knew I couldn't let her live. What I can't fathom is how she lasted this long. In addition to the Formula, I added my own special herbs to a packet she had from Fully Female." Mr. Fisher carefully braked for a yellow light, turned onto Market Street, and shifted closer to the curb to make room for a woman on a bicycle. Her wave said it all: What a gentleman!

"Mrs. Malloy would seem to have been living under a lucky star . . . for a while. She is a no-nonsense woman." My eyes never left the gun. "And I imagine she was expecting a straight-forward knife in the back, not the nix being put on her Healthy Harvest Herbs. But I think I can hazard a guess as to what happened there. The other day she couldn't find her supply, probably because you had moved it, so she borrowed a packet from me. She must have returned the one with the yew leaves because we had a little episode with our cat, which I blamed on someone else. May I be forgiven."

Those last words brought Mrs. M closer than if she had been in the car with me. Was she already interviewing St. Peter and making it plain up front that she wasn't going to get stuck polishing the Pearly Gates? Or could it be that there had been a miracle back at Merlin's Court? Oh, please God! Let Mr. Bludgett come groggily back to life and go stumbling into the dining room to turn off the gas jet in the nick of time.

"We're here, Mrs. Haskell." Mr. Fisher cut short my prayer.

He had pulled into a side alley, and through the tattered veil of rain I saw the sign Fisher Funerals creeking above the door. Cuffing the gun, he came around, helped me out of the car, and ushered me across a square of pavement and through a glass door into a showroom smelling of beeswax and gardenias, with wreaths on the walls instead of pictures and a floor space crowded with coffins—pardon me, cabinets—to suit every taste from baroque to Danish modern.

The unreal part is that I wasn't jibbering with terror. My only explanation is that in my case horror had exercised an anesthetising effect. My mind told me I was destined for the fate which had befallen poor Mrs. Fisher and all those dinners I had burned to a crisp. But I didn't believe it, even when the villain of the piece gave a start which I would have considered artsey-fartsey if Freddy had enacted it on stage.

"Someone's coming!"

I heard it too—the sound of a car pulling into the alley and, breath catching in my throat, the fading throb of the engine being turned off. Whoever it was didn't matter. I wasn't asking for the sheriff or the troops with Rin Tin Tin woofing up the rear, only your off-the-street Joe with adequate hearing. Time for the scream of a lifetime! I had my mouth open and my vocal cords primed when Mr. Fisher reminded me that he had a gun by waving it under my nose. And the next thing I knew, he was hustling me through an archway hung with purple velvet, to where the smell of death was strongest—into the Chapel of Rest.

"Hurry!" A savage poke at my back sent me stumbling towards the altar where Miss Thorn's coffin reposed in all its mournful splendour.

I strained my ears for the sound of the outside door opening and couldn't be sure if I was indulging in wishful thinking.

"Don't let me keep you, Mr. Fisher," I said, "if you have a customer in the back."

"One more peep and I kill you and whoever comes in."

"You won't get away with this."

"And, like all women, you talk too much." Mr. Fisher was now practically treading on my heels and his breath came out in chesty wheezes as he said, "Lift the lid."

"You heard me." A really painful jab this time, as I strained to catch the sound of footsteps. None were forthcoming as I slowly raised the coffin lid. What was I supposed to say to Miss Thorn: Move over and make room for me?

She wasn't there.

"Get in."

Oh, the sick slippery feel of that white satin, but I kept telling myself this wasn't happening, even as Mr. Fisher hauled off his . . . my raincoat and—persnickety man—tossed it in after me. Mustn't raise eyebrows by being caught in ladies' attire, must we, Walter? I hope my jeering smile chilled his blood as he closed the coffin lid. One does so like to have the upper hand at such times.

Darkness. Even when I opened my eyes.

Instinctively, I sensed that the air was rationed and I would have to recycle like crazy. And there wasn't a lot of elbow room (or nose room for that matter), but other than that things could be worse. I could already be dead, instead of waiting for Mr. Fisher to come back and finish the job once he got rid of his customer.

The darkness grew rank with terror, which eased a little when I thought of Ben and his claustrophobia. Thank God he wasn't the one in this pickle. And thank God for my miracle! That thud wasn't my heart. I had jostled my raincoat. And inside the raincoat pocket was Mrs. Malloy's gun. Forget the morning nap, Ellie, there are nappies to wash and the day to be saved. My fingers inched sideways and felt the gun. Any moment now I would weasel it into my hand, and with my finger on the trigger, burst out of my narrow cell, the quintessential Fully Female woman.

So much for heroics. I wasn't to be allowed the privilege of rescuing myself. At least not as planned. Before I could say boo, my coffin lid was inched upward and I found myself gaping into the ever-handsome, if ashen, face of Lionel Wiseman.

"My word! Mrs. Haskell!" He backed down the altar steps, kicking aside a couple of wreaths in the process.

I sat up in my satin coffin pointing the gun at him. "Sorry, Miss Thorn isn't receiving callers."

"What is this? Some kind of dare you cooked up with the other Fully Females?"

"Your questions," I said, sitting up, "are best addressed to Mr. Walter Fisher, who I would assume is currently lurking behind one of those purple hangings."

"My dear lady, I think I should call a doctor."

"Shush!" I silenced him with a lift of the hand, the one holding the gun. I heard escaping footsteps, then a car starting up outside very close to the building, and it dawned on me why I was having this conversation with Mr. Wiseman undisturbed. Walter Fisher, Murderer, had hopped it, possibly because even he thought that getting away with three murders in one day was pushing it, but more probably because he had seen the gun in my hand. "I really don't think you should bother Dr. Melrose," I told Mr. Wiseman. "He will be having a quiet day at home with Flo, talking about his retirement as he poses for one of her paintings. Much better to phone the police, they'll have a grand time chasing down Mr. Fisher. Life is so dull in Chitterton Fells." Stretching my arms above my head I took a deep, reviving breath of gardenias. "Oh,

Mr. Wiseman, before you make that call, would you mind telling me what brings you here?"

"The ring." For a large man his voice was awfully small.

"What?"

"Frightfully embarrassing, Mrs. Haskell."

"Go on."

"If you insist." He straightened up without managing to look as tall as usual. "At the time of Gladys's death I made the foolish gesture of saying I wanted her engagement ring buried with her. However, upon reflection I realized that sentiment has its place . . ."

"In your pocket?"

"My dear lady, it is a very expensive piece of jewelry. Where can it be? Where is Gladys?"

"You didn't . . ." My heart suddenly went out to him. The poor two-timer. "You didn't decide it would be more fitting to have her ashes scattered inside the church organ, and arrange for her to have a Show Case funeral?"

"No! Never heard of such a thing."

"Then my guess is that the next of kin—in this case, Miss Thorn's brother Gladstone—stepped in and requested it in the interests of economy and . . ." I looked away from him. ". . . and making absolutely sure she wouldn't turn up again, twenty years from now.

I reached up a hand and let him help me onto my feet. "Life is very expensive, but dear Mr. Wiseman"—a smile was growing inside me ready to burst out and shine—"it is worth everything you pay for it."

Epilogue

Something had told me Mrs. Malloy would be all right. And so she was, because Ben had listened to his male intuition—that inner voice which told him that I hadn't levelled with him. Halfway to London, he told Freddy he was turning round and they arrived back at Merlin's Court to find Mr. Bludgett busily resuscitating Mrs. Malloy using the plumber's mate—the trusty plunger. It did the trick so well that Mrs. M was able to spill the beans in record time, and before Freddy had the twins out of their coats, Ben was on the phone to the police. They caught up with Walter Fisher a half hour later; by which time neither the car nor he were in one piece. He had gone over the cliff on the far side of the point on the outskirts of Pebblewell. Mrs. Malloy, all stiff upper lip, insisted the case would have been different if the officer in charge had been female. Never send a man to do a woman's job. When I received the news, my feelings were awfully muddled. The horror that I had submerged came bubbling to the surface. There was relief that the bogeyman was gone, blotted out, never to return. And there was sadness for Mrs. Malloy, although I got the feeling she might recover when she telephoned me that evening to say she was dumping every drop of her Fully Female Formula down the sink.

"Good idea," I told her. But much to my surprise, Ben wasn't one hundred percent behind the idea when I told him what she had said.

"I don't know, Ellie." He was lying on the bed, a hand cupped behind his head, a book lying flat across his stomach. "I'm beginning to think I was looking at Fully Female with a closed mind. Just listen to this." He turned the volume over and read in a gloating voice:

> That old saying about an Englishman's home being his castle should be updated. How much sweeter, dear Fellow Female, to say that an Englishman's bed is his castle. Whatever battles he must fight out in the cold, cruel world, between the sheets he is king.

"Give that to me!" I snatched the manual from him. "How *can* you laugh like that?"

"How can I not?" He sat up very still, his eyes turning to darkest emerald. "I have to laugh from the sheer joy of having you safe with me."

"I don't understand why you aren't furious with me for not telling you what I was up to. Particularly when we had just had that go-round about Fully Female."

"This was different." He moved over to make room for me on the bed. "What you did was crazy, Ellie, but I understand why you did it, and why you couldn't tell me."

"You would have stopped me."

"You're damn right."

"I didn't feel I had a choice."

"Oh, Ellie!" He pulled me into his arms and scattered kisses gentle as flowers upon my face. "Don't you see? I never asked for your soul—only your heart."

Breathless, I lifted my face to his. "It's yours, always and forever. I only went to Fully Female because I was afraid. I was afraid that childbirth had made me lumpy and unattractive. I was afraid to want you"—I buried my face against his shoulder—"in case you didn't want me."

His laugh rumpled my hair. "That's funny. Because I felt the same way. I was afraid that the responsibilities of fatherhood had robbed me of my boyish charm."

I wanted to stay in that magic place forever, but suddenly one of the babies whimpered. Not a hungry sound, but a scared one.

"I'll go," I said.

"No." He pressed a finger to my lips, stood, put on his black silk dressing gown, and was off to fight the dragons as knights, bold and true, have been doing for centuries. As for the lady of the manor, she has her role to play in keeping the home fires burning. Stepping over to the table by the window, I started to light the candle that would bathe the sheets with amber light, but all at once I threw down the match and went out onto the landing in a whirl of flannel nightgown. If I couldn't follow my love to the ends of the earth, I could at least follow him to the nursery. Together we would take care of our babies and afterwards . . .

Afterwards is always a mystery.

And sometimes a love story.